Ravishment

JRWalker

Ravishment
Published by The Conrad Press in the United Kingdom 2019

Tel: +44(0)1227 472 874
www.theconradpress.com
info@theconradpress.com

ISBN 978-1-911546-52-8

Typesetting and Cover Design by: Charlotte Mouncey, www.bookstyle.co.uk

The Conrad Press logo was designed by Maria Priestley.

Printed and bound in Great Britain
by Clays Ltd, ELcogRAf S.p.A.

Ravishment

A 17th-century Whodunnit

The first diary of Lady Jane Tremayne

JAMES WALKER

To Jo for her love and understanding.

1

Widowhood

It was, I recall, St George's Day, the twenty-third of April, in the Year of Our Lord 1653, a Wednesday morning, and I was at home at Altringham Manor in East Devon. I could not possibly have known, when I woke, that it was to be a day destined to begin a transformation of my life for ever, both for good and ill.

My home was built three storeys high, in stone, in the early years of Good Queen's Bess's reign, nearly a hundred years previously. With its long gallery and well-stocked library, as well as a pleasing aspect, it was a place of which I had grown deeply fond.

It had been a harsh winter, with snow lingering on the ground even into late March and beyond. However, evidence that spring had properly arrived was now plain to be seen and could be heard everywhere.

I was especially taken by the profusion of primroses that had flowered on the edge of the copse to my left, beyond which lay the southern boundary of the Manor. I remembered that they had been coming up in the same spot ever since I had first arrived there, as an eighteen-year-old bride, nearly a dozen years before. Still, with each succeeding year, they had grown in numbers, and I fancied they had never previously looked quite so dazzling in the morning sunshine.

It being St George's day, I felt minded to celebrate that fact by going for a ride. There could be no dragons to slay, real or imagined, but I still had confidence that a gallop on my seven-year-old mare, Hera, would help to raise my spirits and give me the courage I believe I needed to look the world properly in the eye after long years of war and all the misery it had brought to my country.

Firstly, though, I needed to summon my personal maid, Mary Moffat, to help me dress, so stepping back from the window, I opened my bedroom door, and called out to her.

Mary was a diminutive, pretty seventeen-year-old minx with long brown hair, now respectfully tied up in a clasp, and hazel eyes, who had been a member of my household since she was thirteen. At that tender age she had been engaged as a lowly scullery maid by my cook and housekeeper, Alice Cowper. Mary, possessed of a naturally cheerful disposition, had proved herself to be both competent and conscientious in the performance of her duties. When, six months previously, my maid Jessica Wilkes had married a local tenant farmer and consequentially left my household, Alice had recommended Mary to replace her, and since then she had adjusted well to her new role.

'It's time I got dressed, Mary,' I told her as soon as she appeared. 'The weather looks set fair and I've decided to go for a ride.'

Mary dropped me a curtsey before hurrying to fetch the clothes I required. I knew that I would wish to ride astride rather than side saddle, and in order to do so would put on a man's breeches, over which I would wear a black, velvet riding

8

habit with split skirt. They would not be just any breeches either, but rather ones which had belonged to my late husband, Sir Paul Tremayne, who had died at the Battle of Worcester eighteen months previously, fighting for the forces of Charles Stuart, whom, as a true royalist, he had recognised as his rightful, if yet to be anointed, King.

Mary was also ready to assist me with my toilette, above all the combing of my thick, auburn hair, which would then be bunched up under a white, silk coif. Finally, whilst I invariably preferred to wear no make-up as I still possessed a fair complexion, unblemished by any marks of smallpox, I was content to apply a touch of my favourite jasmine based scent to both my neck and wrists.

Only the briefest of pleasantries passed between us as I was in a reflective humour, and Mary, sensitive to my moods, seemed to know instinctively when she had licence to prattle on and when she did not. She had, after all, taken on her role at a time when I was just emerging from a year of mourning for my late husband, and that my riding habit was black, bore testimony to the fact that I still grieved for him.

Ours could never be a relationship of equals, but all the same there was an easy familiarity between us; an indication that our two personalities complemented each other. I also sensed that she had grown fond of me thanks to my patient forbearance of her and was even somewhat in awe of my good looks. Certainly, I had received enough admiration over the years from both sexes to know that I was something of a beauty. Apart from my hair, I thought my hazel eyes and small, regular shaped nose, my most attractive features although I sometimes wished for more fulsome lips and smaller ears.

My toilette was complete, and I was almost fully dressed for my ride, when I heard a discreet tap on my door. It was one I had been expecting for it formed part of my daily ritual.

'M'lady, may I enter?'

'Of course, Alice.'

Now in her early forties, Alice was somewhat rotund and short in stature but nonetheless carried herself well and combined her duties as cook and housekeeper with an air of calm authority. Like me, Alice was a widow, having lost her husband, Jack, at the battle of Edgehill, nearly eleven years previously. They had originally both been servants together of Sir Paul's father, who had died only a matter of months after I married my husband. Jack had been one of the company of men, which Sir Paul had raised for the king at the outset of the civil war with Parliament.

Lost husbands were not all we had in common, for we both had lost offspring to the ravages of illness, which so readily afflicted infants regardless of their status in life. In one respect, however, Alice was more fortunate, as she still at least had a son, who had survived to reach the cusp of adulthood, now being the same age as Mary, whereas I had been left completely childless, thus compounding the loss of my husband.

'I shall take a little breakfast in the dining room and then, as you can see, I have dressed to go riding,' I told Alice. 'You'll need to tell the stable lad, Toby, to have Hera saddled and ready to depart in half-an-hour.'

'Of course, m'lady. And will your ride be a short one?'

I looked Alice in the eye while I pondered this question. 'I've a mind to ride over to Lady Olivia's so I may not return before evening. I will be back in time for supper, though.'

'Shall I prepare a sack posset for you then, m'lady.'

'Certainly, that'll do me very well.' By now I was walking out of my bedroom towards the staircase, leaving both Alice and Mary to follow on behind. 'And are there any household matters that require my attention?' I asked.

'Not today, m'lady. I believe I 'ave everything in hand.'

I turned my head towards her and smiled. Particularly since my husband's death, I felt immense gratitude for her loyal service. Sir Paul, an only son, had left Altringham Manor to me in his will, and, as I had struggled with my grief, it had been a considerable relief to know that I could always rely on Alice to ensure that the household was efficiently run. Likewise, I felt a similar measure of gratitude towards my steward, Harry Parsons, whose job it was to manage my estate as profitably as my straitened circumstances would allow.

I still found myself waking in the middle of the night in great distress in fearful memory of the evil day, the previous September, when I had received a most unwelcome visit from one of Parliament's Local Commissioners for the County of Devon. He had come with the intention of sequestering all of my estates on behalf of the Parliamentary Committee for Compounding with Royalists and Delinquents, and in order to save myself from this disaster I had been given a mere six weeks to pay a massive fine of three times the estate's annual value.

Six years previously, at the end of the first civil war, the Committee had imposed a similar fine, which had come very close to leaving Paul and myself destitute as we struggled to meet it. This experience had proved a major factor in restraining Paul from taking up arms again on behalf of the king at the onset of the second civil war in 1648.

Yet, after the King's martyrdom the following year, none of my pleadings, nor the threat of yet another sequestration, could constrain my beloved husband from taking up arms on behalf of the man he regarded as his rightful monarch. The consequence had been not only his tragic death, but also another visit from the Commissioner although for whatever reason this had come blessedly later than I had feared it might.

This time, in order to meet the fine, I had had to sell every valuable piece of jewellery I possessed, save for my wedding ring. Even then the money raised had been insufficient, so, as a last resort, I had obtained a loan from a goldsmith in Exeter at a six percent rate of interest, the maximum which the law permitted, and the repayment of which still left me in dread of the poor house.

Fortunately, the harvests of the last two years had been good, tenants' rents had not, with a few exceptions, fallen into arrears, and Harry's hard work had surely also made a difference too. With a fair wind I knew I might therefore manage to repay the loan over the course of the agreed period of five years and so preserve my late husband's estate intact, although for whose benefit was quite another matter entirely.

Certainly, with the arrival of my thirtieth birthday two months previously, I no longer felt young and had a keen sense that I might not live to see fifty. After all, neither my mother or mother-in-law had done so, and I knew from the bottom of my soul how close the death of my beloved daughter and then that of my husband had come to breaking me, both in mind and body. From somewhere had come the resilience to endure, and even revive my spirits somewhat. Yet I felt no desire to marry again and especially in such hard times saw no prospect of anyone seeking to court an 'old maid' whose estate was mortgaged to a goldsmith.

2

Olivia

It was with such sombre reflections that I set out on my ride, mounted on Hera. I had donned a peaked, wide-brimmed, black hat, and thought, not for the first time, how much the Puritan both this and my black riding habit made me appear. I was confident that my late husband would have shuddered to see me looking so dowdy although under my black skirt, his breeches were an altogether more colourful Lincoln green.

In truth, I firmly believed that the person to whom I owed the most gratitude for seeing me through the last eighteen months of pain was my oldest friend, Lady Olivia Courtney, whom I had known since infancy. Our fathers before us had been good friends and I felt a greater affection for her than my own, twenty-six-year old sister,

Caroline was married to a doctor, John Thorpe, and lived in Exeter, some twenty miles away, so a good half-a-day's journey. The problem there lay not so much in either the distance between our homes, or differences in either age or personality, though I thought my sister a shade self-righteous, as the dangerous brew of religion and politics; the good doctor being both a Parliamentarian, who refused to condemn the execution of the good King Charles, and a Puritan.

My sister's union with such an individual was one that I felt would have had my parents spinning in their graves. However, passionate love cares little for land, property or river bank, and having observed my sister Caroline and her husband together, I would say that theirs was a union more of their persons than of their minds.

The civil wars had also turned the world we had known so topsy turvy that I supposed it was a case of any safe port in a storm. I also had no doubt of either the doctor's abilities or worthiness; I merely thought him cheerless, in tune with the times in which we now lived. In any event, we contrived to see little of each other, although recent news that Caroline was once again pregnant, having previously suffered a miscarriage, might change that.

In contrast, my younger brother, Francis, aged twenty-four, whom I had not seen in a year, and was now in possession of my family's estate, some fifty-five miles away, near Barnstable, had an altogether more outgoing personality, and was at heart as staunch a royalist as my late husband. Aged barely thirteen when the first civil war had broken out, a riding accident, two years later, which had broken his leg, and left him with a severe limp, had ended the ambition he had undoubtedly harboured of joining the King's cause. Then, when he was still a few months short of his majority, our dear mother had died, worn down, I felt, by five years of widowhood, and the burden of responsibility for a family and home in a time of war.

My ride to Olivia's was one of barely three miles through countryside of which I never grew bored and which always gave me cause to count my blessings, thinking it surely as beautiful as any on God's earth. Admittedly, I had never travelled further east than Salisbury, or further north than Gloucester and had seldom crossed the Tamar into Cornwall, once recalling a visit to Truro. Still, I could not imagine that far-off places anywhere could be more pleasing to the eye than the river valleys which I had known all my life.

I am minded of what Rosalind says to that melancholic fellow Jacques in the Bard's *As You Like It*, an engaging and somewhat riotous performance of which I once saw in Totnes. *I fear you have sold your own lands to see other men's,* I seem to remember Rosalind telling him, *and to do that is to have rich eyes and poor hands.* That encapsulates my own feelings about travel to distant places; well beyond Exeter, that is.

Fetford Hall, which was Olivia's home, whilst not as large as Altringham Manor, was more modern by some fifty years, having only been built thirty years previously in the Jacobean style, and was in a particularly fine location, on the brow of a hill, surrounded on two sides by many mature oak trees. I could see its red brick walls in the distance when I was still a mile away and by the time I reached it my friend had already spied my arrival and had come outside to greet me.

Six months younger than me, Olivia was also an inch or so taller and, most strikingly of all, had red hair with freckles. I thought her very pretty and was particularly drawn to her naturally solicitous personality as well as her sparkling eyes.

I thought it sad that she seemed fated to remain a spinster for the rest of her days, but then her life had been as touched by tragedy as my own when the man to whom she was betrothed to be married had been killed at the battle of Langport, fighting for the royalist cause towards the end of the first civil war. Then it had fallen to me, Lady Jane Tremayne, to offer what moral support I could in my friend's hour of need and, as the

16

fates would have it, five years later Olivia had come to my aid when I had been left devastated by the death of my husband.

In one vital respect, however, our circumstances did not mirror each other's. Whereas, upon Paul's death, thanks to the terms of his will, I had found myself the sole owner of Altringham Manor, in contrast Olivia had a brother, Sir James, seven years my junior, who had inherited Fetford Hall and its estates along with a baronetcy upon the death of their father only the previous year.

Olivia's mother, Constance, was also a still vigorous woman in her late fifties, and I sensed that as an unmarried daughter Olivia lived somewhat in her shadow, unlike her younger sister Claire, who had married a clergyman, and at twenty-five was already the mother of two seemingly healthy sons. I doubted, though, if any such reflection concerned Olivia much, if at all, and I rather envied the close ties of family affection which she was able to enjoy, living under the same roof with her handsome younger sibling and her good-natured mother. That I myself was treated like an honorary member of their family, and felt at home in their embrace, also encouraged me to visit Fetford Hall two or even three times a week.

I daresay it had often occurred to Constance that I and James would make an excellent couple. However, the impediment to that lay not so much in the fact that I was so much older, or even that I looked upon James more as a younger brother than a possible suitor, but rather in the simple reality that I knew his heart was set on marriage to a girl not yet twenty-one, named Rebecca Trowton, though she was more usually known as Becky.

He had indeed already asked for her hand in marriage,

17

which she had gladly agreed to, save that her father, a staunch Parliamentarian, had refused to give the necessary consent, thinking James too much of a renegade sympathiser. Once Becky was of age, though, in only a few months, that would count for nothing as James had declared himself indifferent to the fact that her father would give her no dowry, and had even threatened to cut her out of his will if the marriage went ahead.

I knew from Olivia that Constance, mindful of the difficult times in which they lived, and the precarious nature of their family's financial position, had tried to persuade James to put his head before his heart and look elsewhere for a bride. However, he had simply become irritated, and in the end shouted at her that he would rather be dead than give up the woman he loved. This heated exchange was not one that Olivia had been meant to be privy to, but she had overheard it nevertheless, and had then seen fit to tell all to me. She had, in truth, never been good at keeping secrets, which along with her delight in small talk and gossip, represented perhaps the greatest weakness in her otherwise estimable character.

It had been in my mind to suggest to Olivia that we go riding together but by the time I reached Fetford Hall, the morning sunshine had been replaced by threatening clouds and there was more than a hint of rain in the air. Looking behind myself, in the westerly direction from which the weather was advancing, I decided that it was likely to turn wetter still, so instead I thought we could remain indoors and indulge in what was our other most favourite pastime, the playing of music.

Olivia was an accomplished harpsichord player with every opportunity to practise her skill. My own ability, by my own admission, was more modest, but I, too, liked to play as often as possible, and I also possessed a reasonable soprano voice. Olivia's was more contralto, which meant that our voices complemented each other quite well and Constance, in particular, who derived real pleasure from hearing us play and sing together, actively encouraged us to do so. James, although he possessed a more than adequate tenor voice, was far less musically inclined, and even as I dismounted from my horse, Olivia was quick to inform me that he had gone out immediately after breakfast and was not expected back until evening.

'I suspect he intends an assignation with Becky,' Olivia said, 'although, of course, he would never admit to that. All he'd say vaguely was that he had business to attend to in Honiton, but I know what he has on his mind.'

'But I thought Becky's father kept her on a tight rein and never more so since he refused his consent to their marrying.'

'Perhaps,' Olivia replied, 'but I have it on good authority that he's had to take to his bed and there's no keener horsewoman than Becky. She's also strong-willed in her own right, and we both know that she and James are smitten with each other. If I'm right, I expect she'll have her maid in toe to prevent any suggestion of impropriety.'

'Even so, maids can be told to look the other way. They should be more patient. In only four months she'll be twenty-one, after all.'

'My dear Jane, I admit I could be wrong but I do believe I'm right. Now, I'll summon the stable boy to attend to your horse, and then you must come indoors out of the rain. Will you be staying long?'

'A few hours; if you'll have me?'

'Of course, you know you're always welcome.'

'I can't stay too late, though. I need to speak to my steward about certain matters.'

'I completely understand, Jane,' Olivia said, with a smile. 'I shall be glad of your company while I have it.'

3

Shocking news

We enjoyed our music-playing very much that day. I had been practising a new piece, a galliard by my favourite composer, Orlando Gibbons. I had struggled with it at first. However, never easily deterred, my persistence had borne fruit and I now believed that I had developed a fair mastery of it, a feat I was keen to demonstrate to my friend.

She did appreciate my playing of the piece, and we were able to pass a distracting few hours, with me playing the galliard and then other pieces together, interrupted only by the simple meal of bread and cheese washed down with watered beer, which Constance had prepared for the three of us. Meanwhile, outside the rain clouds had passed away to be replaced by the warmth of the sun, its rays streaming in upon us through the hall's west facing windows. Eventually, the spell was broken when I stood up and announced that I needed to be going.

'I shall come again soon, of course.'

'Please do, dear Jane,' Constance told me. 'You know we are always delighted to see you.'

The three of us embraced and once I had departed with a smile and a wave of the hand, my thoughts turned once more to James's relationship with Becky. She was certainly a pretty young thing with her pert little nose, rosy cheeks and curly hair, and appeared to be perfectly good natured. It was just that if she and James were determined to marry, I somehow doubted that Becky would ever make such a good companion for Olivia, as apart from any other consideration it was my understanding that Becky had little musical ability.

The closer I came to Altringham Manor, the more I did my best to focus on the matter I wished to discuss with Harry. I had not wished to elucidate on this with Olivia, for it primarily concerned the distasteful though vital business of money. I needed to hear from him what progress he had made in completing the estate's accounts for the year. What mattered most of all was that the monthly repayments to Babbage the goldsmith were fully up to date, but if by some good fortune we could actually do more than break-even then I would have dearly liked to reduce the debt still further as I sometimes felt as if it was like a veritable noose around my neck.

I had barely dismounted from my horse when Harry stepped out of his cottage door to greet me. He was not the most handsome of men, possessing too large a nose and large ears too, but he had an honest, dependable face, had survived the first civil war with nothing more than a flesh wound to his name, and at thirty-five was still in robust, good health . I could tell, though, from the merest glance that something was seriously amiss as his normally calm features were a picture of anxiety.

'What's wrong, Harry, has something terrible happened?'

'I'm afraid it has, m'lady. Melanie Tunnicliffe says a man has ravished her entirely against her will.'

4

Poor Melanie

Melanie was the oldest of five surviving children, and David Tunnicliffe, her father, was my gardener. 'The gal's very distressed, m'lady,' Harry continued. 'She says she doesn't know the man who attacked her at all. Indeed, she says he was masked. Her dress is certainly torn and her mother tells me her virginity's been taken.'

'Oh my God, how awful,' I exclaimed . 'And where did this happen, Harry?'

'In the woods, m'lady, just behind us. She was gathering wild flowers for the table...'

'Yet no one heard her screams?'

'She says the man came up behind her and put a hand over her mouth. He then threatened her with a knife.'

I felt sickened by the thought that a sixteen-year-old could be defiled in such a way. The valleys of South Devon were normally free of criminal activity. There was some occasional petty thieving and poaching, but it was still a place where people felt safe, doors were left unlocked, and Melanie, whom I had known since she was an infant, would have seen no danger in walking alone into the woods in daylight.

'Harry, I would like to speak to Melanie and offer my sympathies.'

Harry immediately led me to the simple, two-storey, thatched cottage that was home to the Tunnicliffe family. David was normally a quiet man, of few words, but as he opened the cottage door in answer to Harry's knock, I was able to detect a look of intense anger on his face, for all that it was quickly replaced by a far more deferential expression the moment he recognised me.

'This is dreadful news, David. How is your daughter?'

'She's mighty tearful, m'lady. If I could lay me hands on the man who did this to 'er, I'd gladly throttle him.'

'That I can well understand. Let us pray that he will soon be brought to justice. May I speak to Melanie?'

'As you wish, m'lady.' He stood to one side to let my enter. I had to duck my head slightly in order to be able to do so. I had been in this cottage and others like it before, but even so it was still darker than I had been expecting, the cottage's only downstairs window being tiny and the light from outside beginning to fade a little. I also couldn't help but wrinkle my nose at the smell, which came from a combination of cooked food and seven human beings living in such a confined space.

Melanie was sitting in front of the hearth amongst the rushes, her hands thrown around her knees, which she had drawn up towards her face, which looked as pale as death. She was quietly sobbing while her mother, Judith, who had clearly been trying to comfort her, was hurriedly getting to her feet in an effort to offer me a curtsey.

'I am sorry to disturb you, Judith,' I said. 'Harry Parsons has told me enough of what has happened to make it clear to me that your daughter has been the victim of a heinous crime. Melanie, my child, can you confirm to me what you told him.

I understand that a stranger came up behind you, put his hand over your mouth, and threatened you with a knife?'

At this question Melanie looked up, her state of distress all too obvious, her eyes tear-stained, and then nodded her head. 'Yes, m'lady,' she added, but so quietly that I barely heard what she said for all that I was virtually standing over her.

'And I understand the man wore a mask?'

Again Melanie managed to nod her head and mumble the same words as before.

'What did the mask look like?' I asked her.

'It was black, I think.'

'Did it cover his whole face?'

'Yes. There were holes for his eyes and mouth, and a small one for his nose.'

'And it was made of what material, would you say?'

'I don't really know, m'lady. Leather, perhaps, and I think 'e was quite young.'

'Why d'you say that?'

''Is voice sounded young. And 'is hands; they didn't look like those of an old man.'

'And do you also recall how he was dressed?'

'Like a gentleman, m'lady,' she answered more audibly.

'Really... why do you say that?'

''E was wearing boots, m'lady, and... and 'is doublet had lots of buttons. Oh yes, and I think 'is cuffs were made of lace. For sure, that's what they looked like. And, 'e also spoke like a gentleman.'

'You didn't recognise him from his voice?'

'... No, m'lady, I'm sorry.'

'No matter. And there was nothing in his voice to suggest that he might be a foreigner or from a different part of the country?'

'No, m'lady. From how 'e spoke I think 'e was a gentleman of this county.'

'And was there anything else in particular you remember about him?'

''E was wearing a dark hat... but that... came off... 'is hair was quite long, I think...'

'What, shoulder length?'

'Perhaps, and it was brown in colour, I'm sure of that...'

'Light or dark?'

'I think dark, m'lady, but... oh, I'm not really sure...'

The recollection of what she had endured again threatened to overwhelm Melanie and she began to sob once more. Even in the poor light I could also see how torn and stained her dress was, whilst above all else I felt satisfied that I was being told the truth, and that this was no fabricated story.

'There was one other thing m'lady... I know I scratched 'is neck. It was then I realised that 'e had a beard. I thought 'e might kill me for doing so but 'e just swore at me instead.'

'Did you draw much blood then?'

'I think so, my nails are long.' In confirmation of which she held up her right hand.

'And which side of his neck did you scratch?'

Melanie again held up her right hand. 'The left, m'lady.'

'So afterwards he just fled, I suppose?'

'Yes, m'lady, I was too upset to see which way 'e went.'

'Thank you for what you have been able to tell me, Melanie. I am going to report this crime to the Justice of the Peace. Whoever was responsible for it must be apprehended.'

'I do hope so, m'lady,' Judith interjected. 'What he did to

my daughter was terrible... terrible wickedness.'

'And there's one further matter,' I said. 'I would like to see the place, Melanie, where you were attacked. I don't expect you to take me there, if you can just tell me where to go?'

'I think I know where it happened, m'lady,' Judith again interjected. 'I heard Mel coming back towards the cottage, crying out in distress, and went to meet her. She told me he had his way with her at a spot where we often pick flowers in the spring and summertime. It's not far from the lane leading to the village.'

'You'll show me then?'

Judith nodded.

5

A crime scene

Leaving Melanie in the care of her father, Judith led Harry and me along a narrow but clearly well-trodden footpath that rapidly entered a small wood, forming part of the estate. I even thought I knew the spot where the attack had taken place, and we reached it in little time at all. I was not looking for anything in particular, but it occurred to me that it was just possible that Melanie's assailant had accidentally left something at the scene of his crime that might help identify him. I also thought a careful inspection of the general locality might just throw some light on whether he had come on foot or by horse.

'I believe this must be the place m'lady,' Judith said, pointing at a profusion of wild flowers, particularly blue bells.'

'And look,' Harry added, pointing towards the ground ahead of us. 'Isn't that a bundle of picked flowers? They must have been dropped when the attack took place.'

'The ground also looks to have been somewhat flattened,' I said. 'Let's look around carefully. Melanie's attacker might just have left something here, which could help identify him.' Harry immediately gave me a sceptical glance. 'I know it's not likely,' I added, 'but we still need to make certain. And look for footprints, too. The ground is still soft from recent rain so as he was wearing boots he'll have left his mark, of that we can be sure. He's also most likely to have come from the direction of the lane, don't you agree, Harry?'

'I do m'lady. And if he was a gentleman, he could well have arrived by horse, I would imagine. He took quite a risk, too. Both the lane and footpath are well used...'

'True enough. But tell me is there anywhere between here and the cottages where the footpath is visible from the lane? You see, I'm thinking that this must have been an opportunistic attack. After all, he can have hardly known in advance that she'd come here.'

'Unless she's not being entirely truthful, about what happened m'lady... Forgive me, I'm not doubting she was ravished, but it could have been by someone known to her whom she is choosing to protect with this... this...'

'... far-fetched tale.'

'Yes, m'lady.'

'My daughter's an honest girl!' Judith protested.

'Even more to the point, I don't believe Melanie had the guile in her to have made it up,' I added. 'No, I think the events are as she's described them to us. So, what do you think; is there somewhere where the footpath is visible from this lane?"

'Um, yes, m'lady. I believe there is,' Judith answered.

Our search of the scene of the crime then failed to produce anything, and nor was it easy to distinguish any particular foot-prints as it was apparent that several people must have passed the same spot in the recent past. However, as we then walked towards the lane, I could see a distinct set of what looked to be recently made footprints, which were well spaced out, suggesting that whoever had created these had been running. Then, as we approached the lane, we came upon a spot where there was a young sycamore tree and the first signs of a horse's shoes marked out in the earth.

'He must have tethered his horse to this tree,' I said. 'Look, the hoof marks extend towards the lane. Now, if you can show me where he might have had a view of the girl.'

We walked on towards the lane, and then along it until we reached a spot where some tree felling had opened up a view that extended as far as the footpath. I thought that he could have got a sight of her, whichever direction he was travelling in, and I said as much.

'As needs must he could just have turned his horse about,' I added. 'Mind you, I think it likely that he had some knowledge of the locality. Otherwise, by the time he'd found a suitable place to tether his horse, he might still have struggled to find her.'

'M'lady, do you think he could be a highwayman?'

'Yes, possibly, Harry, that would make some sense, I agree. However, I've heard no reports of any highway robberies in this area, but he could have come some distance, for all we know.'

Both of us were also aware that the straitened times in which we lived had turned some men, former cavaliers, who had fought for the King and lost everything as a consequence of years of war, to a life of crime. It also occurred to me that they would certainly be hardened and perhaps even depraved by their experiences. For the present, though, this could be nothing more than speculation, and feeling both physically and emotionally drained as well as in need of something to eat, I decided that any talk of finances with Harry could wait for another day.

Come the morning, I would keep my promise to Melanie

and report the crime against her to William Crabb, who was the local Justice of the Peace, for all that it was not a prospect that I welcomed as I thoroughly disliked the man. In the meantime, my last act before going to sleep that night was to offer a fervent prayer to God that Melanie was not now with child.

6
Local knowledge

The following morning brought more rain and an apparently strengthening wind, and with it a distinct ebbing in my resolution to report the previous day's crime. In better times, before the established order had been turned on its head by civil war, I would have expected Olivia's brother, James, to have been appointed Justice of the Peace for the area. Now, however, under the rule of Parliament, that position had been bestowed upon a mere merchant, and all because he had fought on the Parliamentary side and was a devout Puritan.

Not surprisingly, therefore, there was no love lost between us. I thought him a small-minded individual with a squeaky voice, which I found thoroughly irritating. I would also have to ride through the rain to Ottery St Mary, two miles away, with no guarantee of finding him at home. Even supposing that he was, I also strongly suspected that he would be unresponsive to my report, and certainly incapable of doing anything positive to bring the perpetrator of the crime to justice.

The alternative possibility was to report the crime to the deputy parish constable, Josiah Watts, who lived no more than ten minutes brisk walk away in the nearest village of Tipton St John's. He was an altogether more amenable individual, albeit that he had too great a liking for his beer and was getting on in age. This left me to reflect sadly that whoever had committed the attack on Melanie might well continue to roam free unless he attempted to ravish another woman and was caught in the act.

'My greatest concern is that he'll strike again,' I confessed to my maid, Mary, as I sat in front of my walnut framed mirror, allowing the girl to comb my hair. 'I see no point in informing the likes of William Crabb of what has occurred, but we must walk into the village together so I can seek out the deputy constable. He needs to spread the word that every woman and girl living here must be on their guard. I've also a mind to speak to the vicar. Sunday will be with us in two days time and he can reinforce the same message from the pulpit. Now, fetch me my pale-blue day dress and walking shoes. Oh yes, and I will need my broadest rimmed hat and also my thickest woollen scarf to help keep the rain and wind at bay.'

Fortunately, by the time we were ready to depart, the rain had slackened to nothing more than a slight drizzle and the wind also fallen away to a gentle breeze. 'The sky is brightening from the west, Mary. I expect we will soon have some sunshine.'

'I do hope so, m'lady.'

'We must also call on Melanie to see how she is fairing. And I need to speak to Harry, but let that wait until we have returned from the village.'

'Yes, m'lady.'

As we then walked along I grew pensive. I was still wondering whether the man responsible for the attack on Melanie was likely to have possessed some local knowledge. A passing stranger on a horse might, of course, have simply happened to spot her walking along, but, as I had declared the previous evening, by the time he had reached the sycamore tree to dismount, he would surely have been left guessing as to where to look for her. However, luck might again have been in his favour, and nor would he have had to go far in order to find her, so in truth I could not be certain that my supposition was correct. All the same, he would now be bearing a scar on his neck where Melanie had scratched him, and as she had drawn blood it would surely be a few days at least before the scar faded away.

'You know, Mary, I've been thinking that Melanie could well have been ravished by a man with local knowledge, and I told you she scratched the left side of his neck. So, if we could find a man bearing such a scratch mark, he'd likely be our culprit. Mind you, there's no time to lose before the scar's gone.'

7
A well-dressed stranger

The village of Tipton St John's was an ancient one with a population of only about a hundred souls, including children, in addition to which there were perhaps that number again living on the surrounding farms and upon my own estate. I knew pretty much all of them by sight and I could think of no man who would possibly fit Melanie's description. However, there were also two other villages, each less than two miles distant, Venn Ottery to the south west and Harpford to the south, with somewhat smaller populations. A little further distant, there were yet more villages, I could name, but I thought it less likely that any of their inhabitants would possess any intimate knowledge of the lanes and foot-paths around my estate.

Although it was by now mid-morning, I still found Josiah at home and we had barely exchanged greetings before he mentioned Melanie's ravishment.

'It was the talk of the ale house, last night, m'lady.'

'Was it indeed?' Not that I was really that surprised as I knew that word of mouth was capable of carrying such news throughout the village in no time at all. 'In any event, I would like you to spread the word, especially to outlying farms that won't yet have heard what's happened, that for the time being it's dangerous for any woman to be out on their own. I fear this man is capable of striking again. According to Melanie, he was dressed in a gentleman's attire, was young, and wore a brown beard. I also believe he may well have possessed a horse.'

'Right, m' lady.'

'There's something else you should know. The girl tells me that she scratched the left side of the man's neck so I would ask you to spread word of that, too, and, of course, be alert to any man you might see, either bearing such a scar, or keeping his neck covered.'

'Yes, m'lady, I'll gladly do so.' He then smiled at me deferentially, revealing a number of missing teeth.

'And one more thing; can I rely on you to pass the news of what's occurred to the constable in Ottery St Mary, Thomas Godsall?'

'Yes, m'lady.'

'It's not as if it's all that far from here, so I think women living there should be made aware of the risk of another attack, and Thomas also needs to be told about the scratch mark on the neck. He'll need to be spoken to quickly, mind.'

'As it happens, he's due here tomorrow.'

'What, in the morning?' Watts nodded. 'All to the good, then. Tell him when he arrives. And I can alert your fellow deputy, Matthew Smith, in Harpford, when I next visit Fetford Hall. I was only there yesterday but I'll still call again tomorrow. That just leaves Venn Ottery. Am I right in thinking there's no deputy serving there at the moment?'

'Ye are, m'lady, but again as it happens, Thomas and me 'ave work to attend to there...' He dropped his voice. 'It's the village's miller; he's behind with his taxes, you see. In any event,

I'll spread the word at the same time, don't you worry.'

'Thank you. Let us just hope that whoever committed this foul crime was just a passing stranger and will never return.'

I then walked on in the direction of the church rectory where I was told by the vicar's wife that he had been gone an hour or more with the intention of giving the last rites to one of the oldest women in the village, Kate Samprey, who had been ailing for some weeks and was now very close to death.

'I expect he'll be back soon.'

I was disinclined to wait, and was about to ask the good woman to relay a message to her husband when, sure enough, he appeared, looking as affable as ever. William Darcy, now in his early fifties, had been vicar of St John's church for the best part of twenty years and was a kind-hearted soul whom I had grown fond of with the passing years. His sermons were also never pompous or too long-winded and he possessed a dry sense of humour, which did not take either himself or the world too seriously.

I thought that it was such an outlook that had probably helped to preserve his faith, even through the dark years, which had seen the execution of not just the King, and with it the disestablishment of the church, but also the execution of the Archbishop of Canterbury. Parliament, too, had sought to replace the Book of Common Prayer with the Directory for Public Worship. However, to his credit, so far as I was concerned, William had calmly refused to have any truck with this change and still made use of the former.

My only reservation about his character lay in the fact that he had chosen to swear the oath of engagement pledging his loyalty to the new commonwealth, even though I knew that in his heart he was a loyalist. That he had done so in order to preserve his living had displayed a certain lack of courage that I had found a shade disappointing. All the same, I could not really blame him, given the large family which he had to support. Having been left a widower at forty with four surviving children, he had quickly re-married, and his second wife had now given him three more children, still all under the age of twelve.

'Good morning, vicar, I expect you may have heard by now that Melanie Tunnicliffe has been ravished by a masked man.'

He looked at me in surprise. 'No, I have not.'

'Forgive me, vicar, it only happened yesterday afternoon but news travels quickly in this village. Josiah Watts was already aware of what had happened when I spoke to him not many minutes ago.'

'Well I have been attending to the needs of the dying. Kate Samprey has now passed away, God rest her soul.'

'I'm saddened to hear that, vicar, she will be missed.' I then went on to explain what exactly had befallen Melanie, as well as my suspicion that her attacker had local knowledge and my fear that he might strike again. 'Josiah has promised to ensure that outlying farms are informed of what has happened and you would naturally expect that all women would wish to be especially cautious. Even so, it would not go amiss for you to emphasise the need for vigilance when you come to preach on Sunday.'

'I shall gladly do so. I must say that in all my years as vicar here, I can never remember such a heinous crime being committed before. Are you certain the girl is telling the truth?'

'Vicar, I think certainty a very precious commodity, but I

38

doubt if she has the wit to have made up such a tale. I must also trust to the evidence of my own eyes when it comes to the footprints and hoof-marks that I discovered.'

'Then I pray that it was merely an isolated event and whoever was responsible will never strike again.'

'Amen to that, vicar.'

Before returning to the Manor, I decided upon one more visit, informing Mary that I needed to see Jacob, the Blacksmith. 'My mare, Hera, is in need of shoeing and I want to see if he is able to do the work for me this afternoon.'

Jacob Potts was another individual whom I had come to know quite well since my arrival at the Manor. At that time he had only recently succeeded his late father as the village blacksmith and he had continued in that role ever since. Undoubtedly hard working and competent, with a wife and five surviving children, he was normally a man of few words and had a rather dour temperament. All the same, he was always polite and I had never seen any malice in his character.

His oldest child, as I recalled, was also a girl, who was close to Melanie in age, having been a two year old infant, when I first set eyes on her. After he had confirmed that he would be pleased to carry out the necessary task for me that very afternoon, I therefore decided to mention Melanie's sad fate and although I had made no plan to do so also asked him a question.

'I don't suppose you happened to see any stranger ride through the village yesterday?'

'More than that, m'lady, one came to me as his horse was in urgent need of shoeing. 'E was nigh on lame, 'e was.

'So it was a stallion then?'

'Aye, m'lady, much like your own horse in colour, 'e was, but two hands taller, I would say.'

'And as to the man, can you describe his appearance?'

'He had a well-trimmed beard. Brown in colour, it was, and 'e was quite handsomely dressed...'

'So you'd describe him as a gentleman then?'

'Oh aye, m'lady, his doublet looked to be best quality to me, and his collar was made of lace. 'E had a fine pair of leather boots, too, and his hat was well made, I'd say.'

'And his age, what would you say to that?'

'Young enough, m'lady. 'E never took his hat off but I doubt if 'e was more than thirty-five.'

'I see. And he spoke well, I take it?'

'Aye, m'lady... I'd say so but still 'e be a man of Devon...'

'From his accent, you mean?'

'Aye, m'lady. It wasn't strong mind, but still I noticed it. 'E mentioned 'e was on his way to Honiton, but didn't tell me where 'e'd come from.'

Such a description so closely matched Melanie's, that I felt an immediate conviction that this was likely to be the same man who had ravished her. I then searched my mind for anything else that might identify him and came up with some more questions. The hat, Jacob recalled, had been dark-brown in colour, but he was unable to be any more precise, and he had seen no scar on the man's neck. However, it had not been long after midday when he had turned up and it had been much later in the afternoon when Melanie was attacked.

'But wait, I do recall that he 'ad a scar under his left eye. It ran down his cheek as far his beard.'

'Do you now. And was he bearing arms at all?' I finally asked.

'No, I don't think so, m'lady. None that I saw. He had a large saddle-bag, though, but I can't say what was inside it.'

'Thank you, Jacob, you've been most helpful.'

8

Remaining vigilant

The following morning I once again rode over to Fetford Hall. On this occasion, the weather was decidedly inclement with frequent showers, one of which was heavy enough to give me a good soaking before it was borne away on the wind. I very much doubted if word of what had befallen Melanie would yet have spread this far, and I looked forward to telling Olivia the whole intriguing story.

The girl's fate was undoubtedly a sad one, I reflected. Yet, I was honest enough with myself to accept that the mystery surrounding the perpetrator, had, if only for the worst of reasons, brought a little diversion into my otherwise predictable and narrowly focused existence. I also reflected that since my husband's death, without Olivia's friendship and that of her family, I would have gone quite mad; not so much with grief but sheer boredom.

The first person to greet me upon my arrival happened to be James. He was no more than an inch or two taller than I was and stockily built. I had always thought him handsome, with a well-proportioned face and a ready smile, and believed Becky to be a fortunate girl to have won his heart. What at first made me stare at him, though, was the thought that at first glance he could easily have fitted the blacksmith's description of the stranger who had come to his forge on the day of Melanie's ravishment. Not only was he young, but he also wore a neatly trimmed light brown beard and, as was to be expected of a man of his station, was dressed like a gentleman. I was fairly certain, however, that the blacksmith would have known him, and above all I quickly realised that he possessed neither any scar on his face or scratch mark on his neck.

'Good morning, Jane,' James said to my brightly. 'I trust you are well? You're looking at me as if you've just seen a spectre.'

I felt an instant flush of embarrassment. 'Oh James, do forgive me, I was lost in thought. You accomplished everything you wanted to in Honiton, I hope?'

James smiled at me, a little mischievously, I thought. 'Why, yes, very much so, thank you. And I am sorry to have missed you. Mother and Olivia told me you had paid us a visit in my absence. In any event, it's good to see you back again so soon.'

'It's partly because I wanted to see Deputy Constable Smith in Harpford and perhaps your vicar, too. You see, a terrible crime has been committed.'

'What, murder?'

'No, thank God, but still bad enough. The sixteen year old daughter of one of my tenants has been ravished by a masked stranger.'

'Really, a masked stranger, indeed. What a rogue. You must tell us more. Mother and Olivia will be pleased to see you, as ever.'

As a stable boy took Hera away to the stables, James ushered me indoors and Olivia immediately came to greet me. 'We did not expect you back so soon,' she declared.

'I'm sorry to impose.'

'Don't be silly, you know perfectly well that you are always welcome here.'

'She has brought us some interesting news,' James suggested, a twinkle in his eye.

'No, James, interesting is not quite the word I would use. Tragic would be far more appropriate.'

'But you spoke of a masked stranger. That, at least, is intriguing, you must confess.'

Olivia looked bemused. 'I am sorry, what on earth are you both talking about?'

I hastened to explain as succinctly as I could, reflecting as I did so on how many more times I might need to do so, and how easy it was for any tale to grow in the telling. 'I thought at first that the perpetrator must have had local knowledge in order to be able to find the girl,' I concluded. 'Yet he could easily have seen her from the lane, and, from what the black-smith has now told me about the well-dressed stranger that came to his forge on the day of the attack, I think it quite possible that he was the villain concerned.'

Later, after the whole sorry tale had also been explained to Constance, Olivia agreed to ride into Harpford with me; the skies having brightened considerably. It was then that I confessed my greatest concern.

'You know, whatever my fear that the man might strike again, it is Melanie who really concerns me. I may never find herself a husband after what has happened, and if by any chance she is pregnant there will be those who will claim that she cannot have been ravished at all.'

'But that's nonsense.'

'Yes, I agree, but you must be aware of the notion that a

woman cannot become pregnant unless she gives herself willingly to a man. In times gone by, this was widely accepted as being true, and even in this modern age there are still those who cling to old ideas, however fallacious. Whatever, she does not want to find herself having to care for a bastard child.'

'Her family will still support her, surely?'

'I expect they shall, so far as they are able. I'll also do what I can to ensure that no one starves and as a last resort there's always the parish fund. Even so, one act of wilful lust could well have ruined the poor girl's life for ever, and no doubt left her in dread of any man lying with her, even if anyone was willing.'

Once we had arrived in the village, it did not take me long, with Olivia's help, to seek out Matthew Smith and make the same request that I had made of Josiah Watts. Matthew, who was ten years younger than Josiah, was not well known to me but on the odd occasion when our paths had crossed I had still formed a favourable impression of him. After expressing a due measure of shock at what I had to tell him he was quick to promise to alert the village to what had occurred and to keep his eyes open for any man he came across with a scar on his cheek as well as a scratch on his neck.

'Mind you,' I told him, 'the likelihood is that this was an opportunist crime committed by a stranger, whom, pray God, will never come again to these parts.'

'Even so, m'lady, we must be vigilant.'

'Indeed we must.'

This task completed, I was in two minds as to whether or not it was also necessary to approach the village's vicar and said as much to Olivia. However, the words were barely out of my mouth, neither of us having yet remounted their horses, when

I saw him walking towards us from the direction of the village church. Stephen Havelock, in contrast to William Darcy, had only held his position for a matter of months, following the death of his predecessor, and was still a young man in his late twenties. Quite tall and angular in appearance, with black hair and a trim beard to match, I thought him handsome but, all the same, didn't much like him.

'I believe he thinks too highly of himself,' had been my remark to Olivia after first making his acquaintance.

'And nor do I like the way he seems to look down on us through that long nose of his,' Olivia had responded.

It was not just his conceit that failed to appeal but also both his religious persuasion and his politics, for he was both an ardent parliamentarian and an advocate of the Directory for Public Worship, which he had immediately introduced upon taking up his appointment. His whole approach had come as rather an unpleasant shock to his parishioners and there had been mutterings of discontent behind his back. However, if he was aware of these at all, he still seemed to be entirely indifferent to them and Olivia found his over-zealousness even more irritating than I. However, neither of us would ever have dreamed of being anything less than polite to him, seeing civility in all things as an essential virtue.

'Good morning, vicar,' Olivia said to him, brightly enough, whereupon he doffed his hat to us both.

'And a good morning to you, Lady Olivia....And to you, Lady Jane....'

I looked him in the eye, which he returned without flinching and once more I briefly told the story of Melanie's misfortune. Yet the moment I described the attack by a masked man wearing gentleman's clothes, he scoffed at me.

'Why that strikes me as being a tall tale. You don't seriously believe such nonsense?'

'I most certainly do, vicar. I saw how distraught she was.,.. and bruised too. I've also known her since she was knee high and there is no guile in her. There were signs, too, of a man wearing boots having run from where she was attacked and then mounting a horse. He may just have been passing through as the blacksmith in Tipton St John remembers a well dressed stranger on a horse coming to his forge on the day of the attack with a scar on his left cheek. All the same, there must still be a danger that he will seek to attack again so I would be obliged to you if, in church on Sunday, you would warn all women in the village to be especially vigilant. Can I also ask that you keep an eye out for any man you might see with that self-same scar as well as a scratch on the left side of his neck, for Melanie was adamant that she scratched him there.'

'I was not aware, my lady, that you had been made a Justice of the Peace to give me such instructions.'

'I am not doing anything of the kind, vicar. I am merely seeking to protect the women of the parish and asking you as a good Christian to assist me in this endeavour.'

He looked at me sharply. 'Very well. I shall do as you ask.'

'Thank you, vicar, I am grateful to you.'

'And now I really must be on my way, I have a parishioner's needs to attend to.'

As he strode on, Olivia scowled at his back. 'Insufferable man,' she said quietly when he was well out of earshot.

I felt inclined to agree with this sentiment and was grateful for the fact that I did not have to endure the sermons that he

47

delivered in church every Sunday. Olivia often parodied them as being full of hell's fire and brimstone as well as tediously long, and also mimicked the vicar's self-righteous tone, into the bargain. In so doing she made me laugh and altogether lightened my mood as well as reinforcing the bond of friendship between us.

I was now satisfied that I had done all that could reasonably be expected of me to both investigate the crime that had been committed and take the necessary steps to protect the immediate parish. Had my late husband, Paul, still been alive, I was certain that he would have done no less, and, although it might not be seen as being a woman's place to take any initiative in such a matter, the fact remained that circumstances had left me in the role of not just Lady of the Manor but de facto Lord also. The likes of Stephen Havelock might look askance at me for seeking to carry out a task normally considered a male preserve, but they had no power over me, and if Paul's death had brought me any benefit, it was the freedom to act as I saw fit, and in so doing stretch the social conventions that placed so many limitations upon my sex.

9

Travesty

Five days later I once more visited Olivia, hoping to find solace in her company after my spirits had taken a downward turn. I had barely dismounted from Hera when Olivia came rushing to greet me, clearly in an animated state.

'Have you heard the news?'

'No... what news?'

'General Cromwell has dismissed Parliament!'

'What!'

'I tell you, it's true. James has been in Honiton again and has a pamphlet that tells all.'

'In God's name, are we to have a tyranny now?'

'I pray not.'

Once we were inside, Olivia was quick to thrust a copy of the pamphlet into my hands and I read with astonishment a report of Cromwell's speech.

'I like this...*defiled by your practice of every vice; ye are a fractious crew, and enemies to all good government; ye are a pack of mercenary wretches....Ye sordid prostitutes have you not defiled this sacred place....In the name of God, go!* Christ, the nerve of the man!'

'Methinks he and the Reverend Havelock would get on famously. It strikes me they're both full of self-righteous condemnation of lesser mortals,' Olivia declared with a grin.

'And Cromwell the worst of hypocrites, too, if he now intends to rule like a King!'

'Perhaps that's how he sees himself. What do you say to King Oliver the First?'

'I say it would be a travesty. Our true King is Charles the Second; there can be no other.'

10

A second attack

Some four weeks later, I woke early after what had proved to be a restless night, disturbed by a dream that had turned into a nightmare as I imagined myself pursued. I had been riding Hera when some mounted stranger had come towards me, and fearing danger I had fled until Hera stumbled and threw me. Miraculously unhurt, I had then lifted my skirt and begun to run until my chest was heaving, after which I remembered nothing; just a sense of unease, which made me toss and turn until I could stand it no longer.

Rising from my bed I threw open the curtains to discover that there wasn't a cloud to be seen and that the birds were singing happily. The last week had been decidedly wet so it came as a relief to see the sunshine and know that I ought to be able to ride over to Fetford Hall without fear of being drenched by some heavy downpour. On my most recent visit Olivia and I had had to remain inside all day long, although I still recalled the experience with pleasure as we had sung and played the Harpsichord together to our hearts' content.

For a few hours I had even felt more at ease with the world than at any time since Paul's death; my happiness only replaced by one of sadness when I realised that the time had come to go home. Part of me had even wished that I would never have to return to Altringham Manor at all and I had begun to realise that my grief at Paul's death was gradually being overridden by feelings of isolation and loneliness whenever I was there. It was not that I was ever totally alone, of course, as I had my maid Mary and to the lesser extent the other servants to provide me with a measure of company, but it was never the same as having Olivia by my side, or how it had been when Paul was still alive.

As soon as I could do so with a clear conscience that I was not dragging anyone out of bed, I summoned Mary to help me dress, and after no more than a glass of watered beer for breakfast, rode to Fetford Hall, hoping that no one would mind my arriving early. After all, on what remained a very fine day , perhaps they too had decided to rise with the lark. I also had in mind suggesting to Olivia that the two of us ride towards the coast, which was barely three miles to the south of Harpford. We could be in the fishing village of Sidmouth in no time and then take our horses down onto the beach for a gallop so long as the tide was out.

Olivia was enthusiastic about the idea and hurried to get ready to leave. However, I was still in the process of changing into my riding dress when I happened to glance out of the window and was sure that I recognised Stephen Havelock approaching.

'I can't imagine what brings that man here?' Olivia said crossly when I pointed him out to her.

'He looks rather anxious to me.'

'Probably because he understands that we do not like him."

'He'll be looking to speak to James, I would imagine.'

'No doubt.'

The vicar was duly shown into the receiving room by a servant, where he was shortly joined by James. Meanwhile, I and Olivia could, if we had chosen, merely left the hall without further ado. However, curiosity certainly got the better of Olivia, and we decided to interrupt the conversation between the two men by informing James that we were about to depart.

'The vicar has some bad news for us, Olivia,' he immediately told her as we entered the room. 'Another innocent woman has been ravished and her description of the perpetrator matches that given by the previous victim.'

'I confess that I was dubious about the first attack,' the vicar added. 'I thought the girl must have made up my story, but this time he has ravished a respectable matron, Joan Tapton, who has three children. And she, too, told me that he was masked and dressed like a gentleman.'

At that moment I caught the vicar's eye and I could tell that my presence was making him uncomfortable. Much as I was appalled by his news, I also couldn't help but feel pleased on Melanie's behalf that no one could now possibly doubt that she had been telling the truth.

'The woman's husband, Tobias, came to the vicarage yesterday evening,' the vicar continued. 'He told me that she was in a distraught state so I went to visit her in order to give what solace I could in Christ's name. It was getting too late to alert anyone else but first thing this morning I went to the deputy constable's cottage only to discover that he was not at home. I thought to therefore come here. The news of what has happened needs to be widely known.' At this juncture he looked pointedly at me. 'Who knows where and when he might strike again?'

'But what was she doing out on her own?' I asked. 'Surely, after the first attack, every woman in the parish would have understood the threat.'

'Yes, that is so, but the weeks have slipped by since then and the poor woman had not even left her farm. I can hardly blame her for thinking herself safe in her own barn.'

'But wouldn't any of her children have been with her?'

'They were all in the fields helping their father. The youngest is ten now, you see.'

'The perpetrator grows bolder, it seems,' Olivia remarked. 'I just hope he doesn't attack again.'

'I pray so, too. My fear is that if there were to be a next time he might kill,' the vicar said.

'Why do you say that?' I asked him sharply.

'I believe this attack has been more violent than its predecessor. The good matron tried to struggle with him so he hit her hard. There's a massive bruise on her right cheek.'

'And whereabouts is the farm, exactly?'

'It's a quarter of a mile to the south of the village, just by the road.'

'So easily accessed and observed by a passing rider?

'Yes, I suppose it is.'

'Well, I can see to it that news of this attack reaches as far as Ottery St Mary,' I said.

'But if the attacker is mounted he could be coming from as far away as Honiton, or even Exmouth or Exeter, for that matter,' the vicar suggested.

'Should we even seek to alert the entirety of South East Devon to the potential danger it faces?' Olivia asked.

James nodded his head. 'When I am next in Honiton, I can certainly try and speak to the Justice of the Peace, William Crabb,' he declared. ' Even if the perpetrator cannot be apprehended, everything possible should be done to ensure that every woman in South East Devon is aware of these attacks and understands that they need to take care.'

'Well, brother, Jane and I are about to go for a ride. We thought of going as far as the coast. Would you care to accompany us?'

'I would like to but I'm too busy with estate matters, this morning. Mind that you stay together.'

'Oh we will, you need have no fear on that account.'

Polite farewells were then exchanged with the vicar while I continued to sense his discomfort.

'I fancy it did not come easy to him to have to eat humble pie,' I said to Olivia as soon as we had left the hall.

'No, I'm sure it did not. Interesting, though, that he should have said what he did...What were his exact words...oh yes, I fear that if there were to be a next time he might kill.'

'I just pray that they do not prove to be prophetic. But tell me, will we be passing the Tapton's farm on our way to the coast?'

'Yes, we will.'

'Then why don't we visit the scene of the crime. We can offer our felicitations and see if Mistress Tapton is well enough to speak to us. I would quite like to have a look at the barn as well. We might just be able to gather some more useful information. Remember I told you what I was able to discover after the attack on the girl, Melanie.'

Olivia gave me a broad smile. 'I think you're enjoying this.'

'I'm sorry, I don't know what on earth you mean.'

'This hunt for....for clues, of course.'

'I admit I find what has happened intriguing. Not, let me

be clear, that I would wish any poor woman to be ravished by some wicked man.'

'Very well; at least I know the family a little. The husband, Tobias, always strikes me as being a kindly individual.'

'And his wife, Joan?'

'Quite timid, I would say, and likely to be even more so after what has happened to her.'

A short ride brought us within sight of the small farmhouse, and we had our first view of it when we were still some distance away. As we came closer, the farmyard along with the barn, where I imagined the attack had taken place, also came into view, until we reached a point where the entrance to the barn was clearly discernible, and, with its doors standing open, it was quite possible to see inside.

'The perpetrator might well have first caught sight of Mistress Tapton inside the barn from this very spot,' I declared.

'Another opportunist crime then?'

'Yes, I think it must have been.'

'But, all the same, he took a considerable risk. How could he have known she was on her own?'

'By how quiet it was, I imagine; much like today.'

'Even so, someone else could have returned at anytime or simply been inside the farmhouse.'

'Yes, I agree. Perhaps he's an individual who is both impulsive and something of a gambler. And I still wonder if he is in fact a local man, not that that could possibly have given him a knowledge of this family's movements.'

'Unless this crime was in fact more calculated, and he bided his time, observing the family's comings and goings.'

'But then he would have run every risk of being observed

especially if he was in fact mounted. No, I still think it more likely that he seized the moment.'

We continued on our way until we reached the farmhouse whereupon, having dismounted and tethered our horses, Olivia knocked on its door. After a few moments a pretty girl, who looked to be twelve or thirteen years of age, appeared, and instantly recognising Olivia, curtseyed to her, whilst nervously looking downwards as she did so.

'Child, I have come to pay my respects to your mother and I have my friend with me..Lady Jane...May we both come in?'

The girl stepped to one side. 'Ma is very poorly...' she said quietly, her eyes still downcast.

'Of course, we understand that. We will not outstay our welcome too long...'

'If she is able, there are just a few questions that we would like to ask her,' I added as we entered surroundings not dissimilar to those which had presented themselves to me when I had visited Melanie. The family was, though, somewhat more prosperous as evidenced by the solid oak kitchen dresser that presented itself to us. Once upstairs, we also discovered Mistress Tapton sitting up in bed supported by two feather down pillows.

The livid bruise on her face that the vicar had described was only too visible even in the half-light and she was understandably startled by our sudden appearance, although Olivia was quick to put her at her ease, stepping forward with a sympathetic smile and placing a hand on her left shoulder.

'Please forgive our intrusion. We wanted to offer our sincere sympathies. What has happened to you is quite awful...'

'And I am Lady Tremayne. I do not believe we have previously met.'

At first the poor woman seemed lost for words, and I thought that she was about to burst into tears, but then she found the strength from somewhere to control her emotions.

'Tis mighty kind of ye...I'm sure. I'm sorry I don't feel well enough to rise from me bed.'

'Of course you can't...There's no need to apologise. I just wondered if you wouldn't mind telling me what happened?' I asked her. 'Don't worry, if you don't feel well enough to do so.'

Haltingly, her voice tired and sometimes falling away to little more than a whisper, Mistress Tapton described an attack that sounded very similar to the one inflicted upon Melanie Tunnicliffe. The man responsible had taken her by complete surprise, placing a hand over her mouth, and bundling her into a dark corner of the barn where he then had his way with her. When at first she had tried to struggle with him he had hit her hard across the face with a fist, and whispered to her that if she resisted him any further, or made any attempt to cry out, he would strangle her. Such a threat had had the desired effect and she had then simply lain still and silent.

Like Melanie she also said that he was masked, and that from the clothes he wore and the manner of his voice, she took him to be a gentleman, whilst agreeing when I pressed her that it still had the distinctive twang of a man of Devon. She could not, however, say whether he was bearded or not, or even recall the colour or length of his hair, and nor did she recall seeing any scratch mark on his neck. However, given the time that had elapsed since the previous attack, I thought it was likely to have faded away to nothing, anyway.

'And do you recall what type of mask he was wearing?' I asked her. 'Did it cover all of his face?'

'Aye it did. 'Twas black, too. Black leather, I'd say.'

Having wished her a speedy recovery, we then withdrew, although I insisted on inspecting the barn before we finally rode away. 'It's just in case the perpetrator left something behind, be it ever so small, that might give us some tiny clue as to his identity,' I explained.

Olivia looked at me sceptically but I remained determined whereupon the two of us searched the building although Olivia with far less intent than I.

'I really don't know what we're supposed to be looking for,' she complained.

'And nor do I, really. It's just on the off chance. Nothing more, I assure you.'

In the event, we found nothing, so were soon on our way again, encouraging our horses into a steady trot, so that it wasn't long before the sea came into view. I was beginning to perspire vigorously on what was proving a perfect spring day, feeling suitably invigorated, and as we dropped down towards the beach also appreciated the cooling sea breeze. Once there, we found it deserted with the tide well out and decided to race each other, knowing ourselves fortunate to be able to indulge in what some might consider unladylike behaviour.

With our backs to the wind conditions were positively ideal, and I now felt a familiar sense of exhilaration at the sight of the beautifully tall, red, sandstone cliffs, stretching away into the distance ahead of us. Hera, too, was a stronger horse than Olivia's, with both greater endurance and a faster head of speed, so it came as no surprise to either of us that I won the race quite easily.

'It's time we headed back,' Olivia said. 'I'm feeling hungry.'

'So am I, and thirsty too. But, you know, I fear that if that ravisher isn't caught, he's bound to strike again.

'And what was it that the vicar said...'

'...The next time he may kill.'

'One thing, though, he didn't bother with any knife when he ravished Mistress Tapton.'

'No, he probably found it an encumbrance so simply threatened to wring her neck instead.'

'Either way, he needs to be stopped before it's too late.'

'But how, though, when we haven't the least idea who he might be? That's the rub.'

'That's not totally true. You forget what the blacksmith told me.'

'All right, but he didn't recognise the man, and he could have come from twenty miles away, or even further.'

'Yet someone must have seen him on his horse yesterday. Think of the number of people we've passed working in the fields. You simply can't ride about and not expect to be noticed. The chances are they can provide a good description of him that I fancy will match that of the blacksmith's. This could then be circulated and if anyone answering to that description is seen in this vicinity in future, they could at least be asked what their business is and perhaps deterred from striking again.'

'If he's any sense he'll surely not come back anyway.'

'Not to Harpford, I agree, or for that matter Tipton St John, but there are other villages nearby, and I still believe that whoever the man is, he's no stranger to this area.'

'Except that the blacksmith didn't recognise him...'

'I've been thinking about that. God knows, we've lived through hard times with fathers and sons going away to war and never returning; many dead and some in exile with the king, or elsewhere.'

'So....'

'What if one of them has recently returned; enough years having passed for no one to recognise him any longer. He might have ridden away to war as a spotty faced youth without a beard and now he's back, ten years later, hardened by war and used to the company of whores. Such a man might be capable of these crimes, might he not?'

'I suppose he might, if his experiences have corrupted him sufficiently, or it was in his blood anyway. But this is only supposition unless... Have you anyone in mind in fact.'

'Not yet, no. Of course, we know plenty of households that lost loved ones in the wars but I am trying hard to think of any wealthy families that might still have any sons who are in exile or simply unaccounted for. They might even have been wrongly presumed to be dead...'

'All the same, the country has now been at peace for more than eighteen months.'

'Quite so; I agree that is getting late in the day for someone to return, Lazareth like, from the grave. Yet wars scatter people far and wide and, who knows, he might have spent that time recuperating from his wounds.'

'And what about our steward's suggestion that it could be a highwayman; do you give any credence to that?'

'I would give it more if we had received any reports of such activity taking place in this area. As far as I am aware, though, there have been none.'

'You still can't be certain of that. When James speaks to the Justice of the Peace he can ask him what he knows.'

'Very well, that would be sensible. And what I would also ask of you, Olivia, is that you seek out Deputy Constable Smith as well as your vicar and ask them both if they will do all they can to encourage people to come forward with any description they may have of a well-dressed stranger on a horse seen riding about in the vicinity yesterday. As I say, someone will have had a good view of him, they must have.'

11

Tatcham Hall

A week had passed and I had come again to Fetford Hall where I and Olivia decided that we would play music together on what had become a wet and miserable day. First, however, Olivia had some news to impart. More than one person had come forward to say that they had seen a well-dressed man riding a horse in the vicinity of the Tapton's farm on the day of the ravishment. No one had had that close a view of him, but no witness had said that he looked more than forty, and all had referred to his trim brown beard. The two of us agreed that this was entirely consistent with the descriptions given by both Melanie and Mistress Tapton as well as that of the blacksmith.

'The word now needs to be spread far and wide for everyone to be on the alert to the presence of any stranger answering to this description,' I said. 'Hopefully, people will pay due heed.'

'I'm sure they will, but I'm bound to tell you that my brother has spoken with the Justice of the Peace and he has no knowledge of any highwayman being active in this part of the county. Have you given any more thought to what you said last week; I mean, about your conjecture that whoever is responsible could be someone recently returned to these parts after a long absence?'

'Yes, I have and one possibility has come to mind. You know the widower, Sir George Sumner of Tatcham Hall?'

'I do but that's well north of here and he must be nearly seventy, if he's a day.'

'True and plagued by gout, so I hear. Even so, it's not so far that you couldn't make an early start and ride there in half a day. There was also a time when he owned a house along with some land near here, which I believe he then sold. In any event, he had two sons...'

'Who, as I've heard, are both dead.'

'Ah, but are they, though?'

'Well one surely is. Didn't he die at Naseby?'

'By all accounts he did and I've no reason to doubt that's true. However, I'm not so sure what happened to his younger brother, or in fact half-brother, for Sir George married twice...'

'And twice left a widower.'

'Yes, sad for him, I know, but my point is that the younger brother, if he lives, would only be in his late twenties.'

'But what reason have you for thinking he's still alive?'

'No positive reason at all, but on the other hand you can't just assume someone is dead simply because you haven't seen or heard from him for several years.'

'True enough, but I thought...well, that like his older brother he was killed. Wasn't it in fact somewhere in Wales in '48 during the Second Civil War. I even recall thinking, when I heard the news, that poor Sir George would very likely be struck down with grief, for he'd very recently lost his second wife, the boy's mother.

'But I think this was only ever a rumour. I've never heard Sir George confirm that he died.'

'Nor I, but then again I don't think I've even set eyes on him for at least two years. What about you?'

'It must be nigh on a year ago now.'

'And even if his son is alive, where's he been all these years?'

'Sir George is a wealthy man and I believe has estates in Ireland. We know that Parliament regarded those who fought for the king in '48 as no better than renegades. If Sir George's son...'

'What was his name?'

'Thomas, I'm sure that was his name. Anyway, if in fact he survived, he might have fled there...'

'If that's the case, I doubt if it would have given him any peace, for we know General Cromwell took an army there three years ago, which crushed those forces still loyal to the king?'

'Quite so; all of which might explain why Thomas could now have returned home. Indeed, he might have done so at anytime in the last year without our knowledge.'

'Well, perhaps that's the case, but even if what you say is true that doesn't make him a ravisher.'

'No, I'll grant you that.'

'And anyway the description is too vague. It could even make James a suspect, couldn't it.'

'Except that we know for certain that he was at home when Mistress Tapton was attacked... And the man at the blacksmith's had a scar on his cheek.'

For a moment Olivia looked incensed. 'So you're telling me you have considered him a possibly suspect!'

'No... I mean I was relieved to be able to discount any such possibility. Look, I'm sorry, Olivia, I swear to you that I have no desire to point the finger at any man without strong evidence.

We must, though, do everything in our power to protect our community, otherwise every woman remains in danger. He may yet grow bolder and even break into someone's home. None of us can therefore lie safe in our beds until he is caught.'

'I suppose you are right. And this Thomas, what if he is still alive and living with his father. Would you have him questioned by the Constables?'

'Yes, I think I would, but first we need to find out whether he lives or not. I thought I'd therefore ride over to Tatcham Hall and pay Sir George a courtesy visit. Will you come with me?'

'I'm not sure. You live that much closer and if we just turn up unannounced who's to say he'd even receive us.'

'I think he would so long as his health is not too bad. As I recall, he still has an eye for the ladies, and he was always well disposed towards Paul.'

'But start asking intrusive questions and he could quickly become angry.'

'We...I...would have to tread carefully, I grant you, but I think I'm capable of tactfully moving the conversation round to the whereabouts of his son, at least. If he then says that he knows him to be dead, or failing that overseas, then that would be the end of the matter.'

'So when were you thinking of visiting Sir George?'

'The day after tomorrow. Hopefully the weather will have improved somewhat by then. Do say you'll come, too.'

'Very well. You'll want me by mid-morning, I take it. We'll have quite a ride ahead of us after that.'

'Yes, come as early as you can.'

'And should we ride side-saddle, do you think, for propriety's sake?'

'I don't see why. Once we've dismounted and our dresses are buttoned up no one's the wiser that we're wearing breaches underneath.'

12

A face at the window

Tatcham Hall was larger even than either Altringham Manor or Fetford Hall and had been built of red brick about seventy years previously, in what one might term the heyday of good Queen Elizabeth, in a position which gave it a dominating presence over the surrounding area.

'I fear Sir George must live a lonely existence in such a place,' Olivia remarked as we came within sight of it.

'He has his servants, of course, some of whom must have been in his service for many years.'

'They're not family, though, are they?'

'Of course not... Unless perhaps he has some company in his bed.'

'At his age and in poor health, too, surely not?'

'I still wouldn't discount it. I fancy he was handsome enough in his youth and didn't I tell you he still has an eye for the ladies.'

'An old lecher then?'

'Perhaps. It's possible anyway. Otherwise, he could indeed be a very lonely old man and either way probably not long for this world.'

Once we had reached our destination and dismounted from our horses, we were quick to button up our dresses, and I then knocked on the hall's stout front door. Meanwhile, Olivia held the reins of our two mounts, both of which were tired and in need of water after their long ride.

At first it seemed as if no one was going to respond so I rapped on the door again. Seconds later I heard the steady tread of feet approaching from within, and then the door swung open. The man who confronted us was all but bald, red faced, and bore a large bulbous nose, which made him look decidedly ugly. It was not Sir George, though, but rather his steward, David Carew, who instantly recognising me, gave me a bow. He had been in Sir George's service since long before I first came to Altringham Manor, and I imagined he must by now be in his late fifties. Further, his ugliness was at least compensated for by the kindly twinkle in his eye as well as his ready smile.

'Good day to you, Carew. Lady Olivia and I wondered if Sir George was at home and well enough to receive visitors? We would not wish to intrude on his hospitality, of course, but we happened to be passing and thought we would take the opportunity of offering him our felicitations. Our horses are also in need of water.'

'The master is presently resting, m'lady, but if you would care to step inside I'll tell him you're here. I'll also see to it that your horses are attended to, m'lady.'

'Thank you, Carew. That's most kind of you.'

The hall we entered was quite a spacious one, with a tall, decorated plaster ceiling and ahead of us a fine, walnut veneered staircase. Unlike my own hall, which was altogether smaller, ample light was also provided by an oriel window behind the staircase. I have a tendency to impatience if I'm kept waiting for too long but in the event this did not become a concern as Carew promptly returned.

'The Master will be pleased to receive you,' he announced. 'If you would kindly follow me.'

We were taken through into the parlour, which possessed even grander proportions than the hallway, with several curtained windows, as well as a magnificent stone fireplace with a coat of arms emblazoned on the wall above it. For all that it was now late May, there was also a fire burning, which was no doubt wise as otherwise I fancied that the room would still have felt decidedly chilly.

The instant Carew announced us, Sir George rose from his chair, which was placed in front of the fireplace and came to greet us. It was noticeable to me that he needed the aid of a stick to be able to stand and walk, and I was immediately struck by how much he appeared to have aged in the time which had elapsed since our last meeting. Like his steward he had lost a good deal of his hair, and what remained was now snowy white, whilst his face had also become deeply lined, especially around the cheeks and eyes, giving him an altogether aged appearance. I also thought that he looked noticeably thinner. All the same he gave my a ready smile and seemed genuinely pleased to see me.

'My dear Lady Jane, this is an unexpected pleasure. And Lady Olivia, too. My, I thought I was destined to spend another quiet day dozing in front of the fire, but how wrong I was. So what, pray, brings you to Tatcham Hall?' he asked with a ready smile that exposed several blackened teeth.

'It is very good of you to receive us, Sir George,' I said. 'We decided to come for a ride in this direction and thought that if you were at home you might not object to our paying you a short visit with a view to enquiring after your health.'

He smiled at us both again although this time more wistfully. 'As you can see I am an old man now and my bones ache, but at least the gout that has been plaguing me of late is not too bad today, so I mustn't complain. Would you care to drink some wine with me?'

Both I and Olivia promptly accepted this invitation and Carew was sent away in search of a suitable bottle from the wine cellar together with some glasses. It was also obvious to me that Sir George was actually delighted to be able to enjoy our company and I made a resolution to visit him again. Further, over a glass of red wine imported from Bordeaux, it proved easy enough to steer the conversation onto the topic of the two recent ravishments about which Sir George showed commendable concern. However, I hesitated over asking any direct question about the whereabouts of his son; still uncertain that the right moment had arrived when I could tactfully do so. I frequently glanced at Olivia, too, sensing that she was willing me to come to the point. Eventually, it seemed she could stand it no longer; Sir George having paused the conversation to take a long sip of wine.

'I hope you have good news of your son, Thomas, Sir George?' Olivia asked. 'Hasn't he been in Ireland these last few years?' The question was enough to cause him to splutter a little and look thoroughly discomforted for the first time since our arrival.

'Yes, he... he's still there,' he replied very hesitantly after a long pause. 'Not, mind, that I've heard from him for quite a while. He's no friend to either Parliament or this confounded General Cromwell, damn the man...'

'Here, here to that, Sir George,' I piped up.

'I'm glad we're of one mind. God save King Charles the Second, I say.'

'Yes, God save him,' I and Olivia both responded as one.

'In any event, communication's far from easy and letters can all too easily be opened. I know many people even think him dead and perhaps it's best that they continue under that misapprehension. One day, though, when our good King is able to sit upon his throne...I fear I shall be long dead by then, of course.'

'No surely not, Sir George. You must still have many years ahead of you,' I declared optimistically.

'You flatter me, my dear. If I see two more years out, I'll be surprised.'

As soon as we had finished our glasses of wine I glanced out of the window and then at Olivia, before announcing that it really was time that we turned for home.

'I have much enjoyed your visit,' Sir George declared. 'Do feel free to come again whenever you wish. You'll appreciate that I don't get too many visitors these days and in your fair company I almost feel young again.'

'Thank you for your hospitality, Sir George, I will certainly do that,' I said and meant it.

'You'll excuse me if my steward shows you out. I have a little pain in my legs.'

'Of course, Sir George, of course.'

A few moments later as we were mounting our horses, I noticed that Sir George had come to a window and I offered him a wave of the hand, which he returned with a smile. I then happened to look up and just for an instant thought I saw another face looking down at me. My view of this individual was so fleeting, however, that I could not even have sworn to their sex although my impression was that it was a man and a fairly young one at that. Assuming that it must have been a servant, I and Olivia then rode away.

'So you were right then,' Olivia remarked after we had travelled only a short distance. 'Thomas still lives.'

'Except that it would seem he's in Ireland.'

'You sound disappointed.'

'Only to the extent that I cannot think of who else might have been responsible for the attacks.'

'Unless the net can be spread yet wider. Look as far afield as Honiton or even Exeter, and the hand of suspicion could no doubt be pointed at scores of men.'

'That I accept. Yet I still cannot believe that the culprit has come so far from any direction, even if it's physically possible.'

'Ah yes, local knowledge,' Olivia observed. 'But that could have been acquired in the past. It does not mean that he has to be living in the locality at the present time.'

'And that's precisely the logic that caused me to be suspicious that it could be Sir George's son.'

'Well, at least our visit seemed to make the old man happy.'

'Yes, we must try and visit him again. I think he really is very lonely.'

13

An invitation

Two days later, I was sitting in Altringham Manor's long gallery with needle and thread in my hands, mending one of my dresses. I was far from being the best of needlewomen and would have much preferred to be riding, playing my harpsichord, singing or reading. However, in these straitened times mending clothes had become a necessity rather than a choice. At least the light was good as the bright morning sun was shining in through the east facing window, next to which I was sitting. When I cared to glance outside there was also, as ever, a fine view over the hall's ornate Italian garden that my late father-in-law had had laid out, and beyond that the rolling countryside, which I had come to love, now in full bloom.

Ever since Julia and I had visited Sir George I had been largely preoccupied with such routine domesticity, and at times had quite put to one side any thought as to what could possibly be done next to apprehend the ravisher. Yet the fear remained that he might strike again at any time and I felt a nagging sense of frustration that his identity remained a mystery. All that I could hope was that the community was now properly on its guard and would continue to be so. In that event, if such a wickedly lustful individual was still driven to attack again, I could only trust that he would overreach himself and either be caught in the act or give away his identity. Of course, unless he moved on to pastures new, the danger he posed to the community might still be present a year hence or more, by which time people might well have become careless once again, falsely imagining that women were no longer at risk.

Losing concentration on the task at hand, I then managed to prick myself in the finger, drawing a tiny amount of blood and causing me to exclaim loudly in annoyance, taking the Lord's name in vain as I did so. It was at this precise moment that my personal maid, Mary, made an appearance.

'Begging your pardon, m'lady,' she said nervously as I looked up rather crossly.

'Yes, Mary, what is it?'

'A letter has come for you, m'lady.'

I quickly took it from her and having broken the seal began to smile even as I read the letter's contents.

'Sir George Sumner has invited me to dine with him this coming Saturday. Is whoever delivered the letter still here?'

'Yes m'lady.'

'Then you may tell him that I am pleased to accept the invitation. And Mary...'

'Yes, m'lady.'

'I shall need you to accompany me. You can ride the pony, Persephone.'

14

Amorous attraction

We were invited for about midday and with still a mile to travel, I was mildly concerned that we were going to be late. I was by nature a punctual individual and when we had set out I had thought that I had allowed us ample time to arrive by the appointed hour. However, Mary was still a novice rider and to compound this Persephone could be a temperamental creature and something had upset her enough to make her difficult to manage. Still, in the last mile or so we had been able to make more rapid progress, and in the event were able to continue to do so.

It was also a dry and pleasantly warm day and by the time we reached our destination I was feeling relaxed as well as hungry as I dismounted and looked towards the house. I was instantly reminded of the face I had glimpsed at the window, before being brought up short by a sharp pain in my back. For this occasion I had wanted to look my best, so had ridden side-saddle, only to suffer the consequences of adopting such an unnatural posture.

'Are you all right, m'lady?' Mary asked me.

'Just a little pain in the back, but I'm better now.'

Once again, we were greeted at the front door by David Carew, who showed us into the day room. As before, Sir George was seated in front of the fire, save that this time it was not alight, and he had taken the trouble to don a smart yellow doublet along with a fine white lace collar as well as matching breeches. His hair had also been well combed, helping to make him look a little younger than on our previous meeting, and not for the first time since receiving his invitation I even wondered if he had some intentions towards me. Marriages between old men and far younger women are, after all, not unheard of and could even result in the arrival of children. As a mature widow invited to dine with a man in his late sixties, I had not exactly seen the need for any chaperone, and had assumed there would be other guests, but I still did not expect Sir George to be either surprised or disappointed that I had chosen to be accompanied by Mary. However, he seemed quite put out by her presence.

'My dear, I'm delighted you were able to accept my invitation. There is, though, something I need to speak to you about... in confidence. Carew, here, can show your maid the way to the servants' quarters.'

'Very well.'

Once they had departed Sir George adopted a more apologetic tone. 'Forgive me, but we will not be dining alone.'

'I never expected that we would be, Sir George.'

'One other person will be joining us.'

'Oh, really. And they're expected soon?'

'No, he's already here and should be joining us very shortly. In fact, I think I can hear his footsteps now.'

I turned towards the door and was stunned to see none other than Sir George's son, Thomas, walk through it. We had not set eyes on each other for several years but I still recognised him instantly and was struck both by his manliness and also by how handsome he was. It brought to mind my memories of him as a youth when he was undoubtedly good-looking, but still callow, possessing barely the beginnings of any beard, and with significant acne. Now he had matured considerably, seemed taller than I recalled, and looked me straight in the eye with undoubted self-confidence.

In truth, I felt an immediate degree of amorous attraction. Yet this was tempered somewhat by the reflection that in his late twenties and with a trim beard he was capable of fitting both Melanie's and Mistress Tapton's admittedly meagre descriptions of the man who had ravished them both. I was reminded, too, of the face at the window and decided that it could well have been him.

'Lady Tremayne... , what a pleasure it is to meet you again after all these years.'

His voice was also as attractive as his features and I almost blushed, stunned at first into a bewildered silence as he bowed to me.

'...Thomas...I don't....'

'I am afraid, my dear, that I owe you an apology,' Sir George said. He had risen from his chair and was now standing by my side. 'I wasn't at all frank with you when we last met. Thomas has been living with me here, incognito, since early April.'

'It is important that as few people as possible know that I'm here,' Thomas added. 'My father, however, assures me that you remain loyal to the Crown and can be trusted not to tell tales. I take it that is the case?'

'Of course. On my honour, I will tell no one you're here except....'

'Personal maids are used to keeping their lady's secrets, are they not, ' Sir George, suggested. 'My servants are naturally aware of my son's presence but without exception have known him since he was a boy and have been sworn to tell no one. You must elicit the same oath from your maid. Can you do that?'

'Yes, I am sure I can. She's a sensible girl and I believe I have her loyalty.'

'Excellent,' Thomas declared.

'There is one other person, however....Lady Olivia is a close confidante and I would vouch for her loyalty to the Crown...'

'Tell her, if you must, but, like your maid, swear her to secrecy,' Thomas said. 'And there must be absolutely no one else. We have already taken a calculated risk by drawing you into our little web. It could be immensely dangerous for me if half the county ends up knowing I have returned.'

'You fear arrest?'

'It is possible. General Cromwell undoubtedly has his spies and I am a known renegade.'

'...And when you returned to this country...I take it from Ireland?' Thomas nodded. 'Might you not have been recognised?'

'I doubt it very much. I came disguised on a fishing boat out of Waterford. We came ashore at Bideford on the north coast of the county and I then slipped away. I was quickly able to purchase a horse.'

'I see...' I was seized by a mounting sense of dread at these revelations, not because the man in front of me was deemed by those I mostly detested as a renegade, but rather by the growing fear that he could be capable of ravishing innocent women. Yet looking at his handsome features and what I found to be honest, intelligent eyes, I struggled to countenance any such possibility especially as I could see no scar on his cheeks. Surely, his presence at Tatcham Hall was pure coincidence and nothing more, I concluded. Whatever the truth of the matter, I was also left wondering what exactly was the purpose of Thomas's clandestine return. Perhaps, entirely laudably, it was merely that he wished to be reunited with his ageing father. However, that didn't seem to me to entirely explain why he should have remained for several weeks, presumably behind, or very largely behind, closed doors.

As I continued to ponder this question, Carew announced that dinner was ready to be served and Sir George led me through into the dining room where pewter plates had been laid. Carew, with Mary's assistance, then served generous portions of cooked mutton together with a claret that I found very much to my taste. This was followed by a course of various cheeses, and a second bottle of claret was drunk, not merely lubricating the flow of conversation around the table but also making me feel the tug of Thomas's amorous allure evermore intensely.

Then I remembered my late husband, Paul, and was almost overwhelmed by a mixture of guilt and sadness. In an effort to compose myself, as much as any call of nature, I went to the privy, and when I returned was immediately struck by the exquisite aroma of coffee, a delicacy from the New World, which I had only tasted a few times before, and had found to be very pleasing.

Up until that moment we had talked of the sad state of the world, of the weather, of food, of farming, of trade, and Sir George, not unpredictably, had grown nostalgic for what he saw as the happy days before civil war blighted the nation and the natural order of things was turned quite upside down. At one point it had even crossed my mind to mention the ravishments, as much as anything to gauge Thomas's reaction. However, I had then lost the moment as well as my courage, not wanting anyway to believe that he could possibly be a ravisher, and had become too inebriated by my share of the second bottle of claret to concentrate on any subtle betrayal of emotion that any mention of the subject might induce in him.

Now, the strong taste of coffee helped to sober us all up. Further, Carew and Mary having withdrawn from the room, Sir George and Thomas began to speak quite vehemently of their detestation of Parliament and of General Cromwell in particular.

'I tell you, I would not be in the least surprised if he seeks to make himself King,' Thomas declared.

'What a travesty that would be,' Sir George responded. 'Can you imagine it, King Oliver the First when our true King is none other than Charles the Second, God bless him.'

'We must at all costs continue the struggle on our rightful King's behalf,' Thomas asserted, turning his eyes on me. For a few seconds he held my gaze and I momentarily felt like a girl again, transfixed by his beauty, much as I had once been transfixed by that of my late husband.

'I'll be honest with you,' he started to say. 'Apart from the pleasure of your charming company, you're here because we are willing to draw you further into our confidence and wish to ask a mighty favour of you. Feel free to refuse, of course, and be assured that I would not blame you, for I'd be lying if I did not admit that what I wish to ask of you carries with it a measure of danger.'

'Well, tell me what exactly it is you are plotting and you shall have my answer.'

'Nothing less than the restoration of our rightful monarchy and the death of General Cromwell as well as every other man who signed the late King's death warrant.'

'A noble objective, I'll grant you, but pray, how do you propose to achieve this with the country still exhausted by so many years of war, and when all the power of the State has been taken by General Cromwell and his all conquering army?'

'It will not be easy, I'll grant you that. I've spent the last few years seeing Ireland laid waste by Cromwell's army and any resistance to it has now been all but crushed. Nonetheless, here in England there are still, I believe, many like your good self who remain loyal to the Crown and would be willing to work towards its restoration. I realise that it may take some time to put an effective force together, whilst Cromwell and those who serve his cause are bound to be vigilant. Yet, if we are patient and resolute, I am confident that it can be done. Then, when the time is right, I would wish to see us look to kill Cromwell. With his elimination the whole structure that sustains the present system of government will surely begin to crumble,'

'And what part would you wish me to play in achieving this ambition. I am but a widow living in straitened circumstances, so I certainly cannot provide money to aid your cause.'

'That I fully understand. I ask only that you be prepared to offer a safe house when asked to do so to those engaged in working for Cromwell's overthrow.'

I clenched my hands together and sighed.

'I don't expect you to give me an immediate response,'

he added. 'By all means give my proposal careful thought. I would ask only that you give me your answer within five days from now.'

'And if I do say yes to it, am I to be expected to vouch for the silence of my servants? I do not say that I have any reason to believe that any of them have any sympathy for General Cromwell but what if I am wrong in that assumption.'

'Anyone you were asked to give a bed to would not reveal their true identity but rather would pose as say a cousin of yours. They should also not have to remain under your roof for more than a few days.'

'Um...that might be plausible enough on the first occasion but hardly a second or a third time unless perhaps the same individual returns. And may I ask why they could not be given a bed under your own roof?'

'As I've said, I'm a known renegade, given my activities in Ireland. Should my return to this country also become known, or even merely suspected, then it would not be safe to use this house.'

'So when can I expect this person to arrive; assuming, of course, that I agree to help you?'

'That I cannot say for certain at the moment, but probably in a matter of only a few weeks. It should be possible to give you a few days warning.'

'And am I to be allowed to know this person's true identity?'

' Both for your own safety and his, I think it best that you do not. Suffice it to say that he is a person of some standing who, for all the world knows, is in exile on the Continent. So, please, I would be grateful if you would give my request all due consideration.'

'I can give it more than that. I will be delighted to assist the King's cause in whatever humble way I can.'

Thomas's face broke into a broad smile. 'Excellent! You do understand, though, that if you were to be caught giving succour to those of us working to restore the monarchy, you would certainly be imprisoned..'

'Are you now trying to dissuade me?' I teased him.

'No, far from it. I just wish to be sure that you appreciate that this is no game.'

I looked at him angrily. 'Sir, my beloved husband died fighting for the King. If I ever imagined that this was some game, as you put it, that tragedy put paid to any such delusion.'

'Forgive me, I intended no offence.'

'And none taken, I assure you.'

'I also think it best that you say nothing of this conversation, even to your maid...'

'Very well but I would absolutely vouch for the loyalty of Lady Olivia...'

'Perhaps her then, if you must, but only on a vow of absolute secrecy.'

.....

'Remember, Mary, you are to speak to no one of Thomas's return to this country. Do I make myself plain?'

'Of course, m'lady.'

'In the eyes of those who now rule our country he is a renegade and could be arrested at any time.'

'I understand, m'lady.'

'I hope you do, Mary. He is here out of concern for his father's health, no more, and I expect will be returning to

Ireland shortly.

After this brief exchange I fell into a pensive silence, which I maintained throughout the remainder of our return ride. I was beginning to fear that I had been too precipitate in accepting Thomas's request and also found it impossible to reconcile the attraction I felt towards him with the dread that he could even be a ravisher. I resolved to talk in confidence with Olivia, comforting myself with the reflection that it was not yet too late to change my mind and refuse to become involved in treasonous activities.

15

All in a good cause

'So what do you think I should do, Olivia?'

Another two days had passed and the two of us were alone in the gardens of Fetford Hall where several rows of tulips, the seeds for which had been expensively imported from Holland, were now in full bloom. After some morning rain, which had given me a drenching on my ride from Altringham Manor, the weather had become increasingly warm and sunny, and Olivia had readily accepted my suggestion that we take a stroll. She had also become intrigued when I whispered into her ear that there was a matter of importance that I wished to discuss with her. Then, as I had explained the course of events at Tatcham Hall, and sworn her to secrecy, this had turned to one of distinct concern on my behalf.

'I am not sure it is at all wise to become embroiled in plots. You could end up in Exeter gaol or, God forbid, even in the Tower of London.'

'But aren't we both of the same mind that something has to be done to put an end to General Cromwell's rule, and all I have agreed to do is give shelter for a few days to some unknown man on the pretence that he is my cousin. That is surely hardly treason?'

'Come, Jane, you are deceiving yourself, when you know full

well that this person's sole intent must be the overthrow of the government. If the truth were to come out, you would be found guilty of aiding acts of treason, and dealt with accordingly.'

'So there is some small risk of imprisonment; that I can live with.'

'I think it could be worse than that. You could even be made an example of and hanged'

'God's mercy, you really think that?'

'It's certainly possible.'

'So I should tell Thomas that I've changed my mind?'

'I think it might be wise, if I were you.'

I grimaced and then flung out my hands. 'I must confess I find him most attractive. I don't want to disappoint him and yet I dread to imagine that he could even be a ravisher.'

'You seriously think that?'

'I don't want to countenance it. Yet, according to Sir George he returned from Ireland in early April, he is a gentleman, he has a horse, he wears a beard, and has a measure of local knowledge.'

'And the Blacksmith you told me about...would he have recognised him?'

'He might have, but then again perhaps not. Thomas has changed a great deal...has grown into a man, in fact, whereas he was little more than a boy when he left. In any event, he cannot have been the man who came to his forge for he carries no scar on his cheeks.'

'It's possible, isn't it, that any such scar has had time to fade away. The chances are, if Thomas was that man, his father along with his servants would have noticed it.'

'That's a fair point, I grant you, but how am I to put the

question? I can hardly go to Sir George, accuse his son of being a ravisher, and demand to know whether he bore any scar on his cheeks before the attack in April. No, I must take him as I find him. He is an honourable man, not a ravisher.'

'But you'll still tell him that you'll have no truck with plotting and treason?'

'I don't know. I'll think on what you've said, of course.'

'Well, whatever you decide, I swear that this conversation will go no further.'

16

A visitor

After leaving Olivia to return home, I was in an increasing quandary as to what to do for the best. I had hoped that my friend's advice would be nothing more than an endorsement of what I had already told Thomas, and had certainly not expected her to be so vehemently opposed to his request.

The possibility of being sent to the gallows for aiding an act of treason was also a particularly sobering one and surely enough justification in itself for a change of heart. On the other hand, I did not like to think of myself as a cowardly female, frightened off by the slightest risk of death, when my late husband had died fighting bravely in the King's cause. Nor, for that matter, did I want to go back on my word, however rashly given, especially to Thomas, for whom I continued to feel a powerful sense of attraction. In the end I resolved to sleep on the matter, only to endure a restless night in which I struggled to fall asleep. Further, when morning came I remained undecided on what course of action it was best to take.

By the time I found the energy to summon Mary to help me dress and comb my hair, I was feeling thoroughly out of sorts. Sensing my mood, I suspect, Mary also suppressed her normal good humour and worked away silently, with barely a word passing between us, until she happened to glance out of the window.

'M'lady,' she said. 'I think we have a visitor.'

'What, this early?' I also looked outside and could barely suppress a gasp. 'My, do you see who it is?'

'No, m'lady, I don't think so.'

'You were serving him at table only a few nights ago. It's Thomas Sumner. Hurry, I must finish getting dressed. What on earth can he want?'

A few minutes later I descended the stairs leading to the hallway, doing my upmost to remain calm but all the while feeling a mixture of curiosity and anticipation, tinged, if I was honest, with more than a touch of fear. After all, I thought it more than likely that he had come to announce the arrival of the mysterious stranger for whom he expected me to provide a bed.

'Good morning, Thomas. This is an unexpected pleasure.'

'Forgive the intrusion. May we speak in private...'

'Come through into the library.'

He followed me to its door, whereupon I stepped to one side and let him enter first before closing the door behind us. We then faced each other and I was immediately struck, yet again, by how handsome he looked for all that his eyes betrayed a clear measure of anxiety.

'They know I am here,' he declared. 'A troop of soldiers turned up yesterday but I was able to hide from them. You know the hall's original owners were Catholics and there is a priest's hole. I came here to tell you that for the time being at least I do not expect to be able to proceed with what I was planning. It's already too late, I fear, to prevent the person of whom I spoke from arriving, but I can still seek to be there when he does and hopefully persuade him to return whence he came...'

'And if he will not do so?'

'Then I will have to think again, but I still expect this part of the county to be too dangerous for him to remain in. Do not be surprised either if the troops who are looking for me come knocking at your door...' I felt instinctively alarmed at this prospect and Thomas held up his left hand in a gesture of reassurance . 'Fear not, I have no reason to think that anyone has reported our recent conversation; it is merely that those searching for me will more than likely be looking to spread their net far and wide and every hall and manor will be seen as fair game. They're likely to know, as well, where your sympathies lie, given the fate of your late husband.'

With that he paused and gave me such a gentle and considerate smile that I couldn't help but smile back at him, albeit somewhat coyly.

'Will you take some beer?' I asked him. 'You look flushed.'

'Aye, I've ridden hard so that would be most welcome. Then I'll be on my way.'

After Alice had brought us both jugs of beer, I invited him to sit with me on a bench in the Italian style garden my late father-in-law had had created. In the morning sunshine, with blackbirds and robins singing in the trees, it was possible to maintain the illusion, if only for a short while, that the world was a peaceful, gentle place, entirely at ease with itself. I felt comfortable, too, in Thomas's presence and had a palpable sense that the attraction I had towards him was reciprocated in kind. We sat in a companionable silence, sipping our beer, while I wished that time would stand still. Instead, it was racing on, as ever, and having drunk his fill he was quickly on his feet once more, thanking me for my hospitality and announcing that it was time for him to depart.

'It may be some time before it is safe for me to return, I'm afraid.'

Although not unexpected, the pang of regret I felt as he uttered these words was still palpable. 'I am sorry to hear that. Where will you go?'

'That depends to an extent on what Lord...the man I go to meet, intends, but suffice it to say there are places I know of that will give me shelter. I can only hope to keep one step ahead of General Cromwell's spies.'

'Take care then. And...I will remember you in my prayers.'

He looked intently into my eyes and I found myself wishing that he would embrace me. 'And I will remember you in mine,' he responded. 'God willing, I will return.'

Let it be soon, I thought but did not say, instead leading him towards the stables. Once he was mounted I then wished him 'God's speed' and raised a hand in farewell as his horse trotted away. I continued to stand and watch until he was out of sight, realising even as I did so that there were tears in my eyes as I recalled having done exactly the same thing when Paul had last departed, never to return. Of one thing I was also more convinced than ever. *Thomas is no ravisher*, I thought. *I'd stake my life on it.*

17

A dangerous renegade?

It was late afternoon, the following day, when a body of cavalrymen, twenty or more in number, appeared, all wearing identical yellow-brown uniforms with breast plates and lobster pot helmets, save for one man with a red sash who was presumably their officer. There was also one other man dressed in the dark clothes of a Puritan with a pointed black hat, riding alongside the officer, and this was the individual who I found myself greeting as he entered my hallway. By then he had removed his hat, exposing a greying head of closely cut hair. He was also clean-shaven with a square jaw, a rugged complexion and above all keen, penetrative eyes. Dispensing with any courtesies, even a nod of the head, he came brusquely to the point.

'Madam, I have a warrant signed by the Justice of the Peace to search this house and all its estate. The men with me will perform this task with all due speed and will not seek to inflict any damage.'

'Sir, on what grounds, may I ask?'

'A dangerous renegade, Thomas Sumner, is known to be at large in this vicinity, and every manor is being searched. Yours is no exception.'

'And may I see the warrant?'

'Of course.' He then reached into his pocket and produced

a document bearing the requisite signature, which I barely glanced at.

'Very well, but I can assure you we are not sheltering any renegades here.'

Ignoring my words, the Puritan merely spoke briefly to the officer at his side and the search began. The fact that I had spoken no more than the truth did little to assuage my intense feeling of discomfort. The fact remained that I could very easily have been sheltering Thomas and I feared the possibility of being questioned about my knowledge of him. At the same time, everything about what was happening seemed to me to be a gross intrusion into my life, and I began to feel resentful of the soldiers' presence.

At first the Puritan who had not even bothered to give me his name, continued to ignore me, preferring instead to go about my property supervising the search. However, once this had ended, at least so far as the house alone was concerned, he was quick to ask the question I had been most dreading.

'Can you tell me when you last had any contact with this renegade?'

'I have not set eyes on him in years, sir. I doubt if I would even recognise him.'

My answer was, of course, nothing more than a bare faced lie and even as I spoke, willing myself to appear as outwardly calm as possible, I feared that he would know this, thanks to some disloyal member of Sir George's household having turned informant.

'Be that as it may,' he answered me with a stony stare, 'remember he is a renegade, intent on nothing less than high treason. Anyone found to be associating with him will be seen in the same light. I trust I make myself clear?'

'Perfectly, sir.'

After another half-an-hour spent searching the estate including all its cottages, the troops then departed, and it was only then that I felt that I could breathe properly once more.

18

Murder!

I groaned, wishing that what I had just been told wasn't true. It was a week later and the deputy constable, Josiah Watts, was standing nervously in front of me, his ashen face a picture of distress at what he had so recently witnessed .

'It's a dreadful crime and no mistake. Strangled in her own bed, and by the looks of it I think he had his way with her, too.'

'And how did he gain entry, do you think?'

'He simply walked in through the door to her cottage. She must have forgotten to lock it, or perhaps even left it ajar. You know how hot it's been these last few nights.'

I was also immediately reminded of the vicar's warning that 'the next time he might kill.' That had proved to be all too prescient and would now cause the entire community to be immensely fearful that even more attacks with fatal consequences could follow.

'I know that things have come to a pretty pass, m'lady, when a woman isn't even safe in her own bed,' Josiah remarked, and I nodded my head in agreement.

Margaret Hodge had been a decent, God fearing woman in her late thirties whose life had been blighted by tragedy when she had lost her husband and her three children to an outbreak of dysentery two years previously. She had been spared, although understandably deeply stricken by grief, and to make ends meet had taken to working as a seamstress. Her plight had also attracted a good deal of sympathy and become common knowledge in the near vicinity.

'I can't see this as a random attack, Josiah,' I said. 'Only someone who knew her, or knew of her, would have picked out her cottage amongst so many others in the village. And have you yet started knocking on doors to see if anyone heard or saw anything suspicious?'

''Twas a woman neighbour who alerted me to the crime, m'lady. She called on Mistress Hodge as she often did, so she told me, and when she didn't answer, she tried the front door and found she could enter. It was still early and she hadn't seen or heard Mistress Hodge go out so she was suspicious enough to enter her bedroom.'

'But she'd heard nothing in the night?'

'No, m'lady, she said not.'

'And what of others?'

'I've had no time to enquire. I decided to come straight here.'

'So the body's still where you found it?

'Yes, m'lady.'

'And you're certain she was strangled?'

'There are marks on her neck, m'lady....In fact I think it was broken.'

'Even so, it would probably be best to have a doctor examine her. The Justice of the Peace will need to be informed as well and...and the coroner fetched from Exeter. My, there's much to be done, Josiah.'

'But you'll help me, m'lady?'

'Of course I shall. And I'll speak to my steward. He can

ride to Exeter while I go to Ottery St Mary to fetch Doctor Gladwell...He'll want paying, of course. Will the coroner meet his fee, do you think?

'I don't believe so, m'lady.'

'Then I suppose I'll have to. No doubt I can speak to the Justice, too. In the meantime, I want you to go about the village and ask if anyone heard or saw anything. I'll wager, too, that whoever did this is the same man who committed the ravishments, in which case he'll have been dressed like a gentleman, and probably have been mounted. Oh yes, and bearded, too, I expect, with perhaps a scar on his left cheek.'

'Yes, m'lady.'

'And one more thing...No one should be allowed to enter the cottage...'

'I thought of that m'lady. I've got my son, Abel, standing guard. You know, he's fifteen now and a strong lad.'

19

The corpse examined

By the time I returned to the village with Doctor Gladwell, it was mid-afternoon and I had not been able to speak to the Justice of Peace as he was apparently on business in Honiton. I had, however, been able to leave him a message and given how little we liked each other was far from sorry to have missed him. True to my word, I had also sent Harry to Exeter to alert the coroner, and felt satisfied that I was doing all that I could in the circumstances.

The day's events helped to emphasise to me more than ever how much I was expected to fit into my late husband's shoes. There was no longer a Lord of the Manor in residence, but there was still a Lady, that I supposed people in the village and its surrounding farms looked up to. I'd also had to haggle with the Doctor over his fee, which I found somewhat distasteful. However, when he'd demanded to be paid nothing less than seven shillings and sixpence for his time, I'd thought that outrageous and told him in no uncertain terms that I could only afford to pay him five shillings. I'd then taken a silver crown from my pocket and somewhat to my surprise he had promptly accepted it.

Now I knew that I would have to steel myself at the prospect of having to set eyes on the corpse of the deceased. It wasn't by any means essential that I be present when the doctor carried out his examination, but I had made up my mind that I wished to be so in order as much as anything to have an opportunity of inspecting the scene of the crime. Much as when Melanie was raped I was determined to see if by any chance the murderer had left behind any clues as to his identity.

Above all else, I prayed that Thomas could not possibly have been responsible for the woman's death. I had no idea, of course, where he was at present, and if he was still anywhere within a day's ride of the village then he had to remain a suspect. All the same, I thought it highly unlikely that he would have had any knowledge of the deceased or the whereabouts of her dwelling. Tatcham Hall, after all, lay several miles to the north, and whilst I supposed it conceivable that one of its servants might be familiar with Tipton St John, and that he could have overheard a conversation concerning the deceased, it was surely beyond all credence that he would then have been able to discover precisely where she lived. As such, I concluded that he could not possibly be guilty. Further, I remained confident that whoever had committed the murder was either a local man, or, just possibly, well acquainted with someone living locally, who had unwittingly revealed to him where Mistress Hodge lived.

I had known Doctor Gladwell, now approaching fifty years of age, ever since I had first arrived at Altringham Manor, and we had always been on polite terms with one another. Certainly, I had never had reason to doubt his professional diligence and I thought him quite good looking, if somewhat sallow in complexion. However, he was also rather aloof and inscrutable with little time for small talk, so our journey passed off mostly in silent contemplation until I told him that I wanted to be present when he examined the body, explaining as I did so my belief that whoever had carried out the ravishments had also been guilty of the murder,

'That might well be the case but I can still see no reason for you to be present.'

'But Doctor, I just want to have the opportunity of seeing if the murderer has left any clues as to his identity...'

At that he scoffed at me. 'He'll hardly have left a message giving you both his name and whereabouts, now would he!'

'Of course not, Doctor, but all the same, I'd still be grateful if you'd let me take a look.'

'Oh very well, if you must, but don't expect it to be a pleasant sight. And I'd rather not have you swooning on me.'

'I've looked on death before now, Doctor, so I promise you that won't happen.'

Upon our arrival, I was then pleased to see that Abel, a gangling lad with a toothy smile, was still standing guard at the entrance to the cottage, and once we had tethered our horses he immediately stood to one side to let us enter. It had remained a warm, sunny day, although the heat had now begun to abate somewhat, and the moment we stepped inside I was struck by the smell of death; noxious to the point of already being somewhat overpowering. It made me shudder and place my hand firmly across my nose but Doctor Gladwell appeared completely unmoved by it as he made his way up the steep and narrow flight of stairs that led to the bedchamber.

The sight that met our eyes was a tragic one, indeed. I did not consider myself a lachrymose creature, by any means, but seeing the poor woman lying on her bed in her torn nightdress was still enough to move me to tears. I managed to suppress these by clenching my teeth and then looking away as the Doctor began his examination.

'The constable was right to say she was strangled and her neck broken into the bargain. Whoever did this was strong, with large hands, I expect, and used considerable force,' he soon declared.

'And was she ravished as well, do you think?'

'As to that, give me a few more moments and then you'll have my opinion.'

I nodded and began to look around the room, which was tiny with only two pieces of furniture in it apart from the bed, namely a chair and a chest. Nothing seemed to be out of place and as I scanned the floor nothing caught my eye, either. I began to wonder what had seriously possessed me to put myself through this ordeal unless it was some prurient desire to bask on the sight of death much as many enjoyed the spectacle of a public execution. Meanwhile, I was conscious that the Doctor was examining the deceased's private parts and also paying close attention to the bed, to which he even put his nose.

'Well, I would say that she was ravished and...look here, I've found a button on the bed. What do you make of it?'

With that he held it up to the light between his thumb and index finger and I was immediately convinced that it had come from a man's doublet and said so. 'It's good quality, too,' I added. 'Only a gentleman would possess one of these.'

'Or someone pretending to be a gentleman,' Doctor Gladwell responded with a snort. 'True gentlemen do not commit acts of ravishment and murder.'

After that it was a relief to walk out into the sunlight and escape the malodorous odours within. I then saw Josiah walking towards us with his rather rolling gait and raised a hand in greeting.

'So, did anyone see or hear anything untoward last night?' I asked him.

'Her neighbour in the adjoining cottage, Mistress Capel, thinks she heard something in the middle of the night. She woke with a start but can't say what is was that roused her. It could well have been a scream but just as easily the hooting of an owl. As she lay awake she then thought she heard a cry coming from nearby but it wasn't loud enough or prolonged enough to cause her to rise from her bed and then she fell asleep again. Her husband also remembers hearing nothing at all but then he's a sound sleeper.'

'And any other neighbours? Did they see or hear nothing?'

'None, I've spoken to, remember anything. It looks to me as if he set upon the deceased after midnight and when it was still well dark, so it's hardly surprising that no one saw him, and only Mistress Capel appears to have heard anything untoward.'

Doctor Gladwell coughed. 'You can tell the coroner that I will be sending him a letter confirming my findings. He ravished and strangled her but I can't say in which order. The state of the body is also consistent with her having died in the early hours of this morning...So, I'll be on my way then. A sorry business, I must say. I knew her from when she was still a child and no one deserves such a fate. And here's the button I found. Perhaps it might lead you to her killer.'

Having handed this to me he then doffed his hat to us both and was soon riding away. I was left feeling quite exhausted, overwhelmed by the emotion of the day's events and in dire need of something to both eat and drink. Then I found my voice and held up the button. It had also not escaped my notice that a small crowd of curious onlookers had gathered.

'This small button may yet help us find a murderer,' I declared boldly. 'Spread the word that if anyone knows of a doublet missing such a button, they are to report this immediately either to Josiah, here, or to myself.'

Two hours or so later, having returned to the Manor to take my ease and enjoy some refreshment, I looked out of the window and saw Harry approaching, accompanied by another rider, whom I assumed must be the coroner. I was impressed with Harry for returning so soon and thought that he must have ridden his horse hard in both directions. He had also obviously lost no time in seeking out the coroner, and found him willing to ride back with him without delay.

The coroner himself was quick to explain that he had been happy to come immediately, being cognisant of the fact that in such warm weather the body would need to be buried quickly. 'I've also nothing else to preoccupy me at present,' he added, 'and I've enjoyed the ride. It's been some time since I was last in this vicinity and I'd almost forgotten how beautiful it is.'

Introducing himself as John Carpenter, he had a ready smile and what seemed to be a thoroughly gregarious personality that went with his size as he was both tall and portly with large hands and a ruddy complexion behind a thick growth of beard. Judging him to be about forty years of age, I took an instant liking to him and was pleased to offer him the hospitality of my manor for the night, it being agreed that the business on which he had come could wait until the morning, given the lateness of the hour. Anticipating the possibility of this eventuality, I had already had Alice make up a bed and ensure that a supper of mutton with black pudding was sufficient for two helpings.

I had felt some misgiving at the prospect of entertaining a stranger who might be as aloof as Doctor Gladwell or as puritanical as the reverend Stephen Havelock, but in the event found the coroner's courteous company a real pleasure. Of course, I knew that we would hardly be on common ground when it came to the matter of politics as I believed that he was bound to owe his position to a sympathy for the parliamentary cause.

Yet, I felt that I could forgive him that and it was anyway a topic that we were both tactful enough to be able to avoid. Instead, we quickly discovered a common interest in both music and horses and when he revealed that he was a widower with two grown daughters, one of whom had recently married, I felt my pulse quicken a little. Not that I found him in anyway as amorously attractive as Thomas and I reasoned that he might also be somewhat older than he looked. Further, I realised that my commitment to the Royalist cause was such that I could not possibly look to enter into any relationship with a man who did not share this. Even so, as we continued to enjoy the bottle of wine, I had had Alice bring to the table, I felt relaxed in his company, whilst he remained perfectly solicitous without revealing any amorous intentions towards me. It wasn't long before I also decided to share with him my puzzlement over who the murderer might be.

'Should he not be a local man, he's certainly in possession of a good deal of local knowledge, and it's apparent that he dresses as a gentleman, is bearded, and has a horse, too, as well as quite possibly a scar on his left cheek.'

'In which case it ought to be possible to identify him, or at least to narrow the field.'

'Yes, you'd think so, but I can identify no one who both fits that description and might have the local knowledge, apart from my best friend, Lady Olivia's brother, James Courtney, and he can't possibly be the culprit. He was in Honiton when the first girl was ravished and he's madly in love.'

In truth there was, of course, Thomas, but I was not about to reveal his existence and anyway I remained convinced he did not have the personality to commit such a series of foul crimes.

'And you're sure that whoever murdered this poor woman also committed the ravishments?'

'As certain as I dare be. The button that's been discovered, which I can show you, must have come from a doublet of good quality. It's also, surely, too much of a coincidence.'

'Well, once I've completed the inquest a hue and cry can be raised and I would suggest that a warrant should be obtained to search Courtney's home. Find a doublet with a missing button that matches the one you hold and he'll have a lot of explaining to do.'

'I'll not raise a case against a man who must be innocent.'

'Forgive me, but if you don't I certainly will. If the man's innocent, he has nothing to fear.'

20

The finger of suspicion

I rode over to Fetford Hall as soon as I was able to, once the inquest had taken place and the coroner had departed, feeling all the while an acute sense of embarrassment. The last thing I had wanted to do was point the finger of suspicion at James, but, unfortunately, once the words were out of my mouth, a seemingly inexorable process had been set in motion. At least, though, I would now have a chance to explain matters to him, and hopefully neither he or any other member of his family, most of all Olivia, would be too angry with me.

Once Josiah, acting in his capacity as deputy constable, had summoned a jury of twelve men from amongst the village's population, the inquest had taken place on the village green, with the corpse being formally identified and a statement provided by the woman who had first discovered it. The coroner had then directed the jury to make a finding of murder, being satisfied that the death could only have been caused by foul play, and, to the relief of all, the corpse had then been released for burial, with most of the village, including me, attending the funeral.

Before his departure, so Josiah informed me, the coroner had spoken to him about the possibility of James being the owner of the button that had been found at the scene of the crime and declared that he would be writing to the Justice of the Peace to recommend that a warrant be issued for Fetford Hall to be searched. I surmised it was likely to take a few days for such action to be set in motion.

In any event, I wasn't far into my journey when it occurred to me that by warning James of what he could expect I was also potentially inviting him to hide, or more likely destroy any doublet that he might possess that would implicate him in the murder. However, the very idea that he could be guilty of such a crime, especially when he had an alibi for the first ravishment, struck me as being so preposterous as to be almost laughable.

In the end, having struggled with my conscience for the remainder of my journey, I decided on a compromise. I would, of course, speak of the murder, news of which might have already reached them anyway, but say nothing of the discovery of the button, save in confidence to Olivia. I reasoned, too, that although a search would be upsetting, it would surely reveal nothing that could possibly implicate James in the murder.

Upon my arrival, I was in the act of dismounting from my horse, when Constance came out of the hall to meet me, looking a little ill at ease.

'My dear, I'm sorry to tell you that Olivia is unwell and has had to take to her bed.'

'I trust it is nothing too serious?'

'A summer cold, I'm afraid. She seems to get them nearly every year. They often bring on headaches, too.'

'I can still see her?'

'Of course, of course, she will welcome your company.'

'And James, is he at home?'

'Oh yes, he's about somewhere.'

'And have you heard the dreadful news?'

'No, whatever's happened?'

'A poor woman has been murdered, three nights ago in her own bed...'

'Oh bless me, how awful. Who was she?'

I began to explain all as Constance led me up the main staircase in the direction of Olivia's bedroom. Almost every year for as long as we had known each other she had been struck down by summer colds so the fact that she was now afflicted with one again came as no surprise. It was not usually bad enough, however, to force her to take to her bed and I was quite shocked by how poorly she seemed. However, sitting propped up in bed, supported by two large pillows, and with her hair allowed to flow freely to her shoulders, she still managed a limp smile.

'I'm sorry that you find me so ill. My headache feels worse and I'm even a little short of breath. Has something serious happened?'

'Jane has just told me that there's been a murder,' Constance said.

'My God, what was it the vicar said...'

'Next time he may kill...and I'm afraid he was right. The woman was strangled in her bed in the dead of night...He got clean away without anyone suspecting anything.'

'And...was she ravished, too...?'

'Doctor Gladwell thought so. I had him inspect her corpse.'

At this moment Olivia began to sneeze whilst her eyes were also streaming and very red. 'Damn this!' she swore.

'I won't stay long if you're really poorly.'

'Nonsense, I'm pleased to see you. I ought to make the effort to get up.'

'No, no, you clearly need to rest.'

'I suppose so. Perhaps you could read to me then.' This was not an idea that caused me much enthusiasm and Olivia knew it.

'Um...What do you have in mind?

'I thought Don Quixote...You know how much I like it.'

'Well, I've got things to do,' Constance interjected. 'I'll leave you both, if you don't mind?'

Once she had departed, I sat down in a chair facing Olivia's bed, looked into her eyes and, for all that she was clearly unwell, was certain that I could see a mischievous twinkle in them.

'Don't worry, Jane, I was only teasing you. We could play cards instead, if you'd prefer.'

I smiled back at her. 'Why yes, that's a much better idea.'

'And draw back the curtains a little more. My headache's not that bad and we need some more light in this room.'

'There's something important I need to tell you, but it must be in strictest confidence; at least for now.'

Olivia looked intrigued. 'What's happened; is it to do with the murder?'

'Yes, you see whoever the perpetrator is left behind a small clue as to his identity. It was nothing more than a button but still one of quality, which you might expect to adorn a gentleman's doublet. It's presently in the custody of Josiah Watts, the deputy constable, and its discovery makes it even more probable that the ravisher has now become a murderer. But that's not all...'

Olivia raised my eyebrows. 'Really?'

'Well, only a man in possession of local knowledge could have possibly committed this murder. Otherwise, how could he have known that the poor woman was a widow, living alone, and still not yet old? And how, too, could he have possibly been able to identify where she lived; if you like, a perfect target for his insatiable lust?'

'Yes, I see that, but yet, why am I only allowed to know this in confidence?'

'Because..., because it narrows the field, indeed narrows it considerably, for how many gentlemen do we know with that sort of local knowledge, or at the very least likely to have heard it from a local person's lips?'

'My God!' Olivia was now sitting bolt upright and clearly angry. You're surely not imagining?'

'No, I'm not, I swear it...but...'

'But what?'

'A process has been set in motion...nothing more...

'In devil's name, what process?'

'This house may be searched. It could yet take a few days but I expect a warrant will be issued. They'll be looking for any doublets with matching buttons. Of course, if they were...'

'That's ridiculous! How can you even imagine such a possibility?'

'I don't Olivia, really I don't. You must just...just try to see it as a...'

'Yes, yes, as you say, a process.'

'I was going to say an...unfortunate necessity.'

'Huh, isn't that what General Cromwell's supposed to have said when he had our gracious King executed! And what about Thomas Sumner, isn't he a suspect, too?'

'Possibly, but for all I know he could be on the other side of the country by now. What's more, the chances of his having acquired sufficient local knowledge to know both the poor woman's circumstances and her place of abode are surely remote.'

'Then who can the murderer possibly be, for I tell you it certainly wasn't James?'

'If I thought I knew that then I swear to you we would not be having this conversation. It is a mystery and no mistake. Please also don't be angry with me, but there is also one more question I need to ask you.

'Olivia glared at me. 'What?' she asked sharply.

'It's just, well, can you tell me...was James at home three nights ago?'

'So, that's when the murder took place, I take it?'

I swallowed hard and nodded my head. Suddenly, Olivia seemed to crumple before my very eyes, adopting an anguished expression and throwing her head back against the pillows.

'No, he wasn't....He was...oh God knows, with drinking friends, even with Becky, or so I imagined. Perhaps, you'd best ask him yourself.'

'Olivia, by itself it means nothing. I only asked because if he had been at home that would have been the end of the matter completely.'

'He could still have slipped away under cover of darkness...'

'Yes, perhaps, although it's far from likely. Look, all I ask is that you don't speak of this, and nor, of course, shall I. When..., if the constables arrive with their warrant, they'll make their search, find nothing, and that will be that.'

'Oh, I do hope so, Jane, really I do.'

We fell into a long silence, which I found increasingly uncomfortable. I also felt a certain guilt for having caused my dearest friend such anguish. It could not, I thought, be much different to the anguish I felt every time I imagined that Thomas might be both a ravisher and a murderer. Of one thing I was certain, and that was that this climate of suspicion and fear was insidiously damaging to relationships that should otherwise be blossoming. Worse, it might well continue to be so until the murderer was apprehended.

'Let's play cards now,' Olivia said. 'You'll find a pack in the top drawer of my dressing table.'

'If you're sure you're well enough?'

'I can't say that what we've just discussed has improved my condition, but I doubt that lying here doing nothing would improve it either.'

'Shall we play ruff and honours then?'

'Yes, why not.'

I duly took the pack of cards from the drawer and we began to play. Both of us were perfectly aware that Puritans were increasingly condemning card games as immoral. However, that tended to assume that every game was played for money, and therefore a form of gambling, whereas we were playing purely for innocent pleasure. I also knew that Olivia was a far more competitive card player than I was and inclined to grow impatient with me if I did not give every game my full concentration. Try as I might, though, my mind kept wandering to thoughts of what could be done to apprehend the murderer and how someone fitting his description could be lurking in the near vicinity without our having any idea who he might be. In the end Olivia did indeed start tutting at me and declared bluntly that my mind was clearly elsewhere.

'I'm sorry Olivia, but I've been thinking that a proper

strategy is required if the murderer is ever to be caught.'

'That may be so but is that really something in which we should be involved? And you've already done all you can, it seems to me.'

'But, if he's not caught, these attacks may continue.'

'If he's any sense at all, I think it more likely that he'll have been scared off by what he's done.'

'You mean, he'll try and escape.'

'I know I would, in which case he could already be far away from here.'

These words had barely been spoken when Olivia began to grow short of breath and declared that she felt too ill to continue with our game.

'You were winning anyway,' I told her. 'I think it wise that I leave you to get some rest, but I'll return in a few days. And please don't be too angry with me concerning James.'

'I'm not, Jane, really I'm not. And I'll send you word when the search has been carried out. Best, I suggest, for you to wait for that to arrive before you come again.'

'Very well then. As you wish.'

21

Thomas returns

It was mid-morning a few days later and I was deep in conversation with Harry over estate business; a boundary wall that was in urgent need of repair, a horse that had gone lame, which cattle to send to market, and a number of other matters, some trivial and others less so. I did not know whether any warrant had yet been obtained and acted upon, but with each day that passed I was becoming more anxious to hear from Olivia that all was well. At least I was pleased to have received confirmation that Melanie had not become pregnant as a result of her ordeal and I could only hope that Mistress Tapton had also been spared.

'M'lady,'

I turned around in surprise to see that Mary had arrived. 'Oh, you took me quite by surprise. Is something wrong?'

'Begging your pardon, m'lady, But the same gentleman who was here a fortnight ago has come again and is asking if he may speak with you.'

'Is he, indeed. Very well, I'll come.' I then turned round to face Harry once more, feeling distinctly ill at ease. I was confident that I had his loyalty along with that of every other person on the estate. All the same, it seemed to me that the situation had become more fraught since Thomas's last visit, for he was now very much a wanted renegade and I could hardly forget that by associating with him I was placing myself in danger. 'We'll talk again soon, Harry.'

'Yes, m'lady.'

I looked into his eyes and saw the same honest, respectful gaze I had always seen. If he was at all curious about my visitor, perhaps even concerned, he was being careful not to show it. I smiled faintly at him and then walked back to the house, deliberately adopting a steady tread, for all that there was part of me that wanted to lift my skirt and hurry along. Above all, I was determined to arrive looking calm and in command of myself.

The moment I set eyes on him there was the same feeling of attraction, of course. That, I accepted, was inevitable, for nothing had changed in his manly bearing and the friendly, open way in which he looked me in the eye and smiled as I approached. I felt compelled to return it and for all that I felt a certain trepidation at his presence, this was largely overridden by a glow of pleasure. He then bowed to me and I offered him a smile, by way of greeting.

'Hello, Thomas, I never expected to see you again so soon.'

'There have been developments. May we speak in private?'

'Of course, let me take you into the library. Will you take some beer?'

'That would be welcome. I've ridden some distance and it continues to be warm.'

I then turned to Mary, asking her to bring two jugs of beer, before leading him into the library.

'We, too, have had developments, Thomas,' I told him before he had a chance to speak a word. 'The manor was searched as you warned me it would be and you were named as a dangerous renegade with whom it would be considered treasonable to have any association. So, you see, you put me in grave danger by coming here.'

'I am sorry, Jane... '

'And we've had a murder, too.'

He looked at me, his face a picture of shock and surprise, bordering on incredulity. It was the reaction I had hoped for and I reasoned that if it was at all contrived he was the very best of actors. 'It must be the same man who committed the ravishments and he remains at large.'

'You think he might strike again?'

'I sincerely hope not. Lady Olivia believes that having committed such a crime, if he's any sense he will have upped and run, in which case he may never be found. The worst of it is that he must have had local knowledge for he murdered a widow, not yet forty, and living by herself in the village, in her own bed.'

'Wherever he might be, I fancy he remains a threat. Such a man must be a monster and no mistake. Anyway, I'm here now because I...we..need to hold you to your word that you would offer the safety of your roof if called upon...'

'I swore no oath, Thomas, and I have been strongly coun-selled that I would be a fool to risk the gallows by giving aid to any renegade...'

'It would be for no more than a couple of nights...and then we would be gone again, I swear...'

'But when we last met you declared that this whole part of the county was unsafe...'

'The truth is that nowhere's safe for Cromwell has his spies everywhere. However, as your manor has recently been searched, I don't think it at all likely that it will be searched again in the near future. We've also been too long in Sidmouth and need to move on into Cornwall, if we can...'

'So you've been in Sidmouth ever since we last met?'

'Nearby there, yes, in hiding, of course. Sooner or later, though, there's always a risk of attracting attention.'

'So, there are just the two of you, are there?'

'Three, I'm afraid. His Lordship has his servant...He's totally trustworthy, of course, although it must be said that his presence means that we are that much more likely to attract attention.'

'And am I to be told his Lordship's name?'

'That I will leave to his discretion, if you will help us?'

I thought of my late husband and of the sacrifice he had made, which was what had motivated me to act with such impetuosity in ever agreeing to offer my support in the first place. Now, I wondered if I had the courage to perhaps risk my very life in furtherance of a cause that, when all was said and done, was probably hopeless.

'Oh very well, but no more than two nights. I doubt if my nerves could stand it if it's any longer.'

Thomas positively beamed at me. 'Thank you, Jane, I am truly grateful to you. I left his Lordship and his servant in the woods, not five minutes ride away. I would like to fetch them, if I may?'

'Yes, of course. But first, I'll need to speak to my servants, and also to my steward, to make it plain that they are not to go telling tales of your presence here. Not that I believe any of them would. Beds will need to be made up, too, and food prepared...We eat but simple fare, and I will need to ask Alice if that can be stretched to feed three extra mouths at such short notice.'

'That I fully understand. Should our stay inconvenience you at all financially then his Lordship also has the means to pay you.'

I shook my head. 'No, no, I am not yet so poor that I cannot offer the hospitality of my house free of any charge.'

'Forgive me, I meant no offence.'

'And none taken, I assure you. Now, please take your ease and I should not be too long. My household, you see, is quite a small one...'

'Might I ask just how small?'

'Oh, I have, what...two household servants, both women. And then there is my steward, Harry, a gardener, Jack Tolson, and also the stable lad. There are my tenants, too, of course, a dozen or more, with their smallholdings. I would not survive without the rent they pay me. But they won't come near the house. Even so I'll still need to speak to the five I've mentioned... If you're worried that's too many?'

'No, no, so long as you're confident they can be trusted to keep their mouths shut?'

'Yes, I am.'

Again he smiled at me and I felt happy to return this. In the back of my mind there was still the thought that Sidmouth was close enough to continue to make him a suspect to murder. Yet, I still could not imagine how he could have ever acquired the necessary local knowledge to be able to commit it, so I put any such idea firmly to one side as highly unlikely.

It then took me the best part of half-an-hour to seek out everyone in turn in order to tell them that an important visitor was about to arrive who would be staying for a couple of nights and that it was vital that they gossiped to no one about either his presence or that of the two other men accompanying him. 'They are no friends to either Parliament or General Cromwell but rather to our true King,' I added. 'However, I trust you to remain silent, knowing that you are loyal both to me and to the King's cause.'

As I had expected they all answered me in the affirmative so suitably reassured I returned to the library, where Thomas had taken down a book and appeared to be reading it.

'All is well,' I told him.

'Right, I will go and give the good news to his Lordship.'

I spent the next half an hour in a state of nervous anticipation, wondering once again if I had made a grave error for which Olivia would be likely to gently reproach me. When I then spied three riders approaching I took a deep breath and went immediately to the front door of the Manor to greet them. Even as they then dismounted I noticed that the leading rider was easily distinguishable by the black eye patch that he wore. This stirred a faint memory in me of a royalist commander who my late husband had spoken of, but I was unable to bring his name to mind.

The eye patch made him look rather sinister, I thought, and this was, if anything, accentuated by his long, somewhat aquiline nose, pale, clean-shaven skin and thin lips.

Like Thomas and the other man with him, whom I assumed must be the servant, he was soberly dressed in dark clothing of no particular quality so was not obviously a member of the aristocracy, but he still walked towards me with the stride and bearing of a man used to giving orders and being obeyed.

'My dear Lady Tremayne,' he declared before bowing to

me, and speaking with a clipped accent that instantly, and no doubt intentionally, betrayed his status in life, 'what an immense pleasure it is to make your acquaintance. You know, I had the honour to serve with your late husband. A fine man of undoubted courage. Please allow me to offer you my sincerest condolences on your sad loss.'

'Thank you, and welcome to Altringham Manor, my Lord.... Forgive me...am I to be allowed to...'

'Of course, the whole world should not know it, of course, but amongst friends I am Henry Hastings, and have the honour to be the First Baron of Loughborough, a title bestowed on me by the late King, of blessed memory.'

I then invited them all inside, before announcing that a midday meal would soon be served in the dining room, consisting principally of a rabbit stew, which Alice had assured my could be stretched to feed three more mouths. I was also pleased to offer my guests one of my best remaining bottles of wine from my cellar and was quite beginning to enjoy the solicitous attentions of both Lord Hastings and Thomas when I happened to glance out of the window and noticed a familiar face riding towards the house.

'Oh my, what timing...'

'Someone you know well?' Thomas enquired

'It is Lady Olivia Courtney of Fetford Hall. We are good friends, especially since my husband's death. I have been expecting a message from her but did not imagine that she would bring it in person. Olivia is a true royalist, though, I can promise you that...'

'In which case she can no doubt join us at the table,' Lord Hastings suggested. 'I see that she is most handsome. Wouldn't you agree, Thomas.'

'I would, my Lord. Indeed, I think, almost as handsome as our charming hostess.' He then smiled flirtatiously at me, and I almost blushed, feeling duly flattered by such a compliment.

'Excuse me, gentlemen, I must go and greet her.'

I then hurried outside, anxious to receive the confirmation I hoped for that nothing had been found to implicate James in the recent murder and also wishing to explain what I had now agreed to.

'Greetings, Olivia, I am glad to see that you are looking well. Do you bring good news?'

A smile from Olivia in response was enough to tell its own story. 'They came late yesterday and, praise the Lord, found nothing.'

'Of course they found nothing. I never doubted it. But Olivia...'

'Yes, is something wrong?'

'No, not wrong exactly, but still I fear you will not be happy. You see Thomas Sumner has returned and brought someone... someone quite important with him.'

'Oh you haven't!'

'It is only for two nights, no more...'

'Oh Jane, what have you done, embroiling yourself in treasonous activities? And I suppose you are now seeking to entice me into this dangerous game of yours?'

'I did not plan for you to arrive here unannounced at this time, any more than I expected Thomas to return quite so soon, if at all.'

'And did he just appear with this...this important person?'

No! He asked me first if I was prepared to give them

both hospitality...'

'And now you are dancing to his tune. Pray God, Jane, you do not end up dancing at the end of a rope. I've a mind to turn my horse around this instant. I want no part of this...'

'But, Olivia, I thought you a royalist...'.

'And so I am...but Cromwell and his army are too powerful. They have this country in the palm of their hand and your friends, I fear, are like mice scurrying towards well laid traps. No, I think it best that I leave. When they have gone by all means pay me a visit. You know you will always be welcome.'

I stood watching Olivia ride away for several seconds, feeling a mixture of regret at her departure as well concern at her reaction to what I had had to tell her. Then I clenched my fists and walked slowly back inside. The moment I entered the dining room I could tell that Lord Hastings was especially disappointed that Olivia was not at my side.

'I am afraid she decided not to stay. She came principally to give me news, which I am pleased to say was most welcome.'

'You told her we were here, I assume?' Thomas asked.

'Yes, I did, though I only gave your name, Thomas. She did not wish to know yours, Lord Hastings, and thought it best you did not meet. That's probably safest for all concerned.'

'I see. Well, I expect she's right enough on that account. Still, it would have been a pleasure to make her acquaintance.'

'In better times, perhaps my Lord, when the King is restored to his throne.'

'I'll drink to that, dear Lady, although how to restore him, there's the rub. It will take much hard work and planning and the seeds must be sown to ferment such discontent that Cromwell is left as naked as Adam ever was.'

'You agree then, my Lord, that he presently has a strong grip on power?'

'Only a fool would deny it and he has the loyalty of an army the like of which I doubt we've seen in these lands since the days of Rome. I tell you in all honesty that I come here merely to see how fertile the soil is for the sowing of seeds of discontent. I would never pretend that our cause is an easy one while Cromwell lives.'

'Is that not our way forward, my Lord,' Thomas suggested quietly in a conspiratorial tone.

'Cut off the head and the body is instantly felled.'

'If it could be achieved, of course it would be. However, I expect Cromwell is as well protected as any King ever was, and we have no secret friends within his camp who could strike the blow for us.'

The three of us then fell into silent reflection until Thomas looked to move the conversation along in a different direction. 'So, Jane, tell us what was the welcome news that Lady Olivia brought you?'

'It concerns the murder I told you about. The perpetrator left a tiny clue as to his identity at the scene of the crime. It was but a button. All the same one of quality and everything suggests that he not only has considerable local knowledge but is also a gentleman, too, or at least dresses like one.'

'And that considerably narrows the field, I'd say,' Lord Hastings interjected.

'Precisely, my Lord, amongst whom is Lady Olivia's brother, James, Suffice it to say that their home has been searched in order to see if he possessed a doublet with buttons that match the one found at the scene of the crime...'

'But no such doublet was found, I suppose,' Thomas responded. 'Mind you, if I was the murderer I would have tossed the doublet off the nearest cliff, or, cut it to shreds and then buried it.'

'Except, Thomas, that supposes that the murderer even realised his mistake. The loss of a single button could readily be overlooked, or, for that matter, thought to have been lost elsewhere.'

'That's true enough, I admit. So are there any more suspects, assuming that Olivia's brother is innocent?'

I felt suddenly a little tense. 'None that I can think of,' I answered as calmly as I could.

'Well, I expect whoever the murderer is they'll have gone to ground by now, ' Lord Hastings commented.

'That's what Olivia, Lady Courtney, thinks. I just worry that he may attack again.'

'Damn fool if he does. You might get away with one murder but try your luck a second time and something's bound to go awry, if you ask me.' And with that his Lordship guffawed with laughter. I was less amused.

'There's every reason, my Lord, to believe he committed two ravishments prior to the murder.'

'Is there indeed, in which case he'd be the biggest fool in Christendom to try his luck a fourth time.'

'What concerns me, my Lord, is that he may be driven by a demon he's powerless to control.'

'The devil's work, you mean?'

'I fear so, my Lord, I really do.'

22

A new suspect

'You have my word, Jane, that I am no murderer, or, for that matter, a ravisher of women.'

'Thomas, I never thought you were.'

'I fancy you still feared I might have been one or the other, or perhaps both. I could see that in your eyes yesterday when I asked you whom else you suspected.'

'Yes, perhaps I have. It's just...'

'I know, I am a gentleman and I know the locality but I swear to God I had not the least idea where the poor murdered woman lived.'

At these words I managed a smile. 'It was for precisely this reason that I discounted any possibility that you could have committed the crime. I couldn't, for the life of me, see how you could have acquired such knowledge.'

After several days of cloudy weather with intermittent rain, it was once again a bright, sunlit morning and the two of us were taking a walk around the Italian garden. It had been Thomas's suggestion that we should do so and whilst I had readily agreed it had still been with a certain sense of apprehension. For all that I found him attractive, there was a part of me that still mourned for my late husband. Indeed, never a day passed when I did not think of him and feel a painful sense of loss.

I was also troubled by Olivia's attitude, feeling most ill at ease at the thought that I might cause irreparable damage to a friendship that had become so important to me since Paul's death. I had therefore stepped out into the garden determined to say no to any suggestion that I should be willing to offer further hospitality to renegades. That Thomas should in fact have chosen to so readily address the most sensitive issue of all between us had then come as both a surprise and a relief. Whatever the future held in store we could at least now remain friends without the darkest of all possible clouds hanging over us.

'We would like to remain here until tomorrow morning,' he told me as we continued our walk.

'I see, and then you will look to travel into Cornwall, I understand.'

'Yes, of any county in England, it is the one that is still most loyal to the King's cause. There are several safe houses there where his Lordship will be made welcome. Firstly, though, I will visit my father. His health is increasingly poor and I am concerned that he may not be long for this world. The drama that ensued when I had to be hidden in the priest's hole at a few minutes notice also did his heart no favours, of that I am certain.'

'Is it safe for you to return there?'

'I will not stay much above an hour, so yes, it ought to be safe enough. Mind you, I still wonder how Cromwell's men came to know I might be there.'

'You were described to me as being a notorious renegade and Tatcham Hall is your home.'

'Yes, but I was a notorious renegade in Ireland. Somehow

they got wind of the fact that I had returned.'

'You must have been recognised on your journey from Ireland and that fact reported.'

'Yes, it's the most likely explanation, I suppose. All the same, I travelled alone, and used a false name, coming into contact with as few other persons as possible.'

'Perhaps it was someone on the boat on which you travelled?'

'They were all Irish and would have sailed for home again the same day I landed.'

'So you were the only passenger?'

'There was one other, but he's a fellow loyalist, as wedded to the King's cause as I am. He hails from Bridgewater and we parted company as soon as we had landed.'

'And your father's servants; are you sure of their loyalty?'

'As certain as you are of yours, I'd say. Most have been in my father's service many years.'

'So what if it was simply suspected that you were no longer in Ireland and the search carried out as a matter of...'

'Speculatively, you mean.'

'Why yes.'

'It's a thought. In any event, I'm determined to see my father but won't trouble him with my Lordship's presence. He and his servant can take their ease at some inn.'

'Isn't he all too recognisable with that eye patch of his?'

'He'll take it off, I expect. His eyeball is shattered but he's not otherwise much disfigured; a scar or two, but they're not that obvious. He's a midlander, too, so no one should know him in this part of the country.'

'And will you stay in Cornwall long?'

'I don't know, a few weeks perhaps. I know that my Lordship

would like to get to the Midlands if he can, but there's danger in that as too many people are likely to recognise him, with or without the eye-patch.'

'And you would travel with him?

'Not necessarily. While my father lives I would prefer to remain close to him.'

I took a deep breath. 'You would be welcome to return here, if it continues to be safe for you to do so.'

He looked at me intently. 'You're sure of that? I fancy that your friend, Lady Olivia, will be less than happy.'

'Why do you say that?'

'I saw the two of you out of the window yesterday. I could not hear what passed between you, but it was obvious to me that she was cross and I can only think of one reason for that.'

'She thinks I will end my days at the end of a rope if I offer you any further aid, but I have made up my mind that it's a risk I am prepared to take.'

'I appreciate that, Jane. We need to find many more men and women with your courage if the King is ever to be restored to his throne.'

'Pray God that you will be able to do so.'

At that moment I had an intuition that Thomas was bent on saying something to me of a personal nature that would reveal the extent of his feelings for me, but in the event this was not forthcoming. I had not thought him to be of either a shy or nervous disposition. However, perhaps he concluded that in such a climate of uncertainty the time was not right for such a conversation. In any event, he fell silent and we soon went inside. Less than twenty four hours later he was gone although I was left with the expectation that we would not be parted from one another for too long. As to Lord Hastings, on the other hand, I thought it quite possible that our paths might never cross again.

Within an hour of their departure I had had Hera saddled and was on my way to Fetford Hall, feeling somewhat anxious. It was open to me to simply obfuscate on the question of whether I would help Thomas and his like in the future. However, I preferred to be honest about the matter, for all that there was a danger that it might damage my friendship with Olivia. At first, though, we avoided the topic altogether, apart from the briefest confirmation that Thomas was gone along with my other unnamed visitor. It was once again a fine, sunny morning and I was happy to take up Olivia's suggestion that we go riding together and head for the coast.

'So long as the tide's sufficiently out, we can go for a gallop along the sands,' I declared, thinking it a pleasing prospect.

James was also at home and I thought he might grumble a good deal about the indignity of having had to submit to a search of his personal belongings. However, whether out of tact or embarrassment, he made no mention of it and was clearly in a good humour, announcing with glee that Becky's twenty-first birthday was now only a week away and that he intended that they should be wed as soon as possible thereafter. I felt happy for them both, although I knew that both Constance and Olivia continued to harbour doubts about his marrying a girl who could bring neither a dowry, or the goodwill of her family, to the relationship.

'They might come round, though,' I suggested as I and Olivia discussed the issue when we first set out on our ride.

'We can only hope so. Mind you, time is running out.'

Then I thought of the topic that was most on my mind and decided that I must speak out about it.

'I have told Thomas Sumner that he is welcome to use my home as a safe house in the future.'

'Oh no, surely not!'

'I have made up my mind that I cannot in all conscience do otherwise. It is what Paul would have done, I am certain of it.'

'Yes, I agree with you there. Had he lived I expect he would have been up to his neck in much the same conspiracy.'

'You should know as well that I feel a certain affection for Thomas...'

'Ah, do you now. And is that reciprocated, do you think.'

'I believe it might be although in truth he's not yet said anything. We are at ease in each other's company. and well, call it a woman's intuition if you like, but I have seen the way he looks at me.'

'And what about the possibility that he's ravished two women and murdered another.'

'We've talked of that. In fact he has sworn to me that he is innocent and I absolutely believe him. I cannot conceive that he would have known both where Mistress Hodge lived and that she was a widow.'

'Unless someone within his father's household was acquainted with her and unwittingly told him all he needed to know.'

'No, that's most unlikely...'

'A conversation overheard, perhaps.'

'No, I don't believe that. Thomas denied his guilt without any prompting from me. I tell you he is an honest, decent man.'

'And as you're smitten by him, you would think that.'

'Whilst you are plainly prejudiced against him!'

'Only because I fear what he might bring you to.'

'On that score, I will take my chance. You will not be involved on any account.'

'Yes, I will.'

'I don't see how.'

'Oh Jane, I did not imagine you so obtuse. I will be forever fretting about what might become of you. And, if the worst were to happen, I would be utterly devastated, I know I would.'

'Nothing need ever come between our friendship, Olivia. You know it matters a great deal to me.'

'Death will come between it.'

'One day, yes, we are all mortal, after all.'

'But let that day be far off when we are both old maids, and let it be in our beds.'

'Amen to that. But whatever the future holds, let us meet again in heaven.'

'Better than hell, I'll be bound!'

And with that Olivia encouraged her horse into a canter as we could now make out the sea and feel its cooling breeze on our faces. We then discovered that the tide was too far in for us to be able to gallop along the sands so instead decided to rest our horses as we sat side by side looking out to sea.

'I still worry that whoever the murderer is he will strike again,' I confessed. 'Yes, I know you think it unlikely and, of course, you may be right, but I believe the man has the devil in him and will just go on until he's caught. Sooner or later, too, he may make a mistake, but that's not to say he won't ravish and murder a good few more women before that happens.'

'So what's to be done then?'

'Didn't you say I'd done more than enough already.'

'And so you have, but clearly you still want to do more.'

'I merely say that every man of any station residing within say half a day's ride of Tipton needs to be identified and questioned.'

'But you can't do that. After all, Exeter and Honiton are no more than that distance , so that would mean having to question scores of men. In any event, it's a task for the Justice of the Peace and his constables.'

'In principle, I agree, but I doubt if they actually have a mind to. I fancy they'll need some encouragement at least, so I believe we could still endeavour to draw up a list of possible suspects and then put it to the Justice that he should act upon it. Perhaps, in fact, we could ask James to put it to him. He's more likely to take heed of his advice, as one man to another.'

Olivia looked at me sceptically. 'We'd still need assistance from persons living in both Exeter and Honiton.'

'True, there's my sister for one. What's more, I'll wager that someone in the village who knew the poor murdered widow, has unwittingly given the man the information he needed in order to be able to attack her. I've also been thinking that it's even possible that someone knows who the murderer is, or, is at least suspicious of him, and yet is choosing to say nothing. After all, in order to commit the crime they had to enter the widow's home in the dead of night when all about it was pitch darkness. That means they would have had to have gone missing from their bed. Perhaps, indeed, even have ridden a horse through pitch darkness though I think that most unlikely.

'Wasn't the moon all but full that night?'

'Yes, I think it was. Yet, unless the perpetrator lives entirely alone, it's probable someone will be aware that he saddled up a horse and then departed for several hours.'

'It's possible he never used a horse at all.'

'Whatever, unless he accomplished everything by dead of night, someone must have seen him on his travels.'

'Would it help us, though, even if they did, unless they actually recognised him?'

'A fair point, I accept, although if they saw he was well-dressed and had a scar on his cheek, it would still be helpful. In any event, every person in the village needs to be asked if they might have spoken of the deceased's circumstances to someone outside the village. Say a relative, or anyone of their acquaintance, for that matter. I also don't see much chance of that happening unless I encourage it, so I must speak to Josiah.'

'And don't you think a hue and cry should be raised more widely, appealing for information on anyone who might have been away from home on the night of the murder?'

'Yes, that has to be worthwhile, I agree. Again, I can mention that to Josiah and as needs be it can be put to the Justice.'

The two of us continued to stare out to sea, my mind turning to thoughts of Thomas and where he might be now.

'Time to head for home?' Olivia then suggested.

'Yes, I suppose we should. Mind you, on a day like this I sometimes wish time would stand still and we could enjoy this vista for ever.'

'If that were possible we would soon begin to feel trapped, I fear.'

'Yes, you're right, of course, though aren't we trapped anyway, I mean by how we find ourselves after all the years of war, the loss of those we loved and now this...this vile series of crimes?'

'We can only trust in God and hope for better days to come.'

On that note we remounted our horses and began our return journey, enjoying a fresh perspective now our backs were to the sea. It caused me to look in a north easterly direction towards the village of Sidford.

'Am I right in thinking that a wealthy merchant built himself a fine house just outside Sidford back in the 1630s?' I asked.

'I don't recall, I'm afraid.'

'Do you mind if we divert in that direction? I would like to take a look at it.'

'What are you thinking?'

'That whoever owns it should be added to our list of suspects. Of course, if the house has been abandoned, or the owner's in his dotage...'

'Very well, as it won't take us far out of our way. But, you know, it seems to me that between Exeter and Honiton there might be another dozen houses, perhaps more, whose owners are wealthy gentlemen; some of which we have no knowledge of whatsoever.'

'We may not know of them but they'll pay taxes and have the right to vote so that will make them identifiable. What's more, how ever many there are, I'll be bound that there'll be only one with the necessary knowledge to have been able to commit the murder.'

As we came within sight of Sidford we also gained a first view of the house I had in mind, standing three storeys tall behind wrought-iron gates and a low wall, about three foot high. The closer we then came to it the more I was certain that it was occupied as two of its upstairs windows were slightly open

'I suggest we ride into the village and see if anyone there can tell us who exactly owns it,' I said.

As luck would have it we soon came upon a forge where its blacksmith was at work so I decided to put the question to him. He looked at me morosely through large brown eyes, his face smudged by soot. 'Why d'ye want to know?'

I was taken aback by such a curt response, which I thought rude. However, this I chose to ignore.

'Simple curiosity. It looks very fine.'

'That's as maybe. I see the gentleman who owns it from time to time.'

'With his horse, I take it?'

'Aye.'

'And do you know if he's at home at present?'

'I doubt it as he works out of Exeter. He's another house there, so he's told me.'

'But this one looks well kept.'

'And so it is. He can afford a housekeeper and a gardener too.'

'But no wife?'

'Not that I know of.'

'And his name, will you give me that? He sounds an interesting gentleman.'

'It be William Pemberton.'

'Would he be the same gentleman who built the house?' Olivia asked.

'Nay, he sold it to this Master Pemberton, who owns it now.'

'Well, thank you for your time.'

The blacksmith merely grunted before returning to his work, and once we had ridden out of his earshot I exclaimed that he was a surly fellow.

'Men of his trade often are, I think.'

'True enough but at least my village blacksmith is always

polite.In any event, what this man's just told us makes me think that Master Pemberton should definitely be a suspect.'

'If it's really the case that he's unmarried then I'd agree.'

'We need to speak to his housekeeper. If she's any knowledge of the murdered woman's circumstances and has spoken of these in her master's presence, then that would surely implicate him...'

'Or she could perhaps even have mended his doublet...'

'Indeed, that would be the most damning evidence of all. But we can't just demand that she answers our questions. We have no such authority... '

'And what's more, if we were to try, she's more than likely to tell her master, in which case he might flee.'

'And good riddance if he did. No, I think we should be bold and say frankly to her that we are investigating a murder and have reason to believe that she knew the deceased. That's bound to draw some reaction, even if it's merely to deny any knowledge of her.'

'There's his gardener, too. Shouldn't we also try to speak to him?'

'As needs be, yes, of course...And don't worry, Olivia, you won't have to say anything. In fact, remain with the horses, if you like, and I'll speak to her on my own.'

'No, no, I'll accompany you.'

Although able to maintain an outward display of confidence, I in fact felt a certain measure of trepidation as I made my way through the gate and up to the house's front door, surmounted by its elaborately carved, semi-circular arch. What I was embarking upon certainly represented an intrusion into the lives of strangers, which they would have every right to question. All the same, I was convinced that I had to seize the opportunity while I could, for all that I kept reminding myself of the adage, act in haste, repent at leisure.

Taking hold of the door knocker, I tapped twice with a firm hand, but after a wait of perhaps half a minute heard no sign of anyone approaching from within.

'The house is large. It's worth another try,' Olivia suggested and so I tapped twice more. However, again there was no response and I was reluctantly coming to the conclusion that no one was in when finally I heard first the sound of approaching feet, and then a voice.

'Who's there?'

It was not the question that I had wished to hear before the door was even opened to me, but still I was determined not to be deterred.

'I am Lady Jane Tremayne of Altringham Manor. Is your master at home?'

'I'm afraid he's not, m'lady. May I ask what you want with him?'

'It concerns a matter of some importance. There's been a murder, you see, in Tipton, and I am giving assistance to the constables...'

The door was then opened to reveal a waif of a woman, barely five foot tall, with a lined face, which suggested that she would never again see fifty.

'You see,' I pressed on, 'we are seeking to alert as many people as we can that this murderer is still on the loose and that every woman is in danger. The poor victim, Mistress Hodge, was asleep in her own bed when she was attacked. Perhaps you know of her?'

'Was she now. Well, her name means nothing to me, and I can tell thee the doors to this house are always kept firmly bolted. The master's most insistent.'

'And when is he likely to be returning?'

'In a few days, I expect. He comes and goes. Shall I tell him ye called?'

'It... It's not essential. The information was intended more for your benefit and that of any other women who may be residing here. Well, I'm obliged to you for your time. Good day.'

'And a good day to thee.' And with that the woman closed the door.

'That was well done,' Olivia remarked as we passed through the gate. 'You were more tactful than you said you'd be.'

'Yes, I suppose I was. In any event, she seems to have no knowledge of Mistress Hodge and whose to say what she'll tell her master. Nor, when it came to it, could I see any justification in demanding to speak to the gardener.'

'Whatever, I think you were right to come here.'

'I hope so, and now I must put aside my dislike of the man and speak to William Crabb. Hopefully, I can persuade him to pursue a course of action that stands some chance of leading to the murderer's arrest.'

'Didn't you suggest that it would be best if James spoke to him?'

'Yes, I did, and perhaps it still would be, but call it pride if you like, I'm the one who feels strongly about this matter, so I shall not shy away from seeking to do myself what I believe to be right. If I fail then James could always be asked to try instead.'

23

Deepening suspicions

I decided that it was best to undertake the journey to Honiton riding side-saddle, and also to dress as plainly as possible . The day following my ride to the coast with Olivia, I had written to William Crabb requesting a meeting at his convenience to discuss matters of importance concerning the recent murder. I had then had Harry deliver it for me whereupon I had had to wait nearly a week before receiving any reply by which time July was almost upon us. To my satisfaction this told me that he was prepared to accede to my request and indicated that he would be at home to receive me if I should care to call on him in four days time.

The prospect of the meeting made me nervous, given the undoubted antipathy that existed between us, but nevertheless, having requested it, I was not about to back down. While I had waited to receive his response to my letter I had also successfully persuaded Josiah to make enquiries around the village of any person who might remember speaking of Mistress Hodge's circumstances to anyone living outside it and still awaited the outcome. I would have liked nothing better than to be able to tell Crabb that vital information pertaining to this had been passed to a member of William Pemberton's household, or failing that at least a resident of Sidford, but for the time being at least this was not to be.

Crabb's house was a large one built of stone, on three storeys, as befitted his position, much like William Pemberton's, and was situated in the town's High Street. It also possessed a courtyard and stables, too, so when I arrived shortly before the appointed hour of noon a stable boy appeared and took Hera from me. I was then met at the door of the house by a young maid who politely showed me into a wood-panelled room with a small open fireplace and a minimal amount of furniture, consisting of a small mahogany table and two chairs. On the former there was also set a vase of roses, which looked to be past their best, whilst on the wall above the fireplace there was a portrait of an elderly woman with a severe expression. I examined the likeness and thought that I might well be Crabb's mother.

'Good day to you, Lady Tremayne.' The voice was abrasive in tone and as I turned I saw that Crabb was looking at me with narrow, bloodshot eyes that betrayed no emotion. In his forties, his shaven face pale and lined with a receding hairline, his lips thin, and his nose rather large, there was nothing in his appearance that I found at all prepossessing.

'And good day to you, Master Crabb, I am grateful to you for agreeing to see me on the matter of Mistress Hodge's murder.'

'I take it you have some pertinent information for me?'

'Not exactly but I have a certain suspicion. You see it is clear to me that the murderer is the same man who carried out the two previous ravishments. That being the case he will be a gentleman, or certainly dressed as one, and will also possess a horse. What's more, it's probable that he was wearing a doublet of some quality when he committed the murder, and must also have local knowledge, for how else could he have known that his victim was living alone. That, as I am sure you would agree, reduces the number of possible suspects significantly.'

Crabb looked at my testily. 'Perhaps it does,' he conceded in a grudging tone.

'Well, I have looked in particular at a certain William Pemberton....'

Crabb immediately cut me off. 'You're not possibly suggesting that he is a suspect, are you?'

'I think it possible, yes.'

'No, that is quite out of the question. He is an eminently successful merchant...and a staunch parliamentarian.'

'But he is unmarried, is he not?'

'That's as may be; it certainly doesn't make him either a ravisher or a murderer.'

'No, but might I be allowed to explain my reasoning?'

'If you must.'

'Thank you...Both women who were raped were clear that their attacker wore gentleman's clothes and it is probable that he was mounted too. Then, as you will already be aware, a button was found at the scene of the murder that can only have come from a gentleman's doublet. Mistress Hodge was also ravished and it surely follows that the same man perpetrated each of these crimes, which after all took place within a short distance of one another over the course of only a few weeks.

'All this I will grant you, but how does that implicate Pemberton?'

'Only in the same way that it implicates any gentleman who lives within half a day's ride of the scenes of these crimes. The finger has already been pointed at James Courtney and I merely say that it can equally be pointed at the likes of Pemberton. You also appear to be acquainted with the man so I would ask you, does he wear a beard?'

'Yes, to the best of my recollection he does.'

'As did the man who committed the first of the ravishments. But look, Pemberton's home should be searched in the same way as James Courtney's was, and he and his household questioned.'

'No, I will not countenance it. Will you have me issue warrants against every gentleman residing between Honiton and Exeter?'

'Yes, as needs must, I would. You'll not apprehend the murderer otherwise, of that I'm certain.'

'No, no, you bring me no evidence. This is nothing but vague suspicion.'

I felt a growing swell of frustration. In the light of what Crabb had just said it seemed to me that he was choosing to favour Pemberton because of his political sympathies and had been prepared to act against James on the same basis, knowing his family to have always favoured the King. I decided, remaining as calm as I could, to advance one more argument.

'Please, if you will not act against Pemberton, at least consider who else might fall under suspicion because of their rank and then act against them. If you do nothing you may have more deaths on your hands.'

Crabb snorted, clearly moved to anger. 'How dare you suggest any such thing. I can assure you that I already have a suspect and every effort is being made to apprehend him.'

I was taken aback. 'And who might that be?'

'Why, Thomas Sumner. I believe you know him?'

'...Yes, though it has been many years since we last met...'

143

Crabb's eyes now seemed to be boring into mine and I felt terribly afraid.

'Has it now. Well, you'll know from the search of your house that he is a renegade and believed to have returned to this county from Ireland. Not only that, but the reasons you have given me for being suspicious of William Pemberton, could just as easily apply to him.'

'He is a gentleman, I grant you,' I said hesitantly. 'But...but what do you know of his movements to say that he could have carried out both the ravishments and the murder?'

'And what do you know of Pemberton's, might I ask?'

'I don't, but then I am not asserting that he is the villain, merely that he and his household should be questioned. And there's another consideration...'

'Oh yes.'

'Whoever murdered Mistress Hodge must have had knowledge of the fact that she was a childless widow, living alone. I do not therefore understand how a man just returned from Ireland could possibly have acquired that knowledge.'

'The information I am in possession of suggests that he returned to this country before the first ravishment was committed. In that length of time he could have learnt of her circumstances.'

'But how?' I thought whilst being at pains to remain silent, as I could see nothing to gain by embroiling myself in any further debate with Crabb.

'Very well,' I said instead. 'I would merely tell you that the deputy constable in Tipton is presently seeking to establish who might have spoken of Mistress's Hodges circumstances to anyone living outside the village. Should this by any chance lead to the finger of suspicion being pointed at any particular individual, I trust that he will then be closely questioned.'

'I cannot think it at all likely that such enquiries will prove fruitful. Nonetheless, you have my assurance that I will not disregard anything that might lead to the murderer being apprehended.'

'In that case why not raise a reward payable to anyone able to provide information concerning the murder that leads to a trial and conviction. I, for one, would be willing to put up five pounds. Perhaps you'd be prepared to match that?'

Crabb looked uncomfortable at any such suggestion. 'That's generous of you, I must say. All right, I'll give it my consideration, on that you have my word.'

'I'm obliged to you. I've especially got in mind any man who was away from their home on the night of the murder. Unless they live alone then someone else will know of it and could be suspicious. A reward might just encourage them to come forward.'

'Yes, I'll grant you that. I shall sleep on your proposal and then let you know my decision.'

'Very well. I wish you a good day and thank you for your time.'

At that Crabb deigned to give me a supercilious smile. 'And a good day to you.'

I was relieved to be out of his presence whilst at the same time overcome by a profound sense of disappointment at how the meeting between us had progressed. It was bad enough that I had completely failed to persuade him to take any action against Pemberton, but far worse that he should be choosing to accuse Thomas of the crimes. All this was compounded, too, by the realisation that he was unwilling to take any action against Pemberton, not so much because he was wealthy, but rather because of where his political sympathies lay.

It was also scant consolation that he had been prepared to consider a reward being offered as apart from any other consideration I wondered at my folly at proposing an amount that I could not really afford. That I had been provoked into doing so by his attitude was, I felt, little excuse.

I rode back towards Tipton in a mood of introspection, fearful that Thomas would soon be arrested and then brought to trial. Yet, as matters stood, I thought that the evidence against him was no more than circumstantial so surely no jury would convict him, at least on any charge of ravishment or murder. What fate he might suffer as a known renegade was quite another matter. Everything, I decided, might well turn on Josiah's enquiries, always assuming that he was being true to his word and carrying these out. Certainly, if they did not prove fruitful then we would be no closer to identifying the murderer.

I was not far from Tipton when I became aware of a man riding towards me. The road was also straight enough for me to have a view of him when he was still some distance away although at first I gave him little attention, being still absorbed in thought about my meeting with William Crabb. However, as he came ever closer, I became conscious of the fact that he was well-dressed, with a feathered hat and beard and appearing to be in his thirties. For an instant my heart leapt at the thought that it could even be Thomas but then I realised that the individual was a total stranger.

He was riding his horse at a steady trot as was I, so we were very soon within a matter of feet of each other, and I half-expected him to doff his hat to me. Instead, he appeared to be completely indifferent to my existence and rode on, stony faced, without making any attempt to acknowledge my existence. I was instinctively so suspicious of him that I was actually tempted to follow him for all that that might well be courting danger. I even went so far as to bring Hera to a halt and then look back at the rider whereupon he also turned his head round. He had now progressed some distance along the road, but even so I felt his eyes boring into mine unpleasantly and was sufficiently discomforted to urge Hera into a fast trot in the direction in which I had been travelling. All the while I was also left wondering if I had just looked into the eyes of a murderer.

Five minutes later I entered the village, determined to seek out Josiah and ask him how his enquiries had been progressing. I thought, too, that the man I had just passed on the road must have ridden through the village and wondered if he might even have stopped at the inn, or possibly the forge. I was reminded as well of the man whose horse had needed shoeing on the day that Melanie was ravished and it occurred to me that this could be the same individual, though at a glance I hadn't noticed any scar on either cheek. In any event, I went straight to Josiah's cottage and was pleased to find him at home.

'Well, m'lady, I've found no one who remembers speaking to anyone outside the village about Mistress Hodge,' he told me in response to my enquiry. 'That said, one of my neighbours did tell me that Mistress Hodge has a cousin living in Sidford...'

'Really!' The very mention of that village made me excited.

'Yes, m'lady. It seems they exchanged frequent visits.'

'And did he know this cousin's name?'

'He said it was Ann Linley. She came to the funeral, it seems.'

I was instantly reminded of a woman whose features had been similar to that of the deceased and who had also looked to be of a similar age. I had briefly wondered about her at the time but then put her out of my mind completely.

'You have done well, Josiah, very well indeed. You see, I have my suspicions against a certain gentleman residing in Sidford.'

'Thank'e, m'lady.'

I also wished that I had been armed with this information before my meeting with Crabb although I suspected that, of itself, it would not have made any real difference. He would still have demanded much more evidence so what was now vital was that this cousin should be questioned in order to elicit from her whom she might have spoken to about the deceased's circumstances. It was also hardly likely that she would have said anything directly to William Pemberton, or, for that matter, said anything in his presence, but what was perfectly plausible was that anyone she had told had then passed this information on.

What I now debated with myself was whether or not to merely let matters take their course. I could, after all, merely urge Josiah to bring what he had just discovered to Crabb's attention and then allow him to do the rest. However, my meeting with him that morning had left me with little confidence that he would be prepared to take any initiative that might lead to the finger of guilt being pointed at Pemberton.

'Josiah, you must report what you have discovered to the Justice. I was with him this morning and he is already aware of my suspicions.'

'I will, m'lady, I will.'

'The gentleman I have in mind is however quite wealthy and has some influence, I fear. Do not speak of this to anyone, least of all the Justice, but I think I might make some enquiries of my own in Sidford.'

'As you wish, m'lady.'

24

The trail looks promising

I had woken feeling sick. I normally prided myself on my robust health, but perhaps because something I had eaten the night before had disagreed with me I now felt positively wretched. I called Mary to my bedside and barely had time to ask her to bring a bowl to me before I felt the urge to throw up. Three times I then proceeded to empty the contents of my stomach at which point I began to feel better. I was still tired and weak, though, and doubted if I would find the strength to get up for some while, which was frustrating as I had determined to ride to Fetford Hall in order to see Olivia, and to ask her if she would accompany me to Sidford once more.

'I am going to rest for a couple of hours,' I told Mary. 'But do not let me sleep beyond eleven. Provided I am feeling well enough I still intend to visit Lady Olivia today so tell Toby that he must still have Hera saddled.'

I remembered little after that until I heard Mary's voice and also felt her gently touching my arm.

'M'lady, please wake up. It's now past eleven and I have a letter for you. It's come from the Justice of the Peace, Master Crabb.'

I promptly opened my eyes and began to sit up. I wondered if I might feel sick again and was thankful that I did not.

'It must be his answer to my proposal that we put up a reward for any information leading to the conviction of Mistress Hodge's murderer,' I said as I broke the letter's seal before reading its brief contents. Somewhat to my surprise they were reasonably positive.

'What does he say, m'lady?'

'That he thinks my idea of a reward a sensible one and that although he feels unable to match my offer of five pounds he is willing to put up three. He's also prepared to have a notice printed and circulated as widely as possible and we shall just have to see if it brings any helpful response. Now, I must get up.'

Thirty minutes later I was on my way to Fetford Hall on what was a cloudy, muggy morning with a hint of rain in the air. I feared that it might turn to a heavy downpour before my arrival and was grateful that this held off until Constance had welcomed me indoors. She also had news for me.

'The wedding is to go ahead. There is to be a handfasting here on Sunday week with the wedding ceremony three weeks thereafter.'

'And what about her family?'

'Thank the Lord, they've relented somewhat. There'll still be no dowry, it seems, but they've at least indicated that they will not put any physical impediment in Becky's path and she now has her mother's blessing. She may yet bring her father round before the wedding; we'll just have to wait and see.'

'I'm happy for them both.'

'As is Olivia. She's been poorly again with a summer cold, I'm afraid...'

'She's not in bed?'

'No, but she's rather tired. You'll find her in her bedroom.'

'No, you won't.' I turned and saw Olivia walking towards us. 'I saw that you had arrived. Was your meeting with Crabb a success?'

'Not really although he has agreed to a reward being offered for any information leading to a conviction. More importantly, it's now clear that Mistress Hodge has a cousin living in Sidford and that they were in regular contact with one another.'

'Had she indeed! And does Crabb know this?'

'He should do by now. It was Josiah who discovered this and I told him to report the finding. Mind you, I doubt if Crabb will act upon it. Pemberton, it seems, is a wealthy merchant with influence so Crabb made it clear to me that he would not countenance any action against him without firm evidence. Do you think you might be well enough to ride to Sidford with me?'

'Yes, why not. I've been cooped up indoors long enough.'

'A meal will be served shortly,' Constance pointed out. 'At which you are welcome to join us, Jane. That will still leave you all afternoon to ride to Sidford and back.'

James also sat down with us to eat and it was obvious from the moment he entered the room that he was a happy man, laughing, joking, and ready to tease Olivia at the slightest opportunity. I was also as pleased as ever to be part of this family gathering but wondered whether this would continue once Becky took up residence as James's bride. I had only ever met her on a couple of occasions and even then for too short a length of time to gain more than a fleeting impression of her character. Certainly, she was attractive, some might even say beautiful, so I was not at all surprised that James was so in love with her. I recalled, too, her ready smile and easy laugh, and had certainly found nothing to dislike in her.

It also struck me that she must have some strength of character in order to be marrying James in the face of her mother and father's evident hostility, whilst the fact that she seemed to be gradually winning them round to the idea spoke, as well, of some powers of patient persuasion. All this boded well, but nonetheless her arrival would still be bound to herald changes over the course of time, not least, god willing, the arrival of children. Certainly, occasions such as this, with just the four of us together, would soon be but a memory.

'You're looking pensive, Jane,' James remarked. 'In one of your reflective moods, I'll warrant.'

'I smiled at him. 'You were ever the perceptive one, James. I was just thinking what happiness it brings me to be in the company of you all.'

'And long may that continue.'

'Very soon, you will be married...'

'But you'll always be welcome here, have no fear of that. And you and Becky will get on well, I know you will. She has a sweet nature to match her fair looks...'

'I'm sure she does.'

James seized hold of his glass, which was full almost to the brim with red wine from Bordeaux. It came from an old bottle that he had insisted on opening. 'I propose a toast then, to friendship and family!'

'To friendship and family,' we all cried, lifting our glasses.

'And one more besides. To our King in exile. May he one day reign over us.'

Again we all lifted our glasses in unison while I wondered

how many years it might be, if ever, before that hope became a reality. Less than an hour later I and Olivia set off for Sidford.

'Take care,' Constance called out to us with a wave of her hand.

'We will, mother, we will,' Olivia assured her.

The weather remained both cloudy and humid, but, no doubt assisted by the wine we had drunk, I felt in good spirits. Olivia, however, seemed far less so, which I at first put down to her cold. However, there was, in fact, a little more to it than that.

'I think mother is fearful that we might stir up a hornet's nest.'

'Really, and what do you think?'

'That, well...that once again we are interfering in matters that are best left to others to pursue...'

I shook my head vigorously. 'But I tell you, Crabb will not raise a finger against Pemberton unless he is left with no choice. We must take the initiative or the murderer will strike again, I know he will.'

'And you really think he could be Pemberton?'

'No, not yet, but if this Ann Linley has spoken in the past of her cousin's circumstances to anyone who has any connection with Pemberton then I will become mighty suspicious that it could well be him. And there's another thing...'

'Oh yes...'

'I passed another rider while I was returning from seeing Crabb. It was very close to Tipton. I didn't recognise him but he was well-dressed, bearded, no more than forty, and there was something about his manner and the look in his eye which I did not like. I'd certainly know him again if I saw him and I've been wondering if he could even have been Pemberton.'

'So, do you mean to confront him?'

'No, no I don't. Let us merely see if we can locate Ann Linley and then question her. That need not involve any danger.'

'I hope you're right.'

By the time we reached Sidford the threat of rain appeared to have abated and the clouds had lifted completely, making the temperature far less oppressive. Hoping that this was a good omen, I determined that we should ask the first person we saw where we might find Ann Linley and in the event this turned out to be an old man whom we saw walking slowly towards us, aided by a stick. Unfortunately, he proved to be hard of hearing, and despairing of making myself understood I turned instead to a shabbily dressed young woman who pointed in the direction of a row of small cottages.

'She's in the one at the far end. I dunno whether you'll find 'er in, mind.'

I immediately strode up to the cottage door and knocked loudly.

'Hello, who's there?'

'Forgive me for intruding upon you. I am Lady Jane Tremayne of Altringham Manor, Tipton, and I'm here with my friend, Lady Olivia Courtney, concerning your late cousin, Mistress Hodge. I have a question I need to ask you.'

Moments later the cottage door opened to reveal a slightly built woman, looking to be barely five feet tall and with a face that might once have been pretty but which was now blemished by the marks of smallpox. She had alert, intelligent eyes, though, and looked at us both curiously.

'M'ladies, my home is a very simple one and also small but if you wish to come inside...'

'There's no need. It's just that we understand that you and your late cousin used to exchange visits and we were wondering if you ever told anyone living here in Sidford about her circumstances and, if so, who?'

'I may have done. Why d'ye want to know?'

'We have suspicions that a person from this village could have been responsible for your cousin's murder. But we also think they'll have needed to know that she was living alone, and it's possible they could have learnt this through you...'

'What are ye suggesting; that I sit down with villains?'

'No, of course not; you misunderstand me. We merely wonder if what you said could have been overheard without your knowledge...'

'Or perhaps passed on,' Olivia added.

'Well, let me see, my husband, Jacob, and my two lads; they're all working in the fields at present, knew of Margaret's situation. Mind you, I can't see any reason for them to gossip about it. And then there are my other children but they're really too young.'

'But no one else?' I asked.

'I'm just thinking....Yes, there is one other person, Mabel Davenport. She's my oldest friend. We grew up together in this village. She got to know Margaret, in fact, from her visits. Whether, I'd have told anyone else, I can't say...'

'She has family, though?' Olivia asked.

'Oh yes, a husband and three children, still living. She may well have told them.'

'And she lives nearby, I take it?'

'Why yes, just on the other side of the village green. Look, her cottage is the one over there to the right, nearest the beech tree.'

I made eye contact with Olivia. We both understood the need to press on with our enquiries and felt we were tantalisingly close to achieving our objective. Thanking Mistress Linley for her time, we therefore made our way across the green and I prepared to repeat the exercise I had just been through. What Mabel Davenport then told us convinced me that this further visit to Sidford had been worthwhile.

'Oh yes, m'lady, my family knew poor Margaret. She was a good-natured soul and my daughter, Alice, was really upset at the news of her death. You see, she'd known her since she was a babe.'

'And how old is she now?'

'Oh, coming up seventeen. She's become a servant at the big house.'

'What, you mean the one belonging to Richard Pemberton?'

'Why yes.'

'And does your daughter now reside there?'

'Yes, m'lady...But she comes home every Sunday and more often than that when her master is away, which is quite often as he's another house in Exeter.'

'And do you know if he's away at the moment?'

'Alice hasn't come to see me since Sunday so he must be here at present.'

For a few moments I pondered what to do next while once again exchanging glances with Olivia. Then I made up my mind.

'We would like to return on Sunday afternoon in order to speak to your daughter.'

'Should I tell her that you're coming?'

'Yes, by all means, as we would like to find her in, but do not alarm her unduly. We merely need to ask her a few questions. Thank you for your time and I wish you a good day.'

As we then walked back towards our horses I couldn't resist placing a hand on Olivia's arm. 'This grows evermore suspicious, don't you think?' I exclaimed. 'I'll be bound that this girl, Alice, has spoken of Mistress Hodge either directly to Master Pemberton or within his hearing. She has only to confirm that to us and he will have some explaining to do!'

'Have you thought, though, that we might be placing her in some danger?'

'It's on my mind, of course it is, but he'd be foolish to the point of madness to do her any harm. It would be tantamount to an admission of guilt to the crimes we suspect him of. No, what concerns me more, is persuading the Justice to take action. I fear he'll still declare that what I think we've discovered proves nothing.'

'And if he won't act, what can you do then?'

'Perhaps go above his head. The Sheriff of the County might be more open to persuasion. Exeter is also close enough and it's a while since I was last there. As needs must, come with me and we could enjoy some shopping together.'

'Mind you, even if Pemberton is questioned, he's bound to deny everything.'

'Of course he is. If I were him I'd surely vehemently protest my innocence, but don't forget he could have already made two mistakes. Firstly, if he has a scar on his cheek then I'll wager that he was the man whose horse the blacksmith shod on the day of Melanie's ravishment and secondly, there's the button...'

'But won't he have disposed of the doublet by now?'

'Not necessarily and even if he has who's to say that he's done so without anyone knowing about it; his housekeeper for one, possibly even Alice. I tell you, even if Crabb won't listen, I'll put it to the Sheriff that there is sufficient evidence to justify a search of Pemberton's house, together with a questioning of his servants. What's more, the blacksmith must be brought before Pemberton. If he'll identify him that could change everything.'

'Perhaps he made a third mistake, too.'

'Oh yes, what was that?'

'Why, the wearing of the mask. I don't suppose he's destroyed it, in which case it remains capable of being found...'

'Or failing that his possession of it might well be remembered by someone...'

'So, another question to ask his servants then...And I'll tell you this, even if acting against Pemberton fails to lead to any prosecution, it should still discourage him from making any further attacks.'

'Amen to that.'

So, shall we ride to the coast, or return to Fetford?'

'I think we should just go back. It's getting late and I fancy those clouds approaching from the West will soon bring us rain.'

25

And more promising still

Olivia and I were once again approaching Sidford on what had turned into a glorious day with temperatures high enough to give both us and our horses a significant thirst. Both of us, too, were conscious of perspiring in a most unladylike manner but that could not be helped. I would also have preferred us to arrive earlier so that there would be time to ride on to the coast. However, being a Sunday, there had been church to attend in the morning and by the time I had taken my midday meal it had been close to one o'clock before I had been able to depart for Fetford Hall.

'People here will be getting to know us,' Olivia remarked as we arrived at the village well and dismounted.

'And wondering what we're about, I expect. But at least we don't have to pass Pemberton's house. I'd prefer it that he knew nothing of our visits.'.

'He may already know of our first.'

'Quite possibly and if he does that will have caused him some concern, I have little doubt, which is why I'd rather he did not know we've returned again.'

I then proceeded to raise water from the well, first for the benefit of our horses and then for ourselves, having satisfied myself that it was perfectly drinkable. After that we made our way towards the Davenport's cottage, whereupon it was once again Alice's mother, Mabel, who came to answer my gentle tap.

'She's here. I told her you would be coming and why. She's worried that she might get into trouble with her Master for telling tales. She says he has a fierce temper and can fly into a rage at the least excuse.'

'I see. Well, I'd like to assure her that I am not asking her to tell any tales, merely to tell me whether she ever spoke of Mistress Hodge's circumstances to her Master or within his hearing before the murder took place?'

As I spoke I raised my voice, loud enough to be heard inside the cottage and the words had barely left my lips before I saw a waif of a girl, looking every bit a younger version of her mother, appear. 'Well, Alice, what say you?'

'Begging your pardon, m'lady,' the girl said nervously, 'but... well, are ye accusing the Master of murdering Margaret?'

'I'll be honest with you that this depends a good deal on your answer to my question. If you're not minded to give me one then I can summons a constable to demand it of you, but I trust that won't be necessary.'

Alice gulped, her face a picture of anxiety. 'I...I think I did once. It was when Margaret and Ann came to visit the last time afore Margaret died. T'was on a Saturday afternoon and I asked the housekeeper, Mistress Baines, if I might be excused work an hour early so that I could be home when they arrived. We were standing in the hallway and the Master then appeared. He asked me why it was so important that I be there and I told him that Margaret was an old friend of the family who I didn't get to see very often as she lived in Tipton...'And I'm sure I added that I felt sorry for her on account of her having

161

lost her husband and her family.'

'And was that all?'

'No m'lady, I remember him saying that that would be quite a walk for her if she was getting on in years to which I answered that she wasn't yet forty. And then I remember he smiled at me and said I was welcome to be excused. There was also one other thing he asked me...'

'What was that?'

'He wondered what she did to keep body and soul together and I told him she was a fine seamstress and embroiderer and took in work from Exeter. And then he said that he might even know of her through his business and asked me what her name was so I gave this to him.'

'Thank you, Alice, you've been most helpful,' I assured her.

'I do have two more question for you,' Olivia said. 'In the course of your work have you ever noticed if your Master possesses a mask, say of the sort that might be worn to a mask ball.'

Alice looked at me blankly and shook her head. 'No, I can't say I have.'

'And also have you ever seen him wear a doublet with a missing button or perhaps seen a doublet being disposed of?'

Again Alice shook her head.

'Well once again our thanks,' I said. 'And please do not speak of what you have told us when you return to your work.'

'I won't. But tell me, from what I've said, do ye regard the Master as a murderer?'

I looked her straight in the eye. 'Yes, I think it possible, but I'll say to you frankly that there's still one piece missing from the chess board before I can seek to have him arrested. Can you perhaps tell me from whom Margaret received her work and how it was delivered to her? After all, Tipton is but a small village deep in the countryside.'

Alice shook her head but her mother was able to provide an answer. 'I believe it was from her brother, Will, in the county. He's a Master Taylor, you see. I believe he valued her skills as I'd say there was no one better than her in the county when it came to embroidery work. From what she told me he used to visit regularly, bringing material and clothes with him that required her attention. He'd also collect finished work, I'd imagine.'

'But Pemberton has never said anything in your presence, Alice, to suggest that he knew Will?'

'No m'lady, not as I can recall.'

'He did, of course, say that Mary might be known to him,' Olivia interjected, 'and how else save through Will.'

'Quite. I take it, Alice, that your Master trades in cloth and other such materials?'

'Yes, m'lady, I believe he does.'

'I think then, Olivia, that we need to pay this Will a visit,' I said, looking first at my friend and then at Alice and Mabel. 'And tell me, do you by any chance know Will's surname and whereabouts in Exeter we might find him?'

'I recall Margaret telling me that it was something like Thomson,' Mabel said, 'and that his shop was near the Cathedral, but if she ever mentioned the name of the street I can't recall it.'

'No matter, I'm sure we'll find it.'

26

A chance meeting

'So, do you fancy a day in Exeter? I asked Olivia as we rode back to Fetford Hall, having decided that it was too late to head towards the sea. 'It's a while since I was last there and I'm sure we could do some shopping together. We can also pay my sister, Caroline, a visit.'

Olivia smiled at me. 'Yes, why not. With every step we seem to be getting closer to the truth.'

'Indeed we do and I'd wager that this Will Thomson told Pemberton exactly where in Tipton his sister lived. I'm sure it would have been done in all innocence and he has only to confirm that to us and the net will well and truly have closed around Pemberton. I still worry that Crabb won't be convinced but as I've already told you I'm prepared to go above his head if I have to.'

'So when do you propose that we make this visit?'

'The sooner the better. Tomorrow's not an option as I must give my attention to estate business but we could go the day after...If you would come to stay tomorrow night we could then make an early start the following morning.'

'Yes, all right, so long as you're sure that we are taking a path that it would not be better to let others follow?'

'I'm sure. We've come too far to give up now and you must

agree that if we do not do this no one else will. Certainly not Crabb, of that I'm certain, and I have no authority over the constables. In any event, I see no danger in what I'm suggesting. We will merely seek out this Will Thomson, hopefully obtain from him the information which we require, and then enjoy the remainder of our day.'

Olivia seemed persuaded by my argument and we began to talk about what we might purchase together in Exeter. It was then Olivia who first noticed a rider coming towards us and saw that he was dressed in gentleman's clothes and was mounted on a fine, black stallion.

'My, what a beautiful horse,' I declared whereupon I was struck not so much by the appearance of the animal as by my realisation that I recognised the rider as being the same man I had passed on the day I had visited Crabb.

'I've seen him before,' I hissed. 'I wonder if he might just be William Pemberton?'

Olivia looked at my in surprise. 'You really think so?'

'Well, there's one way to find out for certain.'

We were now no more than a twenty yards apart and I called out a greeting. 'Good day to you, sir. Might you be William Pemberton?'

The man immediately looked discomforted and was slow to reply by which point I was able to look him in the eye. 'I am.... What do you want with me?'

'Nothing more than the pleasure of making your acquaintance. I am Lady Jane Tremayne and this is my friend Lady Olivia Courtney.'

'Yes, I know of you. I wish you both a good day. Now, if you'll excuse me.' And with that he encouraged his horse into a trot and rode away.

'I'm not sure that was wise,' I said reflectively once he was out of hearing. 'But curiosity got the better of me.'

'Well, at least you now have confirmation of what you suspected.'

'Yes, his age and appearance are exactly as I hoped and what's he doing riding around in such a random fashion?'

'That you can't be so sure of. He could just be returning from Exeter.'

'I doubt he'd be doing so on this road. No, I tell you he's up to no good and needs to be brought to justice!'

'I saw no scar on his cheek, though.'

' ...True, but there's nothing conclusive in that, either way.'

27
Humiliation

Olivia and I, riding side-saddle, entered Exeter through its medieval east gate. As intended, we had left Altringham Manor by seven o'clock in the morning, and it was now approaching noon.

'We should first visit my sister, Caroline,' I had suggested. 'She'll give us hospitality and we can ask her if she knows where we might find this Will Thomson.'

It was with some sense of nervousness on my part that we then approached Caroline's house, which stood in close proximity to the city's cathedral. We had not seen each other since Eastertide and since then had done no more than exchange letters once.

That our relationship was somewhat strained saddened me, but I was inclined to see that as a consequence of my sister's marriage to John Thorpe, a man I did not like, and hoped that we would not find him at home when we arrived. In this I was, however, to be disappointed as once my knock on the door was answered by a maid, whom I had never seen before and looked to be even younger than my own maid, Mary, it was John who then came to greet us. Dressed entirely in the black garb of a Puritan, he initially frowned at both me and

Olivia, making it instantly clear that our presence was far from welcome. However, he seemed to reluctantly appreciate that it would be discourteous in the extreme not to show some measure of politeness towards his own sister-in-law so managed to step forward and offer a half-hearted embrace.

'Well sister, this is a surprise, I must say. I take it that you would like to see Caroline, but I am afraid she has not risen from her bed today.'

'It is nothing serious, I trust?'

'I think not. She complains of a headache and needs to rest. Her confinement is fast approaching.'

'A month or more, surely?'

'Even so, one cannot be too careful.'

Upon that at least we could both agree and I then introduced Olivia, whom John greeted with what seemed to me to be perfect coldness, managing no more than a curt 'good day to you' and the briefest of handshakes without any smile.

'I hope that I might still be able to see Caroline? I asked.

'I will, of course, tell her that you're both here...'

'As needs be, we can always return later. We have some shopping we wish to attend to.'

'Yes, that might be best but let me speak to her first.'

A few minutes later he returned to announce that Caroline would be pleased to receive us in an hour's time whereupon I enquired of John if he knew where we might locate the shop of the Taylor, Will Thomson.

'You mean Will Thompson, I assume. He and his wife are patients of mine. What do you want with him?'

'I believe that he may be able to give me some information that could help bring a ravisher and murderer to justice.

Perhaps the news hasn't reached you that a woman was strangled in Tipton.'

He looked at me in astonishment. 'Sister, what in the devil's name are you involving yourself in? This is constables' work.'

'That's as maybe, John. I only know that the murderer is still at large and may strike again at any time, leaving yet another poor woman dead or ravished. I've also already tried to persuade the Justice of the Peace to take action and he's refused so I've felt I have no choice but to garner more evidence myself.'

I spoke vehemently enough to make him look almost contrite. 'I see. Well, if you must, you'll find his shop's no more than two streets away. You can be there on foot in less than five minutes.'

He then proceeded to give us more detailed directions and added that he would ensure that an eye was kept on our horses, if we decided to walk. I thanked him for that and with the aid of his directions we were quickly able to locate the shop on foot. Even as we then proceeded to enter it, however, I felt a twinge of unease as I thought I recognised the figure of a well-dressed individual standing with his back to us. When he quickly turned to face me I couldn't resist a sharp intake of breath for it was none other than William Pemberton.

'Well Lady Tremayne, we meet again.'

'I don't understand,' I stuttered. 'What, may I ask, brings you here?'

'I might ask the same of you.' Something between a smile and a sneer crossed his face. 'No, I know your purpose. You are trying to fabricate a case against me of ravishment and murder... I know you have visited my house in Sidford, I know that you have made accusations against me to the Justice of the

Peace. In fact, I decided that I could not put up with any of this a day longer and so called on you this morning at Altringham Manor, only to be told you had not long departed for Exeter. I thought I might catch up with you on the road but in the event thought that I might find you here. Master Thompson and I are old business acquaintances, aren't we Will...'

And with that a short, rather rotund individual, with a red face and lank, grey hair, stepped forward and introduced himself.

'You can confirm, can't you, Will, that I offered to deliver some material on your behalf to Mistress Hodge in Tipton...'

'Yes, that's so.'

'You knew exactly where she lived then?' I asked.

'Yes, I did. However, the conclusion you appear to have reached that this makes me her murderer is, I can assure you, totally mistaken. You see, I know that she was killed on the night of the 15th June, and you're able to vouch for the fact that I was then in Exeter, aren't you, Will?

'I can certainly confirm that I invited you to dine with me and that you did not depart until a little after midnight.'

'And if you are imagining that I then rode through the night to Tipton you are much mistaken as my manservant can confirm that I retired to my bed here in Exeter.'

By now I was beginning to feel uncomfortable, appreciating that what I had imagined was a strong case against Pemberton, now seemed to be disintegrating. As if to rub salt in the wound, he also asserted that he had yet more witness evidence that could vouch for his whereabouts when the two ravishments were committed.

'I suggest, my lady, that you therefore withdraw your

allegations against me and cease your meddling in matters that are best left to Officers of the Law.'

'I...I am indeed sorry to have thought you capable of these crimes. My only desire has been to bring the perpetrator to justice.'

Olivia, however, was still looking at him sceptically. 'May I ask you one question?'

'If you must.'

'When we met on the road two days ago where were you coming from?'

He snorted. 'That is really not your concern.'

'But you were nowhere near the Exeter Road...'

Pemberton glared at her in an exasperated fashion. 'I had been visiting my uncle, Erasmus Cooper. He owns a farm nearby.'

'Yes, I know him,' I responded. 'Again, I can only offer you my apologies for having caused such offence.'

'Accepted,' he said, though in a tone that was none too gracious.

After that I couldn't wait to be out of his sight and hastily withdrew, sighing deeply the moment we stepped out into the open air.

'I fear we have been humiliated,' I confessed.

'Yet, how do we know Thompson wasn't lying on his behalf?' Olivia retorted.

'I can see no reason why he should, especially on such a grave matter. Nor can I believe that Pemberton would have cited other alibis if they were not in fact willing to speak on his behalf.'

'They are his servants and therefore beholden to him.'

'That does not, of itself, invalidate their evidence. What

so irritates me, too, is that Crabb will now consider himself vindicated in his decision not to investigate Pemberton, and we will just be dismissed as empty-headed females who have chosen to meddle in matters better left to men. Worse, we are now no closer to establishing the identity of the murderer and he remains free to strike again. Oh dear, Olivia, I can do nothing more.'

'I still think Pemberton could be guilty.'

'Even so, we will never prove it.'

I was now close to tears but Olivia squeezed my hand. 'Courage Jane, you have nothing to be ashamed of.'

'Thank you, Olivia, you are ever a comfort to me.'

28

Desire

The weather since the fateful meeting with William Pemberton in Exeter, six weeks previously, had mostly seemed to match my mood, turning increasingly wet and gloomy. The more I reflected on what had occurred, the more I felt a mixture of frustration and embarrassment. I had surely been right to suspect him and he had even gone so far as to admit to an exact knowledge of where Mistress Hodge had lived and yet at the same time his alibis appeared to be impeccable. In the face of this I had to assume that he was innocent, but this left me at a loss to understand who otherwise might in fact be guilty.

After some heart searching I came to the reluctant conclusion that there was nothing more that I could usefully do to discover the identity of the murderer, while, for her part, Olivia continued to insist that Pemberton must be guilty anyway and had somehow induced Thompson to lie on his behalf. I, however, simply could not believe that this was true, and increasingly turned my attention to my sister's pregnancy as well as James's marriage to Becky.

Following my confrontation with Pemberton, I had felt little enthusiasm for another meeting with my brother-in-law and in the event had found his supercilious attitude hard to endure when I had admitted that Pemberton was no longer a suspect. Further, although Caroline had been able to receive both me and Olivia, I had been so thoroughly out of sorts, I had found it a relief to escape as quickly as I could. Yet, within a fortnight, I received news that my sister had gone into labour somewhat earlier than had been expected and been safely delivered of a healthy boy, thus causing me to return to Exeter to attend the child's christening as Michael John Thorpe. Any thought I might have harboured of being invited to act as a Godparent had to be quickly put to one side, and I did my upmost not to appear disappointed, knowing full well John's antipathy towards me.

I had then barely returned home before James and Becky were wed in a service, to which I was pleased to be invited, and which Becky's family, including her father, were able to bring themselves to attend. I was delighted by such a measure of reconciliation, which Olivia attributed entirely to Becky's sweet nature and powers of persuasion.

'She can charm the birds off the trees,' she remarked to me with just a hint of jealousy that I thought unbecoming until I reflected on how uncomfortable Becky's arrival must be for her. It was, after all, bringing her close to being beholden in every way to the goodwill of her brother and sister-in-law, and little better than a guest in the home in which she had grown up. 'To the devil with the war for depriving us of either our husbands or the men who would have married us,' I thought but did not say.

'There's even to be a small dowry,' Olivia revealed. 'Nothing much, mind, just a few acres of poor quality land, fit for grazing and nothing more.'

'But, still, when you think how bitterly opposed both parents were to the very idea of such a match only a few weeks ago.'

'Well, she managed to win her father round in the end.'

I was certainly struck by Becky's good looks, particularly her lush auburn hair, large 'come hither' eyes and beautifully unblemished complexion. She seemed in fact like some delicate piece of glass that might all too easily break and spying her slender figure I wondered how fit she was to bear children. A dark thought crossed my mind that she could all too easily bring James, who was clearly besotted by her, to grief by expiring whilst in the pains of her first labour.

I also quickly came to agree with Olivia's description of Becky, noticing that she had a willing smile for everyone she met and an eager way of looking you straight in the eye that was surely capable of melting the heart of even the most sour faced of souls. She had an innocence about her, too, that was fetching and no doubt added to her amorous allure whilst at the same time making her seem vulnerable and in need of protection. How intelligent she was and capable of meeting the demands of running a household efficiently was something on which I was content to reserve judgement. In any event, for the time being at least, she could count on the willing support of both Constance and Olivia.

My first visit to Fetford Hall following the wedding then passed off well. It was quickly apparent that Becky had successfully ingratiated herself with Constance whilst Olivia, too, seemed to have succumbed to her charms.

'It is impossible not to like her,' Olivia declared, perhaps suggesting that if she could have found a way, she would. 'I'm sure she will make James a loving and attentive wife.'

Having stayed later than I had intended on what was a pleasantly warm August day, I returned to Altringham Manor, taking my usual route through countryside bathed in sunshine. I had reached a stage where the fate of Mistress Hodge and the two poor women who had been raped was no longer at the forefront of my mind and I could even go for hours at a time without thinking of them at all. I did not now expect that the culprit would ever be apprehended and every Sunday in church was conscientious in offering a prayer to God that he would never strike again.

It was as I was approaching Tipton along a narrow lane that in winter could become virtually impassable because of either mud or snow, but which in its present dried out state was perfectly negotiable, that I saw another rider approaching me from the opposite direction. At first this made me shudder in annoyance, thinking that it must be Pemberton, but as he came closer I realised that it wasn't him at all but rather the vicar of Harpford, Stephen Havelock. It came as a complete surprise to me to see him mounted on a horse as I had never imagined that he had the means to both own and stable one. I felt immediately suspicious of him but quickly checked myself as he was properly dressed in the black cassock of a clergyman with a Canterbury cap on his head, which he briefly doffed in my direction, whilst offering a thin smile and wishing me a good day.

'And to you, vicar. A fine one, is it not?'

'Yes, most pleasing.'

'I did not take you for a horseman?' By the time I asked this question he had almost ridden past me and glanced at me somewhat crossly, I thought.

'I have a small allowance from my father in addition to my stipend.'

And with that he rode on, leaving me to ponder the inconceivable, which I was quick to dismiss from my mind as nothing more than that. Just because the vicar unexpectedly owned a horse, and might, for all I knew, own some gentleman's clothing to boot, did not make him either a ravisher or a murderer and I could imagine being given very short shrift by the likes of Crabb if I tried to suggest otherwise. My fingers had also been burnt quite enough by Pemberton and I possessed no desire to repeat the experience.

I completed my journey home in a mood of sombre contemplation, only to be told by the stable lad, Toby, when he came to take Hera from me, that I had a visitor.

'He came no more than an hour ago m'lady. His horse was in a fine sweat but it's cooled off now.'

I felt my heart give a little leap. 'Who is it?'

'Be Thomas Sumner, m'lady,'

'But not a word to another soul that you know that!'

'No m'lady, I understand.'

I felt an urge to pick up my skirt and run inside. However, I restrained myself and instead walked in calmly. There was a part of me that had been longing for this moment ever since our last parting but I told myself that a few more seconds would be of no consequence and that as a mature woman it would be unbecoming to behave like some love sick girl of sixteen. Anyway, I was by no means certain that I was in love with Thomas; I just knew I had been starved of any relationship with a man for far too long and that I was drawn to him as much by the strength of his personality as the attractiveness of

177

his appearance. As I then stepped inside the hall he emerged from the parlour.

'Jane.'

'Thomas.'

He was smiling at me and I smiled back, but I could see tension in his face and sensed that something was wrong.

'It's good to see you... I've...' He hesitated.

'Yes....?'

'I've missed you...'

I felt the colour rising in my cheeks. 'And I you...I take it you wish to stay?'

'Yes, but there's danger afoot...'

'You're not thinking you've been followed?'

'I trust not but I had to flee my last hiding place. I gave my pursuers the slip by hiding in some woods but they'll still be looking for me, of that you can be certain.'

'And how far have you come from your last hiding place?'

'Near Newton Abbott, south of Dartmoor. Those who were after me will have known I was heading East at the time I got away from them. They're bound to come searching my father's home sooner or later, and here, too, I wouldn't be surprised.'

'And my Lord Hastings, where is he?'

'Gone to the Midlands to garner support and safe enough for the present, or so I hope.'

We were now standing so close to each other that I could easily have flung my arms around him. I felt an almost unbearable tension, wanting so much to do so, but then he brought his lips to mine and we began to kiss. First, in a purely tender, exploratory fashion, but soon with more ardour, holding each other close.

Then we sprang apart, both startled by a nervous cough behind us. It came from an embarrassed looking Alice.

'Forgive me, m'lady, but shall I serve supper?'

I glanced at Thomas and we exchanged mischievous grins, both feeling like children who have been caught doing something they shouldn't.

'I haven't eaten since breakfast,' he confessed.

'Then surely, Alice, do so directly,' I told her.

We sat down to eat an eel and oyster pie, seasoned with salt and pepper, and sweetened with currants and raisins. Having already eaten well at Fetford Hall at midday, I was not all that hungry and felt content to let Thomas devour the lion's share, simply pleased to have his company as well as the sight of him enjoying his meal. I was on fire about the kiss we had just shared and the thought that we might soon be tempted into sharing a bed. This would be hard to accomplish without the likes of Mary and Alice knowing about it, in which case it might soon be the gossip of the whole estate, but I did not much care. What concerned me more was the possibility that any love-making might leave me pregnant although there were ways of preventing that, which I decided I would not hesitate to employ, if necessary.

Soon enough our conversation came round to my abortive attempt to accuse Pemberton of the murder of Mistress Hodge and Thomas was suitably sympathetic when I confessed my deep sense of frustration at the turn of events.

'I was becoming so certain of his guilt, yet once he produced his alibis the whole case against him fell apart. I was left feeling humiliated and now I haven't the least idea who the murderer could have been. I still fear that he has the devil in him and will strike again.'

'Is it really likely he'd take such a risk?'

'He may yet feel emboldened by having literally got away with murder and may not seek to murder again but rather to ravish. I suspect, indeed, that was ever his intention but Mistress Hodge may have recognised him by tearing off his mask.'

'In which case he can't have come out of nowhere. Mind you, he might have simply felt more secure behind his mask, and become angry once that was taken away.'

'That may be so, but, oh, I don't know, Thomas, when all's said and done it's just idle speculation, which I try to put to the back of my mind, though I must confess it's hard. When I saw the vicar of Harpford riding a horse this afternoon that I did not know he possessed, I even began to suspect him. It's almost unthinkable, of course.'

'Why?'

'Oh come, Thomas, he's a man of the cloth and nor do I see him seriously imagining that he could hide his identity behind nothing more than a mask. Why should he also know where Mistress Hodge lived any more than you would have thought Pemberton did until he confessed to the contrary.'

'Perhaps Pemberton is still your man and his alibis are simply bogus.'

'That's what Olivia believes but I simply can't imagine any circumstances in which Will Thompson would actually lie for him on such a grave matter.'

'Unless perhaps he has some hold over him.'

'But what? It would have to be something dire for him to be prepared to make himself a party to murder.'

'But when he told you that Pemberton was with him until

midnight that could have been telling the truth and still left the man time to ride back to Tipton and commit the murder under cover of darkness.'

I shook my head. 'That I doubt, and don't forget, he told me that his manservant could vouch for his having remained in Exeter.'

'That could have been pure bluff on Pemberton's part. He was quite possibly counting on your not having the authority to actually question his manservant. In any event, if he did leave the city at such a late hour, he would have had to rouse a gatekeeper and have him open the gates.'

'You're suggesting that I question the city's gatekeepers then?'

'It might help to put the matter beyond doubt and it's not something they're likely to have forgotten about.'

I struggled to suppress a yawn. It had been a long day and in all honesty I was feeling tired. 'Oh, Thomas, I don't know that I have the energy to play the constable any longer but perhaps when I'm next in Exeter I'll do as you suggest.' Then I smiled at him, remembering our kiss and enjoying our increasing intimacy. It had used to be this way with Paul and I knew that he would not have wanted me to remain a widow for the remainder of my days. As I looked into his eyes, desire for him overcame my lethargy. Assuming he was willing, I would allow him into my bed and nature could take its course except that I would make him withdraw before he could plant his seed in me.

I had already told Alice in his presence to have a bed made ready for him but his bedroom was but three doors away from my own and once we had finished our meal I placed a hand on his and we began to kiss once more.

181

'You are beautiful,' he told me and I was happy to believe that he meant what he said.

'And you most handsome. My bed has been a lonely one since my husband's death.'

'May I come to you tonight?' he asked, whispering the question into my ear to which my initial answer was to barely nod my head and draw him into another lingering kiss.

'I'll have my maidservant, Mary, show you to your bedroom,' I then told him before dropping my voice to no more than a whisper. 'Remember, my room is three doors beyond yours on the same landing. The clock in the hall has just struck ten. Come to me in an hour from now. If you listen out for it, you'll hear the clock again strike out the hour.'

As Mary helped me prepare for bed, I found that a growing sense of anticipation had stolen away any feeling of tiredness. I was reminded of my wedding night and could almost imagine myself a virgin bride once more, excited but also somewhat fearful. In the event Paul had been ardent but gentle and the love we had felt for one another had overcome any inhibition. Now, I wondered if I had allowed myself to be seduced too easily and was being altogether too wanton, only to reject any such idea out of hand. The fact was that I was lonely, that he was most handsome, and that I desired him. Life, I decided, was also too short not to seize the opportunity for a little happiness when it presented itself so readily.

29

Pleasure's cost

Two hours later, I was not so sure that I had made the correct decision when I gave myself to pleasure. It was not that our love-making had failed to be pleasurable, on the contrary he had pleased me greatly. It was just that I had got so carried away in the moment that any thought of making him withdraw from me had slipped away before it was far too late, and now I felt a rising trepidation at the realisation that I might be pregnant. In better times we might have contemplated marriage and I knew I would be far from being the first woman to go to the altar with a child already growing in my womb. That, however, was presently a virtual impossibility. In a few hours, or days at the most, Thomas would no doubt be gone again, perhaps never to return, a dangerous renegade in peril of the hangman's noose, much as I might be myself, if it ever became known that I was harbouring him.

30

They arrive again

I awoke to the sound of banging on the front door of the Manor. I immediately sensed that whoever was making such a clatter posed a threat and glancing at Thomas was presented by his naked backside as he slipped out of bed and hurriedly sought to don some clothing.

'I fear the worst; is there anywhere I can hide?'

I, too, was by now out of bed, and seizing a dress drew it about me before going to the window and peering out.

'Christ, they're soldiers!'

'Come in search of me, no doubt. I say again, is there anywhere I can hide.'

My brain was already racing to come up with some answer to that question. 'Yes, I think there might be. You'll need to get onto the roof. Go up two flights of stairs at the end of the landing and you'll reach the attics. Enter the one furthest from you and go to the window; it drops down to almost the level of the floor and looks out over the rear of the house. Open it and you'll see that it leads onto a parapet. It extends around the entire house. Stay on your hands and knees or you might be seen from the ground.'

'But once up there, I'll be completely trapped.' By now he was dressed and at the bedroom door.

'I can think of nowhere else. Shut the window behind you and it may not occur to them to think that it provides any access to the roof.'

He shook his head doubtfully but was already halfway out of the door and running, just as Alice appeared. By now I could also hear a voice raised in anger, demanding to be allowed entry before the front door was broken down.

'Quickly, Alice, go and let them in. Tell them that the lady of the house will receive them shortly.'

'Yes, m'lady.'

Alice passed Mary on the stairs and I urgently beckoned to my maidservant to help me dress. It was quickly done, and trying to remain as calm as possible I then made my way downstairs. I was confronted by two dragoons, both armed with swords and wearing lobster-pot helmets, one of whom indicated that their commanding officer was in the parlour. As I entered it and he turned towards me I recognised the same officer who had come to search my house before. However, there was no sign of the sinister individual who had accompanied him and for this I gave thanks. The officer had also already removed his helmet and was wearing an apologetic expression on his face.

'Please forgive me, m'lady, I am sorry to intrude upon you once more. However, I have another warrant here authorising a search of your house and estate. The renegade Thomas Sumner is again believed to be in the county and yours is but one of a number of houses where it is believed he could be hiding. My orders require me to search thoroughly but my men and I will do our best not to cause any damage.'

I was tempted to argue, if only to play for time, but reckoned that such an approach would only antagonise the officer and that by now Thomas would have surely found his way onto the roof. Instead, I therefore merely asked to see the warrant, keeping my voice as relaxed as possible, although I could not prevent myself from grimacing when I recognised Crabb's signature on the document. I also tensed ever so slightly when I thought of what personal possessions Thomas could have possibly left in his bedroom and, too, that he might have neglected to properly shut the attic window from the outside.

'Very well, officer, do as you must.'

He nodded to me and the search proceeded with another half a dozen men entering the house and beginning to look in every room whilst orders were also given for every outbuilding to be searched as well. Again I tensed at the thought of Thomas's horse save that it would by now have had its saddle removed and hopefully offer no clue as to its true ownership. There was always a risk, though, however slight, that a careful note had been taken of the number of horses in my stables when the previous search had been carried out, in which case the fact that an extra horse had now appeared would be readily noticed.

Feeling utterly powerless, I remained in the parlour, staring out of the window and expecting with every passing second to hear a cry go up that would lead not only to Thomas's arrest but also my own. I cursed myself for a fool, allowing my heart to rule my head. I had never had the stomach for public executions, considering them detestable spectacles, but now found myself imagining what it would be like to begin the dance of death at the end of a rope.

Time passed with agonising slowness and still I heard nothing but the sound of booted feet growing more distant as they ascended in the direction of the attics. Eventually, when my nerves were so taught that I felt they were fit to snap, I heard the sound returning and the officer then re-entered the room. His face wore the same apologetic expression as before.

'We have finished searching the house, m'lady. Please forgive the intrusion. As soon as my men have also completed their search of the outbuildings we will be on our way.'

In response I managed a thin smile. 'That's all right, officer, I understand that you are only doing your duty.'

The officer nodded and then withdrew, leaving me almost shaking with relief that Thomas had managed to evade capture. I then waited, my heart still racing, until I saw the last of the soldiers ride away, whereupon I made my way upstairs to the attics where I immediately opened the window leading onto the roof. Thomas was crouched next to it.

'They've gone at last,' I told him.

'Thank God. You know one of them even opened the window and came out onto the roof. It's as well I'd managed to wedge myself behind a chimney stack, otherwise he'd have certainly discovered me.'

As he stepped back inside the window, I clung to him and we immediately sought out each other's lips. 'You should be safe here now,' I told him. 'They'll surely not look for you a third time.'

'I'm not so certain. Nor do I want to put you or any of your household at any more risk.'

'It doesn't matter, at least not so far as I'm concerned...I just don't want you to leave me again so soon, not after last night...'

He looked into my eyes and gave me that gentle smile I was coming to love. 'All right, but I still think it would be better if I didn't remain in the house. Is there, perhaps, a cottage on your estate that's unoccupied at present?'

'I don't think so...No, wait, there's one but it's in a very poor state, the thatch is letting water, and the door and shutters will barely keep out the wind and rain...'

'Does it stand alone?'

'Yes, it's an old woodman's cottage, and easily missed. I'm wondering, in fact, if the soldiers will even have found it when they made their search.'

'Then it will suffice for now, especially as it's still summer. In any event, I must be on the move again within a few days.'

'But where will you go?'

'I'd like to visit my father but I fear that's too dangerous. No, I'll look to join up with Lord Hastings in the Midlands. I know enough safe houses on the way.'

'Just so long as they're not already known to those who wish you ill.'

'As to that I'll have to take my chance.'

'In the meantime, whilst you remain my guest you must still take your meals with me... I insist. I'll have a bed made up for you in the cottage, too, and provide you with candles... I could also come to you there... Oh in God's name, must you go?'

At this entreaty I could see a look of hesitation in his eyes. 'Don't imagine that I want to but I have my duty to the cause to consider. I am not free to do entirely as I choose.'

'But what hope have you achieving anything when you are nothing better than a fugitive?'

'I have a plan...'

'Oh and what is that?'

'I'll disguise myself...with your help, perhaps.'

I couldn't help looking at him quizzically. The very mention of the word disguise made me think of the ravisher and murderer, still at large, and think how much everything about him seemed to be a disguise, by which means his true identity was amply protected.

'I'll shave off my beard for a start and I also want to wear my hair like a crop-head,' he continued. 'Then I'll need altogether plainer clothes...'

'I'll see what I can do for you. My steward may have something to spare, which is suitable, and he's about your height and build, I'd say. But what about your horse? You'll want to keep that with you, surely?'

He shook his head. 'Much as I'd like to, it's too much of a liability. It makes me stand out and everywhere I go it requires stabling.'

'Except that it gives you speed and mobility...'

But what good has that just done me when the soldiers came searching? I cannot be for ever on the back of a horse.'

'Your journey to the Midlands will take you far longer without one.'

'Of course, but I believe I'll still travel more safely.'

'And you want me to take care of your horse in your absence, I assume?'

'I would be most grateful to you. Call it my guarantee that I will return as soon as I am able.'

I looked into his eyes and wanted very much to believe that he would come back to me although whether that might be in six months or several years I could not possibly predict. In the meantime, I was determined to enjoy his company for whatever little time remained to us before his departure. In the eyes of some that might make me a wanton woman but having already laid with him once and found it a pleasurable experience I decided that I had little compunction in doing so again. True, I might compound the possibility that I was already pregnant but I was beginning to feel an almost reckless disregard for such a consequence of my desire. I was, after all, still mistress in my own house and reasoned that I could command the co-operation of others in helping me to not merely disguise any pregnancy, but also even the birth itself, although I could hardly dispense with the services of a competent midwife. If the child lived, a wet-nurse could then no doubt be found for it, and as needs must she could be persuaded, albeit at a price, to adopt the child as her own.

Thomas's particular choice of words also made me think again of the murderer. He had surely ridden a horse, he surely would have stood out and yet he appeared to have got away completely with his crime. Further, I remained at a loss to imagine who it might have been unless Olivia was right and it was still Pemberton after all. Yet, I still could not imagine what possible hold he could have on Thompson that would cause him to lie on such a grievous matter. No, it still made no sense at all.

31

Another victim

I was feeling deeply upset at the prospect of Thomas's imminent departure. A further night together, this time in the woodman's cottage, had been enough to convince me that I was really falling in love with him. This, however, only served to make the thought of our separation particularly hard to bear. There was a part of me that would have liked to beg him not to leave, but, instead, I tried to be brave and accept the inevitable, although when he chose to confess his love for me, I was unable to hold back the tears, both of joy and of grief. He then held me close and I told him in turn how much I loved him and wished that we could find some way to be together.

'In time, once we have succeeded in our endeavours and restored King Charles to his rightful throne, but until then we must be patient and live in hope.'

I did not argue with him, but could draw little or no comfort from the reflection that it might take many years to achieve such an aim with no guarantee at all of any final victory. He had also now changed his appearance to such an extent that at a first glance he was barely recognisable. I myself had cut his hair for him, while he had shaved off his beard and moustache before donning the plain garb that my steward, Harry, had been able to make available. Finally, that very morning, he had told me gently that he intended to depart at dawn the following day, leaving me to cling to every hour we continued to enjoy in each other's company. However, in the late morning this was interrupted by Olivia's unexpected arrival.

I caught sight of her out of the window even before she had dismounted from her horse. Normally, I would have been delighted to see her but on this occasion I was unable to suppress a slight feeling of irritation. Of course, I would still be welcoming, and would not hesitate to invite her to join us for a midday meal, but after that I hoped Olivia would be perceptive enough to understand that I preferred to be left alone with Thomas. I decided, too, that it would be best if I went straight out to greet her in order to explain Thomas's presence as well as perhaps giving her some intimation of what had occurred between us.

'Who is it?' he asked me, standing by my side. I briefly explained before placing a hand on his and leaving the room. The moment I then stepped out of the front door and looked in Olivia's direction, I sensed that something was amiss as she appeared unusually anxious.

'Oh my God, Jane,' she called out from the saddle. 'He's struck again. Becky's been ravished!'

I gasped out in horror. 'How can this be? When? How?'

'It was yesterday evening.' By now she was in the act of dismounting. 'It was in the woods. She'd been walking in the gardens and strayed a little too far. She was barely out of sight of the Hall, mind you.'

'Christ, he's bold. But didn't she scream out?'

'She was never given the chance. He came on her from behind and had his hand over her mouth in an instant. Then he threatened to slit her throat if she made more than a murmur.'

'And I suppose she never saw his face?'

'No, not at all. After he'd done his worst, and was running away, she caught a glimpse of him from behind. He appeared to be well attired and his hair was worn long.'

'Then it's our man, for certain.'

'She also said that his voice had a distinct Devon accent. It was harsh, too; possibly in an attempt to disguise it, she thought.'

'So how is she now?'

'Deeply shocked, tearful, frightened...It's as if all the vitality she's ever possessed has been squeezed out of her. I worry that she'll never fully recover. James is angry beyond words.'

'I'm not surprised.' I glanced up at the sky and saw a threat of rain in the ominously dark clouds approaching from the west. 'Well, come indoors...I have another visitor.'

'Oh, whose that?'

'Thomas Sumner....He's leaving at dawn tomorrow.'

'Oh...I see.'

I sensed that Olivia was rather put out by my news. I felt a sudden urge to add that we had become lovers and that I adored him. Instead, even as the stable lad, Toby, arrived, I told her about the recent turn of events and that he was now in disguise. Then I led her into the parlour where Thomas bowed to her in greeting.

'There's been another ravishment,' I announced bluntly. 'And short of murder it couldn't be worse. Of all people, the victim's Becky. Remember, I mentioned she's just married Olivia's brother, James.'

'Whoever this monster is, he's gone too far this time,' Olivia declared heatedly. 'James alerted the constable yesterday evening and has ridden over to Becky's family as well as into Honiton to speak to Crabb. He'll demand a hue and cry, I'm sure.'

I laid a hand gently on her wrist. 'But we know full well, that by itself, it may achieve nothing, even supposing Crabb agrees.'

'Surely, he shall!'

'He might. I know Becky's gentry, but all the same she's chosen to marry into a family of well known royalist sympathisers and Crabb will no doubt take due account of that. More's to the point, I'd say it's vital that everyone living in the vicinity of the Hall is questioned as to whether they recall seeing a stranger yesterday, who would most probably have been mounted and dressed like a gentleman. If we could just have one reliable description from someone who saw him at close quarters for more than the blink of an eye, then there might be some hope of finding him. Otherwise, I fear that we'll be no further forward than we ever were.'

'I'd say that wretch Pemberton needs to be made to account for his movements yesterday,' Olivia retorted.

'Did you tell James to make that suggestion to Crabb?'

'I did indeed and he said he would but, I grant you, Crabb may have none of it.'

'And can the constables be relied upon to make the necessary enquiries, do you think?' Thomas asked.

'If they're properly directed to do so, they'll do their duty. Otherwise, they're unlikely to show much initiative, I'd say.'

'So what about a reward for information then? If it's tempting enough it might bring you the breakthrough you're looking for. After all, I fancy someone may well have their suspicions about a certain person and have failed to come forward out of misplaced loyalty or affection.'

'One is already been circulated for eight pounds,' I said, briefly explaining what I and Crabb had agreed to.

'All the same, the reward could always be increased, couldn't it?'

'Yes, perhaps. James could afford to put it up ten pounds, couldn't he, Olivia?'

'I'd go even higher than that, if I were him...Raise the total reward to twenty pounds, at least,' Thomas suggested.

Olivia raised her eyebrows. 'I doubt if he could afford to put up ten pounds, never mind twelve. In any event, might it not just encourage all sorts of wild accusations with no foundation to them?'

32

Tensions

This was a question that was allowed to hang in the air. Had it not been for Thomas's presence, there was also a part of me that might have happily suggested that I and Olivia waste no time in taking to our horses and riding back to Fetford Hall with a view to not just offering consolation to Becky but also knocking on doors in search of information. I wondered, indeed, if Olivia had ridden over with that very thought in mind.

However, so long as Thomas remained I had no such intention, and, although it was not in any way her fault, began to feel that Olivia's very presence was needlessly intrusive. These were a last few precious hours in which I wanted him exclusively to myself and Olivia was denying me that small and simple pleasure. She also seemed stubbornly unwilling to depart even after a meal in which I had only had eyes for Thomas and he had more than once stretched out a hand under the table in order to place it on mine. Eventually, when I had become thoroughly irritated with Olivia, and thought it amazing that she could be quite so obtuse, she apologised.

'Forgive me, I can see that you have formed a close attachment and that my presence is not welcome. It's just, Jane, that I hoped you might allow me to stay the night. The atmosphere at home has become too depressing. In the meantime, I promise to leave you both to yourselves.'

'Of course you can stay. Thomas has been sleeping in the old woodman's cottage, thinking it safer after the search that was made for him so you're welcome to have your usual bedroom.'

'Thank you. I'll go and lie down then. I feel a headache coming on.'

'I thought she'd never leave us in peace,' Thomas confessed once Olivia had left the room. 'What's more, I'm not sure she approves of me.'

'Why do you say that?'

'The way she looks at me...as if I'm a bad smell.'

'She's a good friend and worries that you are exposing me to unnecessary danger.'

'And so I am, but you don't mind, do you?'

We both smiled at each other mischievously. 'You know I don't.'

33

Declarations of love

Iwas determined to spend one last night in Thomas's arms and I prepared to accompany him to the woodman's cottage. Meanwhile, Olivia had not re-emerged from her bedroom since going to it in the course of the afternoon, so I decided to gently tap on her door in order to ensure that all was well.

'Are you all right, Olivia?' I called out. 'I can have Mary bring you something to eat and drink if you wish it.'

'Do come in, Jane, I'd like to speak to you.'

As I then entered the room, I discovered Olivia lying on the bed fully clothed apart from her shoes, which she had discarded by its side. The curtains were still open but it was now growing dark.

'I see that you're in love with this Thomas Sumner,' she said bluntly.

'Yes...yes I am.'

'Is that wise?'

'Probably not, but aren't we all entitled to seek a little happiness in life.'

'Of course, do not imagine that I begrudge you that for a moment. It's just that if you're found to be harbouring him you could be imprisoned or worse.'

'He's going away tomorrow morning.'

'Yes, but he'll no doubt be back.'

'I do hope so...I don't actually want him to leave at all. In fact I've tried to persuade him to stay but he's determined to remain true to the cause and I admire him for that. I could well be carrying his child, too. After all, we've lain together more than once, and will do so once more tonight.'

'Oh Jane, have you quite taken leave of your senses?'

'Yes, I expect I have, but I really don't care. I want a child, Thomas's child, and I'm ready to hide its birth.'

'Your household will still know.'

'Of course, but I can count on them to remain loyal. None have betrayed Thomas, after all.'

'Or so you hope. Were any questioned when the last search was made for Thomas?'

'No, but even if they had been I'm sure they would have denied his presence.'

'Well, go to him if you must.'

'I do believe you're jealous.'

Olivia looked shocked. 'No, I'm just concerned for you. I wish you every happiness, of course I do.'

'Then do not begrudge me a few more hours with the man I love. We'll speak more of what has befallen Becky after Thomas has gone.'

34

Breakthrough

I tried to remain composed now Thomas had left, but found this desperately hard. I felt so bereft that there was a part of me that would have liked nothing better than to be alone with my sorrow. Instead, I had Olivia for company, trying hard to be solicitous, but in fact only succeeding in irritating me, which I knew was unfair. In the end, I decided that there was only one solution and that was to go for a ride, perhaps even as far as the sea, if there was time. With luck, the tide would be out, enabling us to gallop along the beach with the wind in our hair, and I could hopefully throw off my feelings of despondency.

Olivia was content to agree with this suggestion and at first we trotted along, side by side, in complete silence. I was at first completely preoccupied with thoughts of Thomas whilst, I suspect, Olivia was anxious not to say anything that I might judge too trivial or inane and thus induce nothing better than a frown of annoyance on my face. After a while, though, I turned my mind to Becky's fate and what could possibly be done to bring her attacker to justice.

'You know, Olivia, we can't wait for the law to take it's course, we must seize the moment,' I declared, my words spoken suddenly, as if out of nowhere.

'You mean...?'

'Let's make a start on finding out if anyone recalls seeing any stranger on a horse in the vicinity of Fetford Hall on the day of the ravishment.'

'But I thought you were determined to head for the coast...'

'I've changed my mind. There's not much time to get there and back before nightfall and this is far more important.'

'So where do we begin?'

'Let's assume for the moment that it could have been Pemberton, in which case he would be most likely to have approached from either the direction of Sidford or Exeter. Either way, there are a number of farms we could call on, and I propose that we seek out either the farmer or his wife and ask them to spread the word that we require information from anyone who remembers seeing a gentleman riding by the day before yesterday. If they do then we would welcome any description they might be able to give us of both the man and his horse. They can either give this to the constable or come to Fetford Hall.

'We could also, perhaps, make mention of the reward, don't you think?'

'Yes, although it will be up to James to increase what is currently on offer. I would also like to take a look at the scene of the attack. There's always a possibility that he's left us another clue, however small.'

Once we reached Fetford Hall, having called on a number of farms on our way, we were immediately greeted by Constance. To my eyes she looked utterly exhausted, no doubt as a consequence of the terrible attack on Becky.

'She hasn't come out of her bedroom since you left, Olivia,' Constance declared. "I fear that she will never recover from this foul assault upon her. I can only pray she isn't pregnant. God knows what we'll do if she is.'

'Neither of the women he has previously ravished have suffered that fate,' Olivia pointed out.

'Which means nothing,' Constance snapped. 'And how can you even know we are talking about the same individual?'

'We don't,' I said gently, 'but all the same it does seem probable. Certainly, I'm sure that the same man committed the previous ravishments and, of course, he's still at large.'

'Olivia's convinced that this fellow, Pemberton, must have been responsible, aren't you, my dear.'

'I agree that he remains our only suspect,' I said. 'But you know that there is a difficulty. He claims to have alibis for his whereabouts when not only the ravishments but also the murder was committed.'

'But only one of those supposed alibis has ever been questioned and he could have been lying,' Olivia asserted.

'Yes, but you know my view on that. Frankly, I don't believe that Pemberton is guilty, for all that there was a time when I was prepared to think otherwise. What's more, I believe that this latest attack has all the hallmarks of its predecessors. Further, can it really be credible that we have two ravishers loose in such a small locality? No, we are surely looking for one individual only; of that I am as certain as I dare be of anything.'

Constance glared at me. 'But you've no idea who that individual is, have you?'

'No, I haven't and nor do I have any faith in the ability of the likes of Crabb to ever find him. I take it that James is still not back from Honiton?'

'No, though I expect him at any time. He's already been

202

gone some hours.'

'May I speak to Becky?'

'If you must but she's in no fit state to talk to anyone.'

'Even so, I'd like to try...'

I shortly made my way upstairs and approached what I knew to be Becky's bedroom. Then I tapped softly on its door.'

'May I come in? It's Lady Jane Tremayne.'

My question was greeted by silence but rather than ask it again I turned the handle anyway and entered. The curtains were closed but the room was still not as dark as it might otherwise have been, thanks to a stream of sunlight. Becky, meanwhile, was tucked up in bed, her body in a foetal position with her head, which was turned away from the door, barely visible.

'Forgive my intrusion, Becky, I just wanted to say how sorry I am. What has happened to you is dreadful...quite dreadful.'

For a moment these words seemed to be met by nothing but silence but then I realised that Becky was sobbing, at first almost imperceptibly but then more loudly. I was moved to sit on the edge of the bed and place a hand on her shoulder. 'James will be back soon, I think.'

Becky turned her head and then buried her face in my lap. I began to stroke her hair, thinking how young and vulnerable she seemed.

'I understand you were attacked from behind and never got a view of his face.'

Becky mumbled something.

'Pardon.'

'I think he looked back. Yes, he did, he did. How could I have forgotten? I've been so upset....it was so awful.' As she spoke

Becky lifted her head and then sat up.

'What did you see?'

'That he was wearing a full face mask but I still got the impression that he wasn't old. His hair was also quite long and brown, you see. I expect you've been told that already?'

I nodded. 'And his clothes were fine, I understand?'

'Yes, the clothes of a gentleman, certainly.'

'And was there anything distinctive about his voice? I take it he did speak to you?'

'Yes, but only to say that he'd slit my throat if I didn't do his bidding. It was the voice of a gentleman, I'd say, but still with a Devon accent.'

'That's helpful, Becky, and, forgive me, I've one more question. If the answer's yes all you need do is squeeze my hand. Did he penetrate you?'

The squeeze was slow to come but squeeze it was. She was sobbing again and I hugged her.

'I'll leave you in peace now but James will come, I'm sure, as soon as he's returned.'

A few moments later I was back downstairs. 'She's remembered something important,' I informed both Olivia and Constance. 'It seems he glanced back at her and she could see that he was wearing a mask. She said, too, that he spoke well but with a Devon accent. All that tally's with what previous victims have been able to tell us.'

'You think it's worth trying to find others who may have seen him?' Constance asked.

'Of course. He would surely have only put on the mask when he was preparing to ravish her. Now I'd like to see where she was attacked.'

'I can show you that,' Olivia said.

It then took us no more than a couple of minutes to reach the scene of the ravishment. The ground still looked as if it had been disturbed and I carefully examined it in the hope that something might have been left there that would offer some clue as to the perpetrator's identity. However, this revealed nothing at all.

'He must have been watching the house in the hope of catching sight of her,' I said. 'I imagine he could not believe his luck when she walked into his clutches so unsuspectingly. How, though, did he manage to gain entry without anyone catching sight of him?'

'You know there's more than one way onto our land.'

'Yes, but even so; and perhaps it wasn't the first time he'd come, either. What's more, assuming he arrived by horse, he'll have had to have tethered it somewhere, and quite possibly for a long while, too.'

'Perhaps he has some prior knowledge of this place.'

'What, a former servant, you mean?'

'I was thinking more of our tenant farmers and their families although that doesn't really tally, does it, with his wearing gentleman's clothing?'

'But that could be no more than a disguise, much like the mask he wears. What strikes me most is that he may well have sufficient knowledge of this place to know that Becky had come to live here.'

'You're suggesting then that he specifically targeted her? I've been thinking that it could just as easily have been me that he ravished, or God forbid, even mother.'

'I'm suggesting it's a possibility, no more than that. I'll be bound, though, that what he did know was that this is largely a household of women so for certain he has a goodly amount of local knowledge. But then that was plain enough already from his previous crimes. I tell you, both, it feels as if he's toying with us and that his identity is right under our very noses and yet we haven't the wits to see who he might be! ...Oh, in God's name, Olivia, do not look at me so smugly. I know you still think it's Pemberton.'

'I am not saying that. I see the sense in your argument that it cannot be him...I think, perhaps, that we should continue our questioning.'

Yes, I suppose we should. Certainly, we should speak with every servant and then all your tenant farmers as well as their families.'

'Most of the servants have already been spoken to and say they saw nothing,' Constance declared.

'But it's not just a matter of what they might have seen on the day of the attack but whether they remember seeing anyone acting suspiciously at anytime since the wedding. Have they been asked that question?'

'Not specifically, so far as I'm aware, but all the same you'd think...'

'Sometimes people need to have their memories nudged a little. It's worthwhile making sure. If you'll begin questioning the tenants, Olivia, I'd welcome your assistance, Constance, in speaking again to the servants.'

'You know we'll just be accused of interfering in men's business... ' Olivia responded.

'I don't care about that. James isn't here, or at least not yet, and it's more vital than ever that we find this man. It's possible that his luck is about to run out but only if we act decisively.'

Thereafter, I had not been engaged on my intended task for long before James returned. The moment I set eyes on him it was also plain that he was not merely hot and sweaty from his long ride but also very angry.

'That reprobate Crabb seems unwilling to lift a finger! I told him that whoever this monster is he cannot be allowed to continue committing these foul crimes, and that I wanted a hue and cry raised throughout the county, but he wouldn't have it. I argued, too, that Pemberton be questioned as to his whereabouts when Becky was attacked but he just grew frostier still. All I could illicit from him was a promise that word would be spread again that a dangerous criminal was still on the loose and that women must be vigilant at all times. He also suggested that the notorious renegade, Thomas Sumner, was the most likely culprit and that he was already the subject of a widespread search.'

'That's a preposterous idea,' I exclaimed. 'You see, I myself have been giving him shelter, and can vouch for the fact that he was with me when Becky was attacked.'

James was understandably shocked by this revelation. 'Really?'

'Yes, really, but you must give me your word that you'll tell no one I said so. I was persuaded to provide a safe house to those serving the cause of the King in exile.

'Of course, I'll tell no one. But haven't you even spoken of this to Olivia?"

'Yes, she knows, but is also sworn to secrecy.'

I then told James what task I and Olivia were engaged upon and suggested the possibility of raising a further reward for any information that might lead to the perpetrator's arrest.

'Do you think it would achieve anything?' he asked me. 'I really couldn't afford to raise the reward to more than eighteen pounds.'

'That might be sufficient and I think it has to be worth the money. Someone out there must know the man and could have suspicions. Whatever their loyalties, the prospect of receiving such a sum might well tempt them. Let us see as well what comes of our questioning. I like to hope that someone living nearby will have seen the man and might be able to give us a good description. I've also spoken to Becky, as gently as I could. She's still most distressed, which is entirely to be expected. However, she's now remembered seeing that her attacker was wearing a mask, so he's bound to be the same individual who has attacked before.'

'Well, I must go to her without further ado. We'll talk later about what's happened. You'll stay for supper, I trust.'

'Yes, if I may. Thank you.'

James immediately ran upstairs while I turned my attention once more to questioning the servants. However, I had barely resumed this task when Olivia re-appeared. She was clearly in an animated state.

'I have some very important news,' she declared breathlessly. 'I've just come from the cottage of Matthew Parker and he's told me that he definitely remembers seeing a well-dressed rider pass him the day before yesterday. He's also convinced that he saw the same man about a week before that.'

'Did he get a good view of him?'

'On the most recent occasion, yes he did. But there's more. He could make out a scar on the man's left cheek above his brown-coloured beard and we know the man, whose horse the blacksmith shod on the day of the first ravishment, also had both such a scar and beard.'

I threw my arms around Olivia in sheer delight. 'My, you have done well, very well indeed. I take it he thinks he would recognise the man again?'

'Oh yes. Indeed, he says that apart from the scar he has a fairly good recollection of his general features.'

Then at last we can be confident that we have two positive identifications of the man most likely to have been responsible for these crimes. Indeed a third, if you count the sighting of the rider in the vicinity of Mistress Tapton's home. I'll warrant, too, that there may be others in the near vicinity who have also seen this man so I think it's still worthwhile pressing on with our enquiries, or at least urging the constables to undertake this task. Oh yes, and what about the man's horse? Did Parker remember anything in particular about that?'

'No, he merely says that it had a nondescript brown coat, looked fully mature, and was about fifteen hands tall. That's a description which could apply to literally thousands of horses.'

'True, but all the same it's still consistent with the blacksmith's description.'

I then I heard a sound behind me and turning round saw that it was James. He still looked grim faced but I was quick to impart the good news to him, and felt his mood improve somewhat. I also hoped that Becky might feel well enough to join us for supper, a simple fare of bread, butter and cheese, washed down with red wine, but in the event she kept to her bed. Meanwhile, I remained in a determinedly upbeat humour and decided to initiate a conversation on a question that had been increasingly exercising my mind ever since my last meeting with Pemberton in Exeter.

'You know, I still think the key to who has been responsible for these terrible crimes, lies in the knowledge he had of where Mistress Hodge lived. Pemberton admitted to that knowledge, but we can now be confident, can't we Olivia, that he is not the culprit. After all, he bears no scar on either cheek.' At that the two of us exchanged smiles and Olivia nodded her head. 'We also know from whom he got that information, namely the tailor, Master Thompson...'

'You're not suggesting he could be the culprit, are you?' James asked, his eyes lighting up.

'No, not at all, although it has crossed my mind. If he'd had a scar on his cheek I'm sure I would remember it, and what's more there's no reason to doubt that he and Pemberton spent the evening in each other's company. I've also never believed that any man would have even attempted to ride through the night all the way from Exeter to Tipton. No, what I've been thinking is that Thompson could well know someone else who had dealings with Mistress Hodge. Indeed, he could even have told him where she lived, just as he told Pemberton. If that was so and that man has a scar on his left cheek then he'll have some explaining to do.'

At these words, James thumped the table. 'In the devil's name, Jane, you're really onto something, at last.'

'Yes, I think perhaps I am. I've been meaning to go back to Exeter to visit my sister and nephew and I shall now make haste to do so, if not tomorrow, then certainly the day after. I've another thought as well, you would not expect a tailor to wear a gentleman's clothing but they surely have the means to make it!'

35

To Exeter

I set out for Exeter in confident mood with Olivia by my side, after she had asked that she might be able to accompany me, and returned to Altringham Manor with me for that purpose. Certainly, I would not have wished to undertake the journey on my own and in Olivia's absence would have taken my maid, Mary, with me, instead. I welcomed, too, the moral support she would be able to provide but was wary of the reaction of my brother-in-law to Olivia's presence in his home. In any event, I was determined that we would not outstay our welcome.

'Let us go first to Master Thompson's shop,' I suggested. 'We needn't detain him long.'

'He may be too busy to speak to us...'

'In which case, we'll have to call back when he isn't. We've both come prepared for at least one over-night stay, after all, and should Caroline and that Puritan brother-in-law of mine not be able to accommodate us then we can always resort to one of the city's inns.'

Both of us were grateful that the weather was fine for our journey, although after a few days of intermittent rain, some of it heavy, the road was very muddy in places. This slowed our progress somewhat, but having left Altringham Manor early we still made quite good time, enabling us to reach our destination by noon.

In comparison with the bright sunshine outside, the shop seemed dark and cavernous as we entered it, the tinkling sound of the door bell announcing our arrival. Thompson almost immediately stepped forward out of the shadows, his expression turning from one of friendly greeting to one of irritation the moment he recognised us.

'I hope you haven't come to question me any further about Master Pemberton? I told you all I know and that's a fact.'

I sought to be reassuring. 'No, I'm now sure he's entirely innocent. You see there has been another attack and he does not answer to the description of the man who we believe was responsible.'

'So, how can I help you then?'

'I merely ask that you tell me if you enjoy the acquaintance of anyone else who might also have known where Mistress Hodge lived in Tipton? I have in mind a fellow tailor. He might well have a scar on his left cheek, I believe.'

'Well, let me think a moment....There's Isaac Turnbull. He owns a shop in Queen Street. He inherited it from his father a few years back now...I can't say if he ever had any dealings with Mistress Hodge but it's possible and come to think of it, he has a scar on one of his cheeks. Yes, it could well be his left. Keeps himself to himself, too. A curt *good day* is usually the most you'll get out of him.'

'Is he married?' Olivia asked

'Not so far as I know.'

'Thank you, Master Thompson, you've been most helpful,' I declared with a smile. 'And while we're here I'd mention that I'm in need of a new riding coat...is that something I could purchase from you?'

'Most certainly, m'lady....'

The prospect of a sale had brought about an almost instant transformation in his manner and for the remainder of our stay in his shop he could not have been more attentive. Olivia, meanwhile, grew increasingly impatient to be gone, sighing a good deal and looking cross, until I was moved to whisper in her ear.

'There's really no hurry, Olivia. The last thing we should do is rush to pay any visit to Master Turnbull.'

Once I had placed my order, I strolled out of the shop in the best of humours. 'This time, Olivia, I believe we have our man! First, though, we must find a Justice of the Peace here in Exeter and persuade him that the case against Turnbull warrants the man's arrest. Certainly, I've no confidence in Crabb but with luck the Justices here will be less prejudiced. I suggest we make enquiries at the Guildhall, which we passed on our way here.'

In the event, it took a frustrating two hours before we were finally able to speak to any Justice, by which time both of us were feeling distinctly more out of sorts with the world and also in need of food in our bellies. The Justice in question, Jeremiah Lake, dressed in sombre black from head to foot, also appeared to be just as much a puritan as Crabb. However, his general demeanour seemed kindlier and he looked to be a good ten years older with a beard turned completely white.

'Thank you for your time, good sir,' I began. 'I must tell you that I have every reason to believe that the tailor, Isaac Turnbull, has ravished three women and murdered a fourth and I would therefore urge you to have him arrested without further ado.'

The Justice looked at me aghast. 'That is a most grave

accusation to make against a man whom I have every reason to believe is of good character and also enjoys some standing within the city, being a member of its Council. What possible evidence do you have against him?'

'A man answering to his description was seen in the vicinity of two of these crimes on the days they were committed. Most especially, the man was seen to have a scar on his left cheek, as does Master Turnbull.'

'I see... Nonetheless, the strife our nation has endured has left many men with scarred faces. Of itself, it proves nothing.'

'But there is something even more crucial. You may have heard something of the circumstances of the poor woman who was murdered in her own bed?'

The Justice shook his head. 'I am certainly aware of the murder you refer to but nothing more.'

'She was a skilled embroiderer and took in work from tailors here in Exeter; Master Thompson for one, who's informed me it's quite possible she also worked for Master Turnbull...'

'But he's not certain?'

'No, not certain. However, whoever murdered Mistress Hodge, who was a widow and lived alone, must have had knowledge of exactly where she lived... You see it's inconceivable to me that her death was a random one...'

'How can you be so sure of that? Someone could have entered her home intending to steal...'

'No, with respect, sir, her person was interfered with. The murderer sought to ravish her as he had his previous two victims. She must have struggled with him, most likely recognised him, and so he strangled her. Nor is there any reason to believe that anything was taken from her home.'

214

The Justice's face still wore an expression of scepticism. 'But if she knew Master Turnbull he'd have been mighty foolish to choose her as a victim, wouldn't he...unless I suppose he always intended to kill her?'

'Sir, all three women who have survived attacks have stated that the man responsible was finely dressed and masked. I have little doubt that this was a disguise and who is better placed to create such a disguise than a master tailor like Turnbull. When he sought to ravish Mistress Hodge he was also masked, I'm sure, but when she struggled with him she probably tore it off his face, or recognised him anyway...'

'Yes, I hear what you say, but this is still nothing more than supposition on your part, you must admit?'

'No sir, it goes further than that. You see I have both a blacksmith and a tenant farmer who I believe would be able to identify Turnbull as having been in the vicinity when two of the ravishments were committed. Certainly, both will say that the man they saw bore a scar on his left cheek, and that he was finely dressed. What I ask, above all else, sir, is that you arrest Turnbull so he can be brought before them both. Should neither of them be able to identify him then let him walk free, but if they can then he will surely have to explain what he was doing dressed as a gentleman so far from Exeter and so close to the scene of two terrible ravishments on the days they were committed.'

I had spoken with increasing conviction and began to feel that my arguments were becoming persuasive as the Justice hesitated, pondering my words.

'Um... I know that Master Turnbull dresses well especially since he became a city councillor. Some would say indeed that he dresses above his station... I for one have seen him in a silk doublet.'

'And is he married, sir?'

'Not to my knowledge... He has an elderly mother who lives with him, if my memory serves me well.'

'Then, sir, do you not agree that the evidence against him is strong enough to merit an arrest?'

'These are most grave allegations and the evidence you have laid before me is no more than circumstantial....You will have to give me time to consider. It still troubles me that you have told me nothing that definitely places him at the scene of any of these crimes... Nearby, perhaps, but that is not the same.'

'Sir, as to that there is one other possibility. As I have told you the man who committed these ravishments was masked. If I am right in thinking that Turnbull is the villain then it is probable that he still has that mask in his possession. What is more when the second ravishment was committed, a button was left at the scene of the crime. It was of fine quality and would have come from a doublet that again the villain might still have. I would urge you therefore, to also consider issuing a warrant for a search of Turnbull's home.'

'Very well, I will certainly do that. You may return here at the same hour tomorrow and I will inform you what I have decided.'

'Thank you, sir, I am grateful to you for your time.'

Lake deigned to give me a thin smile and then Olivia and I walked outside into the sunshine.

'You argued your case well, Jane,' Olivia said. 'Surely he'll now agree to act...'

I felt somewhat less confident. 'Perhaps. At least there must be some chance that he'll decide to issue a warrant. What troubles me, though, is that Turnbull's had every opportunity to dispose of the doublet, or at least replace its buttons.'

'Assuming he's even realised he left one at the scene of his crime. And what of the mask?'

'As a tailor he could even have a supply of masks in his shop , of course, but that would be a mixed blessing for certain. I mean, he could then claim that he possessed one perfectly legitimately.'

'Would not everything depend on the type of mask found to be in his possession? What did the women who were ravished have to say about that? I cannot now remember.'

'As I recall, that it covered all of his face and appeared to be made of black leather'

'So if it was one or several of these that were found in his possession, the case against him would become much stronger...'

'Just so long as he can be identified as having been in the vicinity of two of the crimes. Even supposing that the Justice agrees to an arrest, we are still going to have to bring both the blacksmith and the tenant farmer here to Exeter for that purpose. Mind you, even then I expect he'll have his excuses and without evidence that definitely places him at the scene of any of these crime any jury might be reluctant to convict him.'

'And perhaps rightly so. We were too certain, were we not, that Pemberton was guilty?'

'Yes, and you even more than me.'

The two of us then exchanged rueful smiles.

36

Accusations

Twenty four hours later, we duly returned to the Guildhall. Both of us were feeling somewhat tired as our sleep had been interrupted more than once by the wailings of Caroline's baby son, Michael. John had also barely tolerated our presence and had thoroughly irritated me by throwing scorn on my endeavours.

'I do wish that you would learn from your previous experience, and not keep dabbling in matters that are best left to men.'

'But I tell you, this time I'm confident we have found the villain responsible. Everything fits. He has the means to disguise himself through his trade, he has a scar on his cheek, and we have witnesses to the fact that just such a man was in the vicinity of two of the ravishments on the days they were committed. Surely, this is enough to justify his arrest, at least so he can then be questioned and shown to the two witnesses.'

'I don't agree. Apart from being a member of the City Council, he and his mother are both patients of mine and I cannot believe him capable of the crimes you accuse him of. Even if he was in the vicinity when two of them were committed, that doesn't make him guilty of ravishment and murder. I expect he will be perfectly able to explain his movements on the days you have in mind..

'Perhaps so but I still say he should be questioned. My fear has also always been that these attacks will just continue until the perpetrator is brought to justice. I have therefore merely acted in the interests of my sex and, too, of the community at large, much as I know my late husband would have done were he still alive.'

Still John had looked at me with distain. 'Nevertheless, I cannot believe that you have found the right man.'

Now as we re-entered the Justice's presence and he rose from his chair to greet us, I was full of trepidation as to what decision he had come to. It was then that I noticed that his face wore an expression of clear discomfort and my heart sank.

'In the light of your allegations... ' he coughed and refused to meet my eye...'I have already questioned Turnbull and he vehemently asserts his innocence... '

'You've arrested him then?'

'....um, no, I thought he deserved the courtesy of being spared that indignity.'

I could barely believe what I was hearing and stared at the Justice in open mouthed amazement.... 'Of course he'd deny his guilt,' I spluttered

'I asked him if he admitted being in the vicinity of two of these crimes and he said that it was possible as he has a sister who lives in Harpford and he visits her and her family frequently. I then asked him if he recalled visiting the black-smith's in Tipton and he said that he had done so as without the man's assistance he'd have never made it back to Exeter.'

'And did you ask him if he knew the murdered woman?'

'Naturally,'

'And...'

'He said that he whilst he knew of her, he had never had any dealings with her and was ignorant of her place of abode. I felt satisfied that he was telling me the truth.'

I wanted to appeal to him to still authorise a search warrant but a moment's reflection told me that this was now almost certainly pointless as he would no doubt be busy seeking to cover his tracks even supposing he had not already done so.

'How long since you had this conversation with him?' I asked limply.

'It was yesterday evening...'

There remained a faint possibility, I supposed, that he had never realised he had lost a button but he was still bound to appreciate that his three living victims were capable of describing his clothing so on those grounds alone might well have already destroyed it.

'And what about masks. Did you ask him if he made these and had any in his possession?'

'I did. He told me that he's made some in the past...for masked balls...but that there is now little or no demand for them. He couldn't say for certain whether he had any still in stock.'

'So, you're not prepared to take the matter any further, I suppose?'

'I think not...but I still thank you for bringing your concerns to my attention.' His tone had now become a shade condescending and I felt even more irritated. This, however, I did my best to hold in check, deciding that I was in need of fresh air as soon as possible.

'I still believe that he committed these crimes,' I asserted.

The Justice shook his head. 'I really think not. Perhaps he was in the vicinity of them but that of itself doesn't make him guilty. You have also provided me with no evidence that would place him at the scene of the murder.'

'What about the button?'

'A very tiny item, you must admit, that could have come off so many different pieces of clothing...'

'Only clothing of high quality; it's made of ivory. Mind you, now you've revealed your hand I expect he'll have gone home to destroy anything that might still incriminate him. I hope as well you didn't mention my name?'

At this question the Justice became rather shame-faced. He was clearly embarrassed. 'I... I may have done... ' he confessed.

'Why?' I asked angrily. 'You had no right...'

The Justice bristled a little. 'I had every right. You have made grave accusations...'

'But he's a ravisher, a murderer... God knows what he might do next...'

'You've made accusations like this before have you not?'

'Yes...but...'

'And been proved wrong, so Justice Crabb has informed me only this morning...'

'On that occasion, yes...'

'You cannot continue to accuse men of good standing of these crimes. I suggest that you desist...'

'I have merely been in pursuit of the truth. Must more women suffer before anything is done to bring this villain to justice...'

'Enough! I have made my decision.'

I turned on my heel in disgust. 'Come, Olivia, we've no hope of justice here, it seems.'

Once we'd reached the street where the skies had turned cloudy and there was a hint of rain in the air, my anger bubbled over.

'God give me strength, these men are conspiring against us!'

'And what is Crabb doing here?' Olivia asked. 'The trouble is, they hate us because of where our loyalties lie...'

'True... And because we are mere women, seeking to protect our sex. They've closed ranks against us, that's for certain.'

37

Reunion

It was now September and autumn it seemed was coming early as the weather had turned not only wetter but decidedly colder too. This chimed with my mood, much as when Pemberton had so discomforted me. Yet again all my efforts had come to nothing, leaving me feeling tired and thoroughly out of sorts both with myself and with the world in general.

After the short shrift I felt I had received from the Justice, Jeremiah Lake, I had been grateful to be able to leave Exeter without having to confront my supercilious brother-in-law. I would also have welcomed more support from my sister when I railed against the likes of Justices Lake and Crabb but she was too preoccupied with Michael's needs, something I could readily forgive. Now I found myself increasingly missing Thomas's loving embrace and wondering fretfully if I would ever see him again.

Worse still, I was normally a sound sleeper but as the days passed I began to toss and turn more in my bed, constantly replaying in my mind the evidence against Turnbull and on every occasion coming to the conclusion that he was as guilty as hell. Even worse, I remained fraught with anxiety that he would strike again for all that Olivia did her utmost to reassure me that this was really most unlikely. We were strolling together, side by side, in the Manor's rose garden, the rain of earlier in the day having relented.

'He'd surely not want to risk his luck again when he's come under such suspicion.'

'What suspicion! More likely, he'll think he's been given free licence to act as he pleases!'

'Surely not, Jane.'

'He just has the devil in him, I know he has. And worse, that fool Lake has even given him my name as his accuser...'

'He'd never dare to attack you, Jane...'

'Oh wouldn't he... I tell you, so long as he remains at large we must all take special care. So how is Becky?'

'As well as can be expected, I suppose. She still keeps to her bed a good deal and is most subdued. It's as if all her zest for life has been taken from her.'

' Which is no more than I'd expect...I tell you, that monster Turnbull has much to answer for.'

'If only we had the means to bring him to justice.'

'Alas, while he remains so well protected by his friends that's as likely as restoring our gracious King to his throne. Mind you, I've thought of petitioning the present Sheriff of the County, Peter Bevis, but I doubt he'd listen.'

'Might that not depend on how well drafted it is. We could seek legal advice?'

I frowned. 'Perhaps so, but lawyers are expensive and beyond my means whilst I remain in such debt.'

'James could pay. He's still mighty angry after what has befallen Becky.'

'But does he believe that Turnbull's guilty?'

'He certainly believes that there's enough evidence against

him to justify a charge of ravishment. I've even heard him threaten to call Turnbull out.'

'But duelling's been made illegal and the man's nothing more than a tradesman...'

'It was said more in anger than seriously, I'm sure. But look, there's an attorney in Exeter, Gilbert Overbury, who's acted for our family for many years. You and James could both go and see him.'

I pondered this suggestion for a few moments. 'Very well, you can tell James that I'd be willing, provided he's prepared to bear the cost, or at least the overwhelming majority of it.'

'I shall be pleased to do that as soon as I return home.'

The two of us walked on in silence for a short distance before I coughed a little nervously. Olivia looked at me sharply. 'Is something wrong?'

I met her eye. 'I believe that I may be pregnant.' The words were spoken in barely more than a whisper. 'My courses are normally regular and are now three days late. I do not know whether to cry with joy or with fear.'

Olivia seized my arm. 'Whatever, it makes no difference to our friendship.' The two of us then embraced.

'I so wish that Thomas was here... He'll return one day, I pray, but whether in weeks or months I cannot say.'

'Have you thought of a wet-nurse?'

'It's early days for that but yes, I have. Fortunately, my steward, Harry Parson's wife, Melissa, is well into her pregnancy. She's a strong woman and I know I can fully trust both her and Harry. I'll make it worth their while, of course.'

I then sniffed at a red rose and imbibed its scent, wondering even as I did so whether the difficult road I seemed to have embarked upon would end in happiness or tragedy. Upon Olivia's arrival, we had at first intended to go riding together in our usual fashion, but I no longer felt in the mood for such an activity. Instead, I was inclined to suggest that we play music together or indulge in a game of cards. I looked back towards the Manor with that thought in mind when I saw my maid, Mary, hurrying towards us, looking quite animated.

'Yes, Mary, what is it?'

'Begging your pardon, m'lady, a servant has come from Tatcham Hall... He says he has a message for you, m'lady. He's been told to wait at the front door.'

I felt a surge of excitement at this news and cast an eye at Olivia. 'Lead on then, Mary, lead on...'

I had an urge to run but instead restrained myself, walking ahead of Olivia, whom I beckoned to with a finger to follow me. The hall was gloomy and somewhat cold in contrast to the sunlight I had just been enjoying but I barely noticed as I passed through it, reaching the front door within seconds before throwing it open. I instantly recognised the thin face of a young man with only the beginnings of any beard, whom I remembered from my visit to Tatcham Hall but could not put any name to. He promptly took off the wide-brimmed hat he was wearing but seemed lost for words and failed to meet my eye.

'Well,' I said a little impatiently. 'You have a message for me, I understand.'

'Yes m'lady, Master Thomas 'as sent me,' he replied in a heavy Devon accent. ''E sends 'is compliments to 'e and asks that 'e come to 'im at Tatcham as soon as 'e can. I was also told to say that the old Master's poorly and 'as taken to 'is bed.'

At this news I put a hand to my mouth, masking a gasp of surprise and anticipation before turning to face Olivia.

'I must ride there immediately. You know you're welcome to stay here as long as you wish.'

Olivia shook her head. 'No, I'll ride back to Fetford. I'll also speak directly to James about the matter we discussed.'

I hurried to change into my riding habit and, within twenty minutes, having had Hera saddled and brought from the stables, and having said my farewells to Olivia, was ready to depart, with the young messenger for company. It transpired that he was a stable lad and had been entrusted with one of his Master's horses in order to make the journey required of him. I was somewhat puzzled that Thomas had not seen fit to come in person but could only assume that this was because of his father's ill health. Quite why he had returned so soon was also a mystery, for which he would no doubt provide an explanation when we met. Above all, the closer we got to Tatcham Hall the more my desire to be in his arms once more began to reach a fever pitch.

Once through the hall's entrance gates we entered an avenue of beech trees that were just on the turn with the coming of autumn, and which led slightly uphill. Overcome with impatience, I immediately encouraged Hera into a gallop, not caring whether the stable lad was capable of keeping pace with me. Almost immediately, the roof and chimneys of the hall were in view, and as I approached its elaborately carved doorway, I was delighted when I recognised Thomas emerging to greet me. I immediately noticed that he had regrown his beard and let his hair grow long. As I drew closer, he held up a hand in greeting and smiled broadly.

'Welcome, Jane, I'm delighted you were able to come so quickly.'

As I began to dismount he then came forward and in an instant took me in his arms and our lips met in a lingering kiss.

'Well done, Adam,' he then said, addressing the rather embarrassed looking stable lad. 'Here's something for your trouble.' And with that he tossed him a coin.

'How is your father?' I asked as we made our way inside.

'Not good, I'm afraid. He took to his bed three days ago and has not stirred since.'

'Have you fetched a doctor?'

'Father says he's no time for them. He's always valued his health, you know, and now thinks his end has come.'

'And what has brought you back so soon?'

He looked at me sombrely. 'The supposedly safe house I reached just outside Oxford was searched and I was fortunate that they did not find me. You see I'd gone out to visit an old friend. Then when I reached Northampton the town seemed to be overrun by soldiers, which made me very wary indeed. Still I pressed on towards Leicester, hoping to rendezvous with Lord Hastings. However, when I arrived at a hall near there, he'd left a message for me saying that I should look to save myself if I could as he feared we'd been betrayed.'

'Who would do such a thing?'

'An infiltrator, perhaps, or someone tempted by the lure of gold. Be that as it may, I decided to return here . Mind you, to find my father being so ill has put me into a quandary as to what to do for the best. I don't want to leave him, yet with every day that passes I fear that the risk of another search increases. Certainly, I don't want to place you in any further jeopardy.'

'I don't care about that.'

'I think you should.'

'I can hide you, just as I did before. And, so long as your father lives, you could still visit him here...'

'It might work for a few weeks, I suppose, but not indefinitely...'

'You'll do it then?'

'Yes, if you're sure?'

'Of course.'

By now we had reached the comparative privacy of the library where once again our lips met in a loving kiss. I was tempted to confess that I might be pregnant but then decided that it was too soon to do so. Instead, I had another question for him.

'What will happen to this Hall should your father die?'

'I won't be allowed to inherit, that's for certain. I fear that the estate will be sequestered and sold off...'

'Unless our true King can be restored to his throne.'

'That day may still be far off... Yes, enter.'

We had both heard a gentle tap on the door, which Thomas had closed behind us, and in walked an elderly looking maid, whom I recognised.

'Master Thomas, yer father's taken a turn for the worse, I'm a feared. He's asking for 'e.'

'Very well, Margaret, I'll come directly.' He then looked me in the eye. 'I don't know how long I'll be. Do you want anything to eat or drink? I can have it brought to you...'

'Thank you. I'll take some beer... I need to quench my thirst.'

I passed the time waiting for Thomas's return staring out of the window at the fine view that it afforded of the countryside for a mile or more to the west and sipping my beer, before turning my attention to the library's extensive collection of books. I knew that Thomas's father had a reputation as an antiquarian and several of the books appeared to date back to the days before the invention of the printing press. I imagined that they would have once adorned the shelves of monastery libraries and wondered what would happen to them once the old man expired.

Perhaps upwards of half-an-hour slipped by before Thomas finally returned, looking distinctly grave. I thought in fact that I had never seen him so close to tears and hurrying forward laid a hand gently on his left arm and looked lovingly into his eyes.

'We have said our farewells. He's not keeping any food down and drinking little.'

'Then have a doctor sent for...'

'Father insists that all doctors are useless charlatans. He says he wants no truck with any of them...'

'Send for one anyway...'

'I know father would be angry with me if I did. While there's an ounce of strength in his body, he'd turn his head to the wall and resist any attempt at bleeding. He's always been mighty stubborn. No, I think it best that I respect his wishes.' Thomas then cast his eye over the library shelves. 'He's still most animated about the fate of all of these books. He says he'd rather be damned in hell than see them sold off by Parliament. He's urged me to hide as many of them as I can and a few other items of value besides. Could you help me do that, Jane?'

'Why, of course.'

He then stared thoughtfully at the shelves of books, many of which I imagined had not been opened in years. 'I'm sure my father would also understand if we don't empty the library completely. One cart load of the best amongst them ought to still leave enough behind to avert suspicion that it's been stripped of its contents. If any prying questions are asked it can be said that some were either sold or destroyed. I'll instruct the servants that that's to be the story and none will contradict it, I'm sure.'

'The fate of his servants must be a concern to your father, too.'

'Oh yes, it is. There are five or more who've served under him all their working lives. The war has done much to denude his wealth, unfortunately, although he's told me there is still a tidy sum in gold and silver coinage that he's kept well hidden over the years. Whatever happens I'm to be the beneficiary of that and he's even given me the key.... See.' With that he held it up to me. 'He's also made bequests in his will to all his long serving servants that should be sufficient to keep them from the poor house...'

His voice had begun to falter and he looked so downcast that I threw my arms around him consolingly and we just stood where we were in this loving embrace for upwards of a minute.

'You won't leave me, I hope?' he asked me gently. 'I know I'm not much company and may have to spend the night at my father's bedside but I'd still appreciate your support at this time...'

'And I give it to you with all my heart, Thomas, you know I do...'

He looked into my eyes and found a smile from somewhere, 'You're a darling, you know that.'

'I love you.'

'And I you, with all my heart.'

38

Sadness

'Father's had a terrible night, I'm afraid. I doubt he'll survive the day.'

Thomas had not long entered my bedroom and planted a kiss on my forehead. It had made me wake with startled pleasure as he smiled down at me in that slightly lopsided fashion of his. He had then drawn back the curtains to reveal a nearly clear blue sky although as my bedroom faced west there was no dazzling sunshine. The night before I had offered to sit with him at his father's bedside but he had declined, insisting that I get a good night's rest and I had reluctantly agreed. More tired than I had realised I had then quickly fallen asleep. Now I felt refreshed whilst Thomas looked anything but.

'Have you managed to sleep at all?'

'Very little,' he admitted. 'I managed to doze for a while in the chair next to my father's bed but anxiety for his welfare made me wake all too easily.'

'Do you want to get some rest now? I could sit with your father, if you'll let me?'

'The servants can do their share of that. In any event, I consider it my duty to remain with him as much as possible until the end. God willing, there'll be plenty of time for sleep once he's gone.'

'I could still sit with you. Have you by any chance told him of our relationship?'

'No, I confess I have not.'

'Might he not be pleased?'

'Probably, yes, for he's always spoken well of you. I fear, though, that he's now too far gone to understand anything I say to him.'

'In which case he's hardly in any state to object to my presence.'

'But I don't want to subject you to such an ordeal.'

'He would not be the first person I have seen die.'

I then rose from my bed and took hold of Thomas's hands while looking up into his eyes.

'Very well, if that's your wish.'

I smiled gently at him, and put the fingers of my right hand to his forehead, which he faintly touched. His response was to draw me into a kiss that might all too easily have led to amorous congress had we not both checked ourselves.

'As soon as I've dressed, I will join you at your father's bedside,' I told him. 'Have you broken your fast yet?'

'No, but I can have a servant bring us bread and beer.'

As soon as I entered the bedroom where Thomas's father lay, it was apparent to me from his desperately laboured breathing that it might well not be long before he expired. The heavy damask curtains were also all but closed, allowing only a modest amount of light to penetrate the gloom and the atmosphere was oppressive for want of sufficient air as, to my astonishment, the window was shut. Thomas, meanwhile, was sitting on a chair next to his father's bed and acknowledged my entrance with just a hint of a smile.

'May I open the window,' I said quietly. 'It can surely do no harm to allow some air to penetrate?'

Thomas nodded his consent and I felt a palpable sense of relief when I was able to open the window wide enough to feel a cooling breeze on my face. I then found myself a chair of my own and sat down next to Thomas, placing a hand on his even as I did so. Time then almost seemed to stand still as we awaited the apparently inevitable and my thoughts drifted towards the conversation I had had with Thomas the night before. I had still said nothing about my possible pregnancy but I had expressed my deep frustration over the attitude that the Justice Lake had adopted and explained the idea I and Olivia had discussed of using a lawyer to petition the County Sheriff.

Thomas had been lukewarm about any such notion, proclaiming that the likes of Lake and Crabb and the County Sheriff were all in league with one another. 'I suspect you'll get just as much short shrift from him, in which case James will have wasted his money,' he had declared.

'Still it has to be worthy of the attempt. We cannot just sit back and allow a ravisher and a murderer to remain at large to attack a fifth time and more besides.'

'Well, you must both do as you see fit. I suppose James has little to lose by simply seeking advice.'

Then I had wondered about telling Thomas about Lake's stupidity in revealing my identity to Turnbull and again had hesitated to the point of saying nothing. After all, he already had enough to concern him, what with a dying father and the constant risk of arrest.

Now I was shaken out of my reverie by the realisation that Thomas's father's breathing had grown more shallow and that the moment of death might be very close indeed. I squeezed Thomas's hand more tightly and we each gave the other a nervous glance. Moments later I was conscious that the breathing had stopped and without a word I hugged Thomas and placed a kiss on his left cheek. It was moist with tears.

39

A marriage contract

The body of Thomas's father was laid to rest in the family vault in the nearby parish church three days later. The funeral was well attended by his servants and tenant farmers and their family members but by few others, Thomas being anxious that the funeral should not be too long delayed out of any desire to give those who lived further afield, including some cousins and their spouses, the opportunity to attend.

'Once word of his death spreads, you can be sure as night follows day that it will bring another search party here,' he had declared.

'Then come back with me to Altringham as soon as he's buried...'

'Aye, I'll do that.'

True to his word we set out on our journey within three hours of the funeral having taken place, armed with two bags full of the most precious books from the library together with a quantity of gold and silver coins, although only after Thomas had acted on his father's wishes by handing over generous monetary bequests to all the servants named in his will. They had been received with all due gratitude and there had been many expressions of regret at Thomas's hasty departure, which he had done his best to calm.

'As you well know we live in difficult times,' he told us. The manor remains in your custody to treat with respect as you have always done. I will return whenever I consider it safe to do so. Should anyone come searching for me tell them nothing of my presence here, let alone where you think I might have gone. I am reliant on your loyalty.'

At first we had ridden towards Altringham Manor in companionable silence, pleased to encourage our horses into a canter as the temperature had fallen sharply and the day felt distinctly autumnal. I, however, now decided that the time had come to speak out.

'Thomas...'

'Yes, my love.'

I took a deep breath. 'I believe I am pregnant. My courses are too late for there to be any other explanation.' This confession was met by a long silence. 'Can you wonder at it,' I added disappointedly. 'We have given ourselves over to wanton pleasure...'

'Of course we have and I do not regret that for a single moment...'

Though you will not be the one to bear the child and with it the pain of labour I could not help thinking although I did not say it. I was beginning to feel exasperated with him. Was he about to treat my like a whore, to cast me off disdainfully and ride away for ever, ignoring the fact that he had played an ample part in my downfall?

'Well, is that all you have to say?'

'I confess, Jane, that I am a little shocked but do not imagine for a single moment that I am displeased. In fact I could not be happier. What is more you have made up my mind that I must make an honest woman of you before it's too late. So, will you marry me? Of course, I've little to offer you; just the gold and silver which I carry on my person as well as my true love.'

'Yes, of course I'll marry you, ' I declared without hesitation.

By now we had brought our horses to a standstill at the edge of the road and leaning across in the saddle Thomas was able to put a free hand around my back and draw me towards him until our lips met.

'I think we should be wed as soon as possible, don't you agree?' Thomas said.

'Yes, most certainly.'

'And, I'm afraid, for both our sakes, with as few people as possible knowing about it. Otherwise, the news is bound to reach the ears of those in authority who would like to see me placed in irons, or worse.'

'I understand. And Thomas...'

'Yes?'

'All that matters to me is that we should be man and wife... I have been wed before, don't forget.'

'Whilst I have not.. Nor would I expect to ever replace your late husband in your heart...'

'There's a special place for him there, for sure, but that does not mean that I don't truly love you and wish to bear your child.'

'My darling Jane...' Yet again we could not resist kissing each other even at the risk of falling from our horses.

'Of course, if our marriage is to be kept as secret as possible, we could simply have a spousal contract drawn up,' I suggested. 'It would be as valid as any church ceremony, would it not?'

'Yes, if you're sure that would be acceptable to you?'

'I am.'

'Would we require a lawyer's services to have it drawn up?'

I pondered that question for a few moments. 'Not necessarily. I still have my contract with Paul in my possession. All we need do is adapt it.'

'And witnesses to our signatures?'

'Probably, but that's surely no issue. There's my steward, Harry. Olivia, too, of course. Think, if we act promptly we could be legally man and wife within hours.'

My excitement at this prospect was however somewhat tempered by Thomas reminding my that he was still essentially a fugitive and as such determined to maintain his disguise as nothing more than a humble tenant farmer. There could be no question, therefore, of our residing together openly as man and wife and with every day that passed we would also have to live in fear of exposure. Still, I was undaunted, resolving that I would far rather be married in secret than not at all. Further, the pretence we would have to maintain would still be vastly preferable to total separation.

Within an hour of our reaching Altringham Manor, I had located my spousal contract to Paul in the old chest in which the deeds to the hall were also to be found, and with a quill pen, ink and paper, sat down to write out a contract between myself and Thomas. There would be no dowry, as such, but the very act of marriage would give him title to all I possessed, a reflection that gave me further pause for thought. Yet, still I was undeterred. Meanwhile, Thomas proceeded to shave off his beard and when he presented himself to me I thought him most handsome.

'You need your hair cut short again,' I suggested. 'Allow me to attend to it, if you will. And that shirt you're wearing is still too fine, I think. The lace trimmings give you away, I'm afraid.'

He smiled at me in assent. 'Mind you, it irks me that I must look like a crop-head.'

'It's worth it if it helps to keep you safe, but you must still spend as much time as possible with me here in the house. It will now be yours, after all.'

'Remaining here may be too dangerous. Soldiers could come searching for me at any time.'

'Given this house's position anyone approaching can always expect to be seen well before they arrive, especially if they come as a party by horse. That should always allow you plenty of time to slip out the back of the house and across the fields. We must also invent a new name for you as well in case they decide to spread their search wider and you're unable to hide from them.'

'How about Ned Tattershall then. I had a manservant by that name once but he died of the pox.'

I grinned at him. 'Ned it shall be then.'

By nightfall the task of writing out the contract was complete and I showed it to Thomas.

'What's this I read about a jointure?' he asked.

'It ensures that if you die first Altringham Manor will come back to me in its entirety. Do you not think that reasonable?'

He hesitated a little but then smiled. 'Why yes, perfectly reasonable. Consider it agreed.'

I had already summoned Harry and taken him into my confidence, asking him to act as witness to the contract's signing. The thought that such a simple act carried out with the aid of candlelight in the comfort of my own home, would make me and Thomas man and wife made my feel quite giddy with what verged on disbelief. I worried, too, that Harry's signature alone would not be enough to make the document legal, seeing that my contract with Paul had been witnessed by both my late father and Paul's. Olivia would have been an ideal choice, of course, but that would involve inevitable delay and Thomas was full of reassurance that one witness would be quite sufficient.

'I wonder, indeed, if it even needs witnessing at all?'

'I still think it should be, and what's more I believe it would be wise to have a second witness. I'll ask my housekeeper, Alice, to act as one. I know she can write her own signature.'

'Very well, if you insist. Mind, are you content that this contract will make me sole owner of this estate?' he asked me.

I looked him in the eye. 'Of course, given that in return you will love and protect me, will you not?'

'So far as it is in my power to do so, yes, always.'

'Come then, let's sign it.' I declared, and once both Harry and Alice had been summoned into our presence I took a quill pen in my hand and placed my signature on the contract without hesitation. Thomas then did the same.

40

Master Overbury

We now had a fine view of Exeter Cathedral before us after what had not been the pleasantest of journeys thanks to more than one heavy shower. The temperature, too, had turned distinctly autumnal and I felt grateful for my riding coat to help protect me from the elements. Beside me rode James and also Olivia, the purpose of our journey being to seek out the attorney, Gilbert Overbury. Once that had been accomplished I also intended to visit my sister, Caroline, along with my nephew, Michael.

Allowing, as well, for the possibility that the attorney might not be immediately available, we were prepared to seek over-night accommodation at one of the city's inns and for that reason had travelling bags slung over our horses. The possibility of seeking to impose ourselves on the hospitality of my sister and brother-in-law was also one that I had contemplated, but then decided against, reflecting that we would be bound to receive a frosty welcome from John.

Meanwhile, Thomas remained at Altringham Manor, his hair cropped and his attire suitably plain, like the tenant farmer he pretended to be, yet in reality, following our marriage, none-theless lord of all he surveyed. He continued to worry that news of his father's death would bring more soldiers to the Manor but as yet there had been no sign of any. Furthermore, no news had come from Tatcham Hall of any search being carried out there, notwithstanding that he had been given a pledge by his father's steward to send him word if it were to occur.

All the servants at Altringham were also now aware of Thomas's new status and were willing to defer to him as such. However, his position was still an unusual and rather awkward one to say the least and I worried that he would grow increasingly bored in my absence. The Manor might also have become both his home as well as his property but my steward, Harry, was still very much in command of the running of the estate and nor could Thomas risk travelling anywhere for fear of attracting undue attention. For all that, within two days of the signing of our marriage contract, he had encouraged me to visit Fetford Hall, and that very morning had been in an equable humour about my departure for Exeter.

Olivia, meanwhile, had initially greeted my revelation that I and Thomas had wed by means of a spousal contract by putting her hand to her mouth and staring at me in amazement.

'Oh my, Jane, have you really?' she had spluttered.

'You don't approve then?'

'No, no, not at all. I'm very happy for you, really I am. And...'

'Yes...and what?'

'Do you still think you're pregnant?'

'Yes, more than that...I'm certain...'

'And he knows?'

'Oh yes. It was when I told him that he proposed...'

'That's honourable of him, I must say...'

'It goes much deeper than that. We both love each other, truly we do.'

'I don't doubt it.'

'We will still be the best of friends, Olivia. That will not change, I promise you.'

At that we had embraced each other and all had been smiles. All the same, we had surely both understood perfectly well that, whilst our friendship might endure, our easy intimacy in which we had both come to depend upon one another for emotional support would not be the same. The loser in this regard was also bound to be Olivia and I could understand if she was somewhat jealous of my own good fortune.

'And am I to take it that you have now allowed him to become Master of Altringham Manor and all its estates?' Olivia had then asked quizzically.

'We are married, so yes I have.'

'Forgive me, was that wise?'

'I don't know what you mean?'

'I rather imagined that you had come to value your independence, but more than that, if word ever got out that you had married a renegade everything you possess could be seized by parliament.'

'Then it's important that word does not get out...'

'But that's not entirely within your control and the risk will very likely grow once you have given birth...'

'I don't see why...'

'Well there's your sister for one... Won't you tell her the truth?'

'I'm not sure, perhaps not, though if I did, she'd have to swear to say nothing to her husband, John, or anyone else for that matter. In any event, the deed's done and there's no going back now.'

Olivia's comments had in fact felt like a sting of reproach and irritated me a good deal. The thought that she might actually be right was also the most painful to bear as, not for the first time, I recalled the old adage act in haste, repent at leisure. Love is blind had also come to mind but I had done my best to ignore such reflections and above all had held my tongue in check out of a desire not to sour my friendship with Olivia.

Instead, I had concentrated on the central purpose of my visit, which was to propose that we seek the advice of an attorney and had been pleased to receive an enthusiastic response from James. He was still seething at the thought that the man most likely to have been responsible for Becky's ravishment was being allowed to go unpunished.

'I'll see that swine rot in hell, whatever the cost,' had been his words and the moment I had set eyes on Becky once more I had shared his palpable sense of anger. Although she had at least risen from her bed, it was clear that all her *joie de vivre* had been taken from her and that she had been reduced to a sad, timid creature, still much given to outbursts of weeping.

Her sad fate also served to strengthen my resolve not to give up my quest for justice and this remained as resolute as ever as our party entered the city, and, after leaving our horses at livery stables, made our way on foot to the attorney's chambers in Fore Street. There, an obsequious clerk of middle years, with greasy looking hair and a squat nose, informed us that Master Overbury was presently in court, but was expected to return at shortly after four o'clock whereupon he would no doubt be pleased to assist us.

'It could have been worse,' James declared. 'I feared he might not be free at all today. Let's see if we can find ourselves a meal. That ride has given me quite an appetite.'

I did not demur though in truth the ride had had quite a different effect on me as I was beginning to feel as if I might be about to be sick. I immediately thought of the child I was carrying and remembered the bouts of sickness I had experienced in the early stages of my previous pregnancy. I certainly felt that I would be unable to keep much food down and so determined to eat as little as possible, only nibbling half-heartedly at the meal of bread and cheese with which we were provided before realising that I had no choice but to seek out the privy.

This unedifying experience made Olivia extremely solicitous towards me to the point that I grew quite irritated. 'Please, don't fuss,' I snapped. 'I'm perfectly well now.' However, no sooner had the words left my mouth than I wished I had never spoken them as Olivia looked positively mortified. 'I'm sorry, Olivia, please forgive me,' I hastily added. 'I do understand that you are only concerned for my welfare, really I do.'

'You're not yourself, of course you're not.'

'I am still recovered enough to see Master Overbury, that I can assure you.'

At that, I had smiled reassuringly at both Olivia and James, thinking it just as well that I had drawn him along with Constance and Becky into the secret of both my marriage and my pregnancy. The consequence was to make him just as solicitous towards me as Olivia, although somehow I found his attentions less irritating.

There was still upwards of two hours to wait before four o'clock came round so I suggested a visit to my sister beforehand, to which both Olivia and James were agreeable. The route we chose took us past a number of shops and with a sinking feeling in my stomach I happened to notice a sign bearing the name *Turnbull, Master Tailor*. What was more as we came closer a man emerged from the premises wearing a dark cloak along with a tall hat, who then glanced in our direction. My eyes were immediately drawn to the scar on his cheek.

'Are you Master Turnbull?' James shouted out in a threatening tone.

'Aye, I am, what of it?'

'I believe, sir, that you ravished my wife and as God is my witness I will have justice against you.'

Turnbull looked aghast at these words, as well he might, and I had a moment to study his features. He was wearing a well-trimmed beard, which of itself, of course, proved nothing, whilst his skin was pale and his nose fairly small and stubby. However, what struck my most apart from his somewhat large ears, were his distinctly blue eyes. I decided that he could almost be described as handsome if it were not for the fact that his chin fell away a little and that when he opened his mouth this revealed two or three missing teeth.

'How dare you, sir,' he spluttered. 'That's a foul calumny.'

James response was to shake his fist. 'It's nothing of the kind. We mean to have you arrested for your crimes and then we'll see you hang as you deserve.'

James was a good two or three inches taller than Turnbull and stockier too, so as he advanced on him Turnbull began to back away in fear for his safety.

'Leave me be, sir, or you'll be the one to be arrested, I can assure you!'

'Damn you, if you were any kind of gentleman I'd call you out.'

'Duelling, sir, is illegal.'

I placed a restraining hand on James's left arm. 'Come away,' I whispered in his ear. 'There's no point in this, we've a meeting to attend, remember.'

'Ha!' James still strode towards Turnbull as if he intended to strike him but at the last moment simply carried on his way with Olivia and I following on behind. As we passed Turnbull by, I glanced at him and wondered. He didn't look like any kind of monster, just an ordinary man.

As I had hoped would be the case, when we reached Caroline's house she was able to inform us that John was out on his rounds. This encouraged me to think that I should seize the opportunity to reveal my secret to her but hesitated to do so, preferring instead to make much of Michael as did Olivia. Thomas had needed to be persuaded that Olivia's family should know that we were now married and that I was pregnant. We had also discussed the wisdom of telling Caroline and in the end he had agreed to leave it to me to make the decision.

'She must swear not to tell her puritan husband, mind,' he'd insisted.

Now, when it came to it, I wondered if Caroline could be trusted and decided that perhaps she couldn't, having come too much under John's influence. Sooner or later, hiding the truth from her would be bound to be problematical but that was a concern for another day.

We were about to leave when John returned. He was barely polite, offering no one a smile, and in so doing making it abundantly clear that he didn't welcome our presence. Caroline's mood also instantly changed and she appeared cowed by her husband's foul temper. It made me wonder if their relationship might be on a downward spiral. Unhappy marriages were a cross to be borne, I supposed, but that did not stop me feeling sympathy for my sister's fate, if that was indeed the situation in which she found herself.

When we then returned to Master Overbury's chambers it was only to be told that he had still not returned from court but was expected at any time.

'We'll wait then, if we may.' James said, whereupon the clerk directed us towards some chairs and there we sat for upwards of ten minutes with only a very limited view of the street outside through windows with square-leaded panes. Meanwhile, the clerk sat opposite us; his desk, along with much of the floor immediately surrounding it, strewn with documents as he scribbled away on the preparation of one with his quill pen. I thought that it must be mighty tedious work and hard on the eyes, too, given the limited amount of light that the windows allowed to enter the room. I imagined that as autumn passed into winter there would be a great need for candles but none were lit at present.

After upwards of half-an-hour's wait, during which time I began to doze-off more than once, an imposing figure of a man came bustling into the room. He was tall and angular with a clean-shaven face and an unruly mass of black hair reaching to his shoulders, which was streaked with grey. His face, too, was beginning to show signs of ageing, but everything about his manner suggested that he was a man still possessed of considerable energy and purpose. He also almost instantly recognised James and came bounding towards him, thrusting out his hand, and smiling broadly in a thoroughly ingratiating fashion.

'Courtney, this is an unexpected pleasure, I hear you're recently married. And who are these charming ladies you've brought with you?'

'Allow me to introduce my sister, Lady Olivia...'

'Delighted to make your acquaintance, my Lady.' And with that he swept her a bow.

'And our dear friend, Lady Jane Tremayne...'

'Delighted too. ' Again he bowed before finding my eye with unflinching self-confidence and what I suspected was a considerable intellect. James then proceeded to briefly explain the purpose of our visit, whereupon Overbury encouraged us all to enter his inner sanctum, as he chose to describe it, apologising all the while for what he confessed to being a state of organised chaos. There was indeed such a mass of documentation strewn in all directions that for the life of me I could not understand how he could work in it and retain any measure of sanity.

After we had all sat down with Overbury continuing to beam at us like a contented cat from behind his desk, James began to explain matters in greater detail but to his credit quickly deferred to me...

'Y'see Overbury, all the credit's due to Jane for getting to the bottom of this. I've had nothing to do with it until Becky was so brutally ravished, and she's far more able to explain our case than I am.'

'Except, sir, that as a woman I doubt if the likes of Lake or Crabb were prepared to give much credence to anything I said. Lake, too, was crass enough to not merely inform Turnbull of the allegations I raised against him but in doing so even tell him that I was the informant. I think that outrageous and still believe that it may have exposed me to the risk of attack. Worse, if he had not already done so he will surely have now destroyed anything in his possession that might possibly implicate him in the crimes....'

'Y'see Overbury, we were hoping that representations you could make on our behalf would be taken more seriously,' James added.

Up to now Overbury had mostly heard our tale in silence although he had not hesitated to express his deepest sympathies for Becky's sad state, the words 'terrible' and 'how tragic' most readily passing his lips. Once our tale was told, however, he became much more loquacious.

'In principle, I'd be delighted to act on your behalf, but there are difficulties. You've said yourself, Lady Tremayne, that your evidence against him is circumstantial and I would agree. Further, I'd agree, too, that he's hardly likely to have left anything in his possession that might possibly incriminate him. Equally, whilst he admits that he might well have been in the vicinity of two of the crimes when they were carried out, the very fact that he has done so nullifies much of the purpose behind having him identified... It would , though, make a significant difference if it could be proved that he's lying when he claims not to have known where the murdered woman lived. Should he in fact have had any direct dealings with her then I'd imagine someone else is likely to know of it; a servant or an employee, perhaps. There could even have been some paperwork, though, if so, that's probably been destroyed by now. Have you thought of returning to the village and questioning the neighbours again?' I and Olivia shook our heads. 'You could nudge their memories with a description of Turnbull, if you have one...'

'We didn't before today,' Olivia said, going on to explain the circumstances of our chance meeting with him.

'And what was your impression of the man?' Overbury asked.

'That apart from the scar on his cheek, there was nothing striking about him, ' I answered. 'He had rather piercing blue eyes but I can't say he looked at all sinister. But look, to me, it's stretching credulity to think that another well-dressed man with a beard and riding a horse was in the vicinity of a small village on the day of the first ravishment...'

'I'd agree with you that it seems unlikely but all the same it's not impossible. Certainly, if I were judging Turnbull, I'd think it a travesty to hang him on the basis of the current evidence against him only to discover a few months later that the real offender has resumed his foul activities.'

'So you're telling us there's nothing you can do for us?' James asked.

'I didn't quite say that. Of course, I could prepare a letter to the Sheriff setting out your case against Turnbull. However, he'll more than likely consult with Lake and Crabb before replying and I'd be less than confident of that being at all positive unless I can bring something new to the table, as it were. That's why I'm suggesting you make further enquiries. I will also add one other thing...'

'Oh yes, what's that?'

'Should you find the evidence I'm suggesting and an appeal to the Sheriff still fall on deaf ears then you could consider pursuing your own private action against Turnbull. I mean you have that right but it would involve bringing a bill of indictment before a Grand Jury.'

'That sounds as if it could be a somewhat expensive option?'

'Yes, most certainly, and I appreciate that like many of my clients you may have fallen on difficult times since the war.

Nonetheless, it remains a possibility that you may wish to consider, if necessary.'

James looked at both I and Olivia. 'Are we agreed then that we should seek further evidence?'

'We can certainly try,' I said. 'With luck, our further efforts may yet prove fruitful.'

41

Another search

I returned home in a determined mood. There could be no certainty that more diligent questioning would nudge anyone's memory, but I was prepared to be optimistic.

After leaving Master Overbury, James had found lodgings at one of the city's inns for the three of us and after an early breakfast we had ridden back to Altringham Manor together. As we had approached the Manor I had invited them both to join me and Thomas for dinner but James had made his excuses, saying that he was anxious to return to Becky's side whilst Olivia had made no suggestion that she wished to do anything other than return to Fetford Hall with him. I was suspicious that Thomas was becoming a barrier between us and that both Olivia and James were reluctant to be seen in the company of a known renegade but I chose to say nothing and accepted their decision without demur. One day, in hopefully happier times to come, I prayed that it would be different and that all five of us including Becky would be the best of friends. Perhaps, too, Olivia might find herself a husband before it was too late and she became an old maid.

Even as I dismounted from Hera, Thomas emerged from the front door of the Manor and the very sight of him lifted my heart. However, as he strode towards me, I could detect an anxious expression on his face.

'It's what I feared would happen. News has come from Tatcham Hall no more than an hour ago that soldiers have come searching for me. I fear they could be here at any time. I've only stayed in the house as long as I have in the hope of your being here soon.'

'I see. You'll be safer in the cottage, for sure.'

He then kissed me lightly on the lips before enquiring about the success of our visit to the attorney in Exeter and at this I shrugged.

'He thinks that no action would be worthwhile without some evidence that can demonstrate that Turnbull was properly acquainted with the widow he murdered. He suggested that we ask more questions of her neighbours so I can but hope that this will prove productive.'

'And what of your sister and her baby?'

I proceeded to explain my concern for Caroline's welfare and how cross I was at her husband, John's, rudeness towards me. We had now progressed into the house and Mary appeared, bobbing me a curtsey. Thomas then turned to close the front door, and gasped.

'The devil, they're here already! I must be away afore it's too late.'

'Quickly then, you can take the path through the garden. And Thomas...'

'Yes?'

'If they search the estate and come upon you in the cottage for pity's sake try and disguise your voice, otherwise the game will still be up for sure.'

'All right, I'll do m'best.'

These words were spoken with a deep west country burr and Thomas had already taken to his heels. By the time a fist pounded on the front door accompanied by a demand for immediate entry, he was well gone, and I imagined within sight of the cottage.

'We have a warrant to search this entire estate,' the grim faced Captain, whose face I remembered from the last search, explained to me without a hint of apology for the intrusion. He then thrust the document under my nose. 'We'll begin with the house.'

Turning to his men, he ordered them to search. 'Be thorough. Leave nothing unturned and remember to pay particular attention to the attics and the cellars. Oh, and there's the roof, too. I recall, you can get to it through one of the attic windows. I'm going to look round the stables.'

This last remark made me tremble slightly. Thomas's horse was there as it had been before when they had searched. It had aroused no suspicion then and ought not to do so now. Yet I sensed that they had come with even more intent than on the previous occasions and knew that I must be ready with my answer if the Captain questioned me. Above all, I knew that I must remain calm and look him in the eye.

'So tell me,' he asked upon his return. 'I see you've two fine horses in stables. They're both yours, I take it?'

'Assuredly, Captain. I allow my steward to ride the stallion. It facilitates his duties, you understand.'

'And how long have you owned them?'

'In the case of the mare, She's born and bred here. The stallion I acquired at market a few years ago now...'

'Very well. As soon as my men have finished their search

of the house, we'll begin on the estate. I've orders to leave no stone unturned...'

It was another ten minutes before the last of the soldiers departed and I knew that my real agony was only just beginning. If Thomas's disguise failed to protect him then the game would indeed be up and I myself could soon be languishing in Exeter gaol. It was a sobering thought, enough indeed to make my mouth run dry and for me to break out in a cold sweat. All I could do was sit and pray.

Forty minutes later I saw the soldiers ride away and allowed myself a long, heartfelt sigh. Ten minutes more brought Thomas back to my door, his face a picture of relief.

'Did they question you?' I asked as I raced into his arms.

'Aye, they did. I put on the best accent I could and that satisfied them. I don't believe they were even suspicious.'

'You've had another lucky escape, that's for certain.'

'And I doubt they'll come again...'

'I sincerely hope not. That's the third time and I don't believe my nerves could stand it if they were to return yet again.'

42

A vital witness

Two mornings later I rode over to Fetford Hall to visit Olivia. Whilst our friendship might no longer be quite what it once was, I remained determined that it should not fall away completely, and in any event wanted to enlist her support in visiting Tipton in the hope of finding more evidence capable of implicating Turnbull in Mistress Hodge's murder. I was immediately greeted by Constance with the not unexpected news that the Hall together with its estate had been searched the previous day.

'It's unconscionable that they keep doing this. Oh, what dreadful times we live in!'

I was quick to agree. Still, it was a relief to me to find Becky looking better than at any time since the ravishment in as much as some colour had returned to her cheeks and she was willing to look me in the eye. Yet the anguish I still saw in hers made me want to weep as well as inducing in me a visceral sense of anger towards the perpetrator of such a foul crime.

'I know I might be overly optimistic of finding any further evidence against Turnbull, but, as Master Overbury believes it to be essential, we owe it to Becky and all his other victims to at least try,' I said to Olivia. 'Will you ride with me into Tipton?'

'Yes, gladly.'

I felt encouraged by Olivia's warm smile and hoped that some of the equilibrium of our friendship had been restored. A pleasant ride on what was a dry, sunny day, with still some warmth in the air as the autumnal equinox approached, also did much to raise both our spirits and gave me the opportunity of expressing my relief at Thomas's narrow escape from capture.

'I still can't quite believe our luck that they didn't recognise him. He says he put on his best Devon accent but if it had been me I would have been shaking so much they'd have been bound to realise who I was.'

'So that's the second time he's come within a whisker of being captured. I mean you thought it a miracle they didn't find him when he went up on the roof...'

'True and I'm fearful his luck wouldn't hold if they were to come yet again. My one hope is that they won't see the need. After all, they've searched three times now without success.'

When we reached Tipton, I then suggested that I go up one side of the street in which the widow had lived while Olivia went up the other.

'I think we should be prepared to knock on every door in the village. Remember, too, that there are two crucial ways in which the good people here may be of assistance to us. Either, they may recall well-dressed men on horses visiting the deceased, in which case they need to be asked if any of them bore scars on their faces, or, just possibly, they might recall conversations with the deceased in which she actually mentioned Turnbull by name.'

'The men will be at work...'

'Naturally, but their wives should be at home and they're more likely to have seen Turnbull, or for that matter conversed with Mistress Hodge. So, are you ready.'

Olivia nodded. 'Yes, let's begin.'

For the next half-an-hour I proceeded to knock on a dozen doors and at all but two received a response. Every person I spoke to was also a woman bar one and without exception they all showed me the respect that was my due as Lady of the Manor and sought to be helpful.

'It's quite dreadful what's happened, m'Lady, quite dreadful, and I'd help if I could,' was the typical response. 'But a well-dressed man on a horse bearing a scar; no, I'm sorry but I don't recall ever seeing any such person in this village. And Turnbull, you say. No, the name means nothing to me.'

I was beginning to feel that my initial optimism had been ill-founded when out of the corner of my eye I noticed Olivia approaching me. It was clear that she was in an animated state.

'I've just been speaking to an old woman. She keeps an eye out for anyone coming or going in this village, but was ill in bed at the time of the murder, and I'm the first person who's ever approached her about it. She says that Mistress Hodge did have occasional visitors, and whilst she wouldn't describe them as gentlemen, exactly, they were still dressed like men of substance.'

'Did she say they arrived on horse?'

'Oh yes, and there's more. She says she'd swear to the fact that one of them had a scar on his left cheek and came more than once. She got a particularly good look at him on one occasion because she was outside her front door cleaning when he rode by.'

At this revelation I seized hold of Olivia's wrist and let out an exclamation of sheer delight. 'My, this is just what we wanted!

Well done, Olivia, very well done. I don't suppose the name Turnbull means anything to her?'

'No, nothing at all'

'Even so, it's still got to be him, it just has to be. And does she believe she'd recognise him if she were to see him again.'

'Yes, she say's she thinks she would.'

'Then we need to take her to Exeter as soon as possible. I must speak with her. You asked her name, I take it?'

'She told me she's Margaret Hurst; a widow. She lives with her son and his family.'

'Yes, I know her. She's always struck me as intelligent and must be over seventy. I've heard her claim she remembers the coming of the Armada.'

'Do you think she might be too old to travel?'

'On the back of a horse, yes, but there's always the back of a cart. We'll get her there somehow, so long as she doesn't become too ill.'

By now we had crossed the street and moments later Olivia was tapping on the widow's door again.

'I'm coming, I'm coming...'

'I've brought Lady Tremayne to speak to you as I said I might...'

'M'lady...'

Mistress Hurst was short and bent over, with a heavily lined face, but still seemed perfectly alert and looked at me with a steady though respectful gaze.

'Lady Olivia tells me that you recall seeing a man of substance with a scar on his left cheek visit Mistress Hodge on more than one occasion and that you believe you'd recognise him again...'

'That's so, m'lady.'

'Then I need you to come to Exeter with me and the sooner the better...'

Mistress Hurst looked fearful at the very idea. 'I... I can't do that, m'lady. I'm too old... And I haven't left this village in nigh on... , it must be ten years or more.'

I felt impatient with her. 'There's a man living in the city who I believe is the same person you saw visiting Mistress Hodge. Identify him as such and there's a chance that we can have him convicted of her murder. Otherwise, he'll continue to be free to commit yet more abominable crimes. If you ride in the back of a cart you should be comfortable enough and I'll pay for your dinner once we arrive.'

I was tempted to also offer a payment in silver but then thought better of it. Should such an inducement ever become known it might well look like bribery and so undermine the credence of her evidence.

Mistress Hurst, however , still looked unhappy and as I glanced at Olivia, I could tell that she was similarly uncomfortable about the idea.

'I'll have my steward bring a cart here tomorrow morning,' I insisted. 'The weather looks to be set fair at present and I'll provide you with a cloak to keep you warm, should you require it.'

'If you really think I should, m'lady...'

'Yes, I do... So, until tomorrow then. I wish you a good day, and thank you.' As we then returned to where we had left our horses I spoke sharply to Olivia.

'What's wrong? I can tell you're unhappy.'

'It's just that I'm wondering how wise this is? Are you seriously proposing to take Mistress Hurst into Turnbull's shop?

You can't even be certain that he'll be there.'

'It's a chance I'm prepared to take. As needs must we can pay him a further visit.'

'But he's going to realise what your game is. There could be trouble.'

'I don't see why. If he attempts to assault either me or Mistress Hurst , it would look like an admission of guilt.'

'Yes, I suppose it might...'

'There's surely no suppose about it. So, will you accompany me tomorrow?'

'Yes, why not. It will be a pleasure.'

43

Frustrations

Overnight the weather broke and it was still raining steadily when I woke up. I felt tempted, as I looked out of the window, to postpone the intended journey. However, I remained determined to go ahead with it without delay, and had already secured a promise from Harry that he would drive the cart for me, while I and Olivia would travel by horse. Of course, if the rain failed to relent it would not be the easiest of journeys, especially for Harry's elderly passenger, but that could not be helped.

Within half-an-hour the three of us were ready to depart and Thomas saw us off from the Manor's front door with a smile and an encouraging wave of the hand. It was still raining steadily, though, and once we reached Tipton St John's to collect Mistress Hurst, she protested at the prospect of having to travel in such conditions.

'I'm sorry, m'lady, but I'm an old woman and I'm afeared that I'll catch me death of cold in this weather.'

'Come, come, I've brought you a thick blanket to drape round you. That and your hat should afford you ample protection from the elements.'

Still, she looked reluctant to set off. 'Can we not wait awhile, m'lady.'

'And what am I and Lady Olivia, not to mention Harry, supposed to do in the meantime? No, the rain will be gone in half-an-hour, most likely. I can already see that the skies are brightening a little from the west, so come, we must be on our way.'

I then took Mistress Hurst's arm and with Harry's assistance bundled her into the back of the cart whereupon we set off on our journey, which was to prove thoroughly unpleasant for all of us. Far from abating the rain in fact became heavier for a while and it was two hours or more before it finally relented completely by which time it was not only Mistress Hurst who felt cold and miserable. I, however, remained undaunted.

'You cannot be born and bred in this country and yet allow yourself to be put off by a little rain. If we were, we'd achieve nothing.'

'That's as may be, Jane,' Olivia said, looking sympathetically towards Mistress Hurst who looked positively drenched. 'But I for one would say that this has been more than just a little rain'

'Well, it's almost stopped now and we've still made good progress.'

Twenty minutes later the skies had cleared sufficiently to allow a weak sun to shine upon us and I felt vindicated in my decision not to be put off by the elements. Nor, in my determined mood, did I intend to be deterred by any of the concerns that Olivia had expressed.

'I still intend that we should go straight to Turnbull's shop and take Mistress Hurst inside. With luck Turnbull will be there and she can make an immediate identification.'

'All the same, I know you don't think he'll do anything stupid, but I'd still take Harry along with you, just in case. I'll look after the cart and the horses, in the meantime.'

' Very well, I agree with that.'

We had set off early enough to ensure our arrival in the city before midday, and I found it a relief to be able to slide out of the saddle and stretch my legs while Harry endeavoured to assist Mistress Hurst to alight from the back of the cart. She had passed much of the journey in silence, making only an occasional complaint when the going became uncomfortable due to the uneven surface of the road. Now, however, she protested loudly that the pains of old age were hurting her so much she could barely move.

Consequently, Harry had to practically carry her from the back of the cart and both he and I then had to support an arm each in order to keep her on her feet. Progress towards the shop's entrance from where we had been able to leave the cart and horses in Olivia's care was thus painfully slow and on two occasions at least Mistress Hurst came close to ending up on the ground.

By the time we reached our destination and prepared to enter, I was feeling quite exhausted by my efforts, and even felt a fleeting concern for the welfare of my unborn infant. Still, I shrugged this off, and summoning my courage opened the door of the shop. Facing me behind a counter, I was immediately confronted by none other than Master Turnbull, causing me to feel a mixture of relief and apprehension. He, for his part, was staring at me with a look first of disbelief and then consternation, his mouth hanging open.

'Master Turnbull, I believe...'

'.... Yes, what can I... ' His words were then choked off by the sight of Mistress Hurst, hobbling along behind me.

'You've been telling lies,' I declared. 'I've every reason to believe that you were well acquainted with Mistress Hodge before you murdered her.' Then I turned to Mistress Hurst. 'So, is this the man you remember?'

Turnbull seemed struck quite dumb as the old woman advanced a couple of steps further into the shop and then fixed her gaze upon him.

'Yes, m'lady, that's the man. I'd swear to it.'

Turnbull now found his voice. 'How dare you bring that old hag into my shop. She doesn't know what she's talking about!'

My response was to simply turn my back on him and guide Mistress Hurst out into the open air.

'I'm not guilty of any crime,' Turnbull bellowed. 'I won't stand for you making false accusations against me. Leave me in peace or you'll regret it, I swear you will.'

Still I ignored him and with Harry's assistance simply led Mistress Hurst back to where we had left Olivia in charge of the cart and horses. Turnbull, meanwhile, made no attempt to follow us.

As soon as I came in sight of Olivia, I smiled broadly at her. 'It went better than I dared to hope. Mistress Hurst immediately identified him and he was simply left fuming.'

'That's good news, indeed.'

'Now we must go straight to Overbury's chambers. Even if he's not there, his clerk can no doubt be persuaded to take down a disposition from Mistress Hurst to which she can place her mark. After that some dinner. I fancy the George in North Street...'

As I had suspected might be the case, Overbury's clerk informed us that his Master was in court but was expected to return by around two o'clock. He then politely declined my suggestion that he take down any disposition.

'M'lady, forgive me, but I can only take instructions from my Master and as you'll see...'

He spread his hands expansively across mounds of parchment in front of him. 'I am somewhat busy with other tasks at present.'

'Oh very well, we'll return at two o'clock then.'

All the while, Mistress Hurst was increasingly complaining of pains in her joints and looked so poorly that I worried that she might be on the point of collapse. It was a fear that Olivia shared.

'This will all have been a waste of time if she dies on us,' she declared gloomily.

I tutted in frustration. 'She needs food in her belly, I expect. As do I.'

Two hours later we went back to Overbury's chambers with I, for one, feeling much revived. Mistress Hurst, too, as I had hoped, seemed better, helped no doubt by the mutton pie we had enjoyed along with some strong beer, and was complaining far less of aches and pains. All the same, she was still so unsteady on her feet that without Harry's support she would have surely collapsed.

'I just hope the beer has not made her drunk,' Olivia quipped.

This time we were in luck and Overbury, having already returned from court, came to greet us the moment we arrived.

'A pleasure to see you again, Lady Jane,' he said with an effusive smile, before bowing to both me and Olivia. 'My clerk tells me you have found a vital witness.'

'Yes. This is Mistress Hurst. I took her to Turnbull's shop this morning and she immediately identified him as the man she saw visiting the murdered woman, Mistress Hodge. I wanted your clerk to take down a disposition from her but he declined to do so without your instructions.'

'You have done well in finding her, I must say.'

'Would you not agree that her evidence changes everything?'

'I would agree that it strengthens it a good deal. But look, I suggest we discuss this further while my clerk takes down her disposition.'

'Harry, I suggest you remain with Mistress Hurst.'

'As you wish, m'lady.

I and Olivia then followed Overbury into his inner sanctum, which appeared to be just as strewn with documentation as on our previous visit.

'I take it that you're now prepared to petition the Sheriff for Turnbull's arrest?'

'I am, but do not imagine that he's bound to agree. Further, even if he does, and this leads to an indictment it doesn't necessarily follow that a jury will convict him.'

'But Mistress Hurst's evidence exposes him as a liar. He knew precisely where Mistress Hodge lived and yet chose to deny it. There can be but one explanation for that: he murdered her.'

'With the greatest respect, I don't believe it's quite that simple. To begin with the witness is elderly and he remains at liberty to assert that she is simply wrong in her identification, or, at the very least, that no reliance should be placed upon her testimony. Furthermore, it's possible that he sought to hide his knowledge of the deceased's abode, not because he killed her, but rather because he was fearful that he might be accused of her murder simply because he had that knowledge. In essence, just because he knew her place of abode, doesn't, of itself, make him guilty of her murder.'

'There's much other evidence, besides, surely.'

'I agree, but all of it is circumstantial. A jury might therefore still be reluctant to convict.'

'Well, I can do no more.' I said with a sigh. 'The chances of any evidence emerging at this late stage, which would definitely place him at the scene of any of his crimes, must be very remote.'

Overbury nodded. 'I also could not possibly recommend that a private prosecution would be worthwhile.'

'That's of no consequence as we could not possibly afford to take such a step.'

'It's worth remembering that what you've already done could be enough to deter him from committing any more crimes...'

'I like to think so but I fear he may be too much the prisoner of the demons which drive him.'

'...In which case he may go too far and be caught in the act or at least observed leaving the scene. Then he would surely swing for his evil deeds.'

'But I would not wish to see any more women suffer at his hands before that happens, if it ever does.'

'Of course not. But look, have no fear, I will petition the Sheriff for you, and, who knows, an arrest and indictment could yet follow. After all, the circumstantial evidence against him is now quite compelling and I will argue that in its totality it creates a case worthy of being put before a jury.'

'How quickly can you prepare it?'

'Return here a week today and it will be ready for your approval.'

'Very well, I will do so... And I expect James will want to come with me.'

'There is one other matter of importance that I need to stress to you.'

'Oh yes, what is that?'

'The case against Turnbull would be strengthened by dispositions from his three victims, who still live, as well as from the blacksmith and the tenant farmer. I particularly have in mind what description the victims can give us of the clothing that their attacker was wearing. By his own admission he was in the vicinity of two of these crimes when they were committed but what we do not know is what he might admit to have been wearing on each occasion. I suspect that he'd say that he was dressed in the plain attire of his trade, but from what you tell me the blacksmith would remember it differently as, of course, would the first of his victims. If their descriptions should match one another...'

'Surely the case against him would be more than circumstantial?' I declared.

'Well I agree that it would be strongly suggestive that her attacker and Turnbull are one and the same individual. I could by all means send my clerk to Tipton but it would add to my fees, of course.'

'You're suggesting that we provide these ourselves, then? I asked

'If you felt able to, it would significantly aid your case; of that I am sure. And I feel that one from your good-self would not go amiss, describing in particular what you discovered at the scene of the first attack. We must do all that we can to convince the sheriff that all of these attacks are only likely to have been committed by the same individual. As they will merely be in support of the petitioning letter they need only relate the bare facts and need not be witnessed.'

'Very well, I will endeavour to do what you ask.'

I parted from Overbury on amicable terms, thanking him for his assistance. The fact of the matter remained that I had accomplished everything I had hoped for, while he had done no more than his professional duty in advising me to be cautious in my expectations. Yet, the thought that it might still come to nothing, and that Turnbull could still walk away a free man, was one that left me feeling somewhat downcast.

Sensing my mood, Olivia tried to be positive, repeating the notion that at the very least we had done enough already to deter any further attack, and I could only hope that this proved to be correct. We also did not leave Overbury's chambers until Mistress Hurst had made her mark on her disposition, and content with that I decided we would go straight home without troubling my sister.

'She'll be preoccupied with Michael's needs, for sure. We'll call on her another time.'

'And try not to worry any more about Turnbull,' Olivia urged me. 'I can't believe he'd ever attempt another attack, for all you think that possible.'

'Yes, I can only hope you're right, Olivia.'

44

Dispositions

A week later, accompanied on this occasion by both James and Olivia, I duly returned to Overbury's chambers. With James's help in providing the necessary disposition from Becky, I had been assiduous in obtaining what had been asked of me, and he was able to present me with a draft of the letter, which he had prepared.

'Please, do read it carefully. I have done my upmost to ensure that it sets out the case against Turnbull as thoroughly as possible. Nonetheless, if you consider that there is anything of importance that I have missed, or failed to give due weight to, now is the time for you to tell me.'

With that he handed the letter first to James, who pronounced himself satisfied with it, and then to me. I could find no fault with it either.

'I believe it puts the case against Turnbull very well. If this doesn't satisfy the Sheriff, surely nothing will. I particularly like the emphasis you have placed not just on Mistress Hurst's evidence, but also the improbability of his being in the vicinity of not just one crime but two, and yet playing no part in either of them. What's more, for all that he's no more than a tailor, he still dresses above his station and as you have requested I have here the blacksmith's disposition, to which he has placed his mark. As you'll see it gives a basic description of the clothes the rider was wearing. Further, if you look at both Becky's and Melanie Tunnicliffe's dispositions you'll see the descriptions are all consistent with one another. Oh yes, I also have the tenant farmer, Matthew Parker's disposition, too.'

Overbury then quickly read the dispositions. 'You've done well to obtain these, and I think the descriptions are helpful. Each of them refers to the doublet being brown in colour although, of course, it could be said that of itself this proves nothing. In any event, I will insert a few more words asserting the similarity of the descriptions and I'll ensure that it is delivered into the Sheriff's own hands tomorrow.'

'And how long before he makes his decision, do you think?' I asked.

'That I cannot say, but the letter will be marked for his urgent attention, that I can promise you. We can only pray that he is not preoccupied with other matters and sees the merits of our case. I'll give him no more than a week to respond.'

'And if he doesn't?' James asked.

'Should that be the case, I'll see to it that a letter of reminder is delivered to him within the hour requesting an immediate reply. In any event, as soon as I've any news for you I will send you a message.'

45

Good news

A week had passed and it was now early October. I was feeling wretched with the nausea that often afflicts expectant women in the morning. I had endured this for several weeks during my previous pregnancy, and told myself it would pass, but that was of little consolation as I started to vomit. Meanwhile, I'd heard nothing yet from Overbury, and in that regard I had decided that I would have to be patient, at least for a few more days. After that, should I continue to hear nothing, I knew I would be tempted, health permitting, to return to Exeter, especially as I was increasingly resolved to also pay another visit to my sister and this time admit to her that I was with child.

'If you must do so, there can be no question of her telling her husband,' Thomas had insisted when I told him what I was now thinking of doing. 'He'd throw up his arms in horror at the very mention of my name and start asking questions about my present whereabouts with a view to reporting this to the authorities. And does your sister have to know either? After all, even if she promises to say nothing, she might find the temptation to reveal all to her own husband irresistible.'

'I thought we'd already agreed that it was my decision to make, and the time will come when the pregnancy will be beyond disguising. She'll have to know then.'

'But will she? After all, she and John never visit you here, do they...'

'No, or very rarely... It must be a year or more since their last visit...'

'Well then, you're surely entitled to make your excuses for not visiting her, without revealing all...'

'Yes, but, she's my own sister... I just feel I owe her the truth, and sooner rather than later. She might never forgive me if I keep this a total secret from her...'

'But does she have to know at all? Then they'll be nothing to forgive...'

'But if the child lives, she'll have to know one day. I'm not ashamed to be having a child by my own husband and, God willing, our King will eventually be restored to his rightful throne.'

'Oh very well , but even if you feel duty bound to reveal both your marriage and your pregnancy to her, why do you have to reveal my name? Surely, there is no need to do that.'

'No, perhaps on that count you're right.'

And so we had left it at that, leaving me to still struggle with my conscience as to what to do for the best. In the end, I had decided, perhaps even against my better judgement, that upon Caroline faithfully swearing to keep the matter secret, I would tell her that I was with child and also married, but at the same time withhold the name of my husband.

Now, as I lay back in bed, having emptied the contents of my stomach into a chamber pot, Thomas was as solicitous towards me as he could be, but was not best pleased when I told him I would be riding back to Exeter in order to visit my sister as soon as I felt well enough to do so.

'I'm sorry Thomas, but I've made up my mind to tell her the truth without further delay. Some days, I feel perfectly well. Hopefully, tomorrow will be one of those, in which case...'

'But I do not like you riding...'

'I shall use a side-saddle.'

'You could still fall...'

I shook my head. 'I am an experienced horsewoman, you know that.'

'As your husband I could order you to remain here.'

I tutted. Was this about to be our first real argument? I was not sure, though, how seriously to take this remark, as he appeared relaxed and there was no trace of anger behind his words. 'You would not do that,' I finally said.

'And would you obey me, even if I did? I understand how much you value your freedom, my love, and I am no better than a prisoner here.'

'No, this is your home...'

'But not one I can safely leave, whereas...'

'I know, I can ride wherever I choose, but it will not always be like this. One day...'

' ...Our King will return and all will be well but we both know that it could be years from now before that happens, if ever. Just think, General Cromwell might live another twenty years.'

'Pray heaven he does not.'

'And pray heaven, too, that no ill befalls you if you're insist-ent upon travelling to Exeter tomorrow.'

'You'll let me go then?'

'Yes, if you must. Truly, my love, I've no desire to deny

you anything.'

These words were enough to bring a smile to my face and we embraced. In the warmth of the marital bed, he soon grew ardent, whilst I, however, still felt far too queasy for any love-making. I therefore gently restrained him before slipping out of bed and making my way to the window to look outside.

'Autumn is well and truly upon us,' I remarked, seeing how much the gathering wind was taking the leaves off the trees. 'In any event, I promise you, Thomas, that I'll only travel to Exeter tomorrow if I truly feel well enough.'

'Thank you, my love, I appreciate that.'

Two hours later, having dressed and taken breakfast, I was feeling more my usual self once more and sitting at the harpsichord, practising, *A Fancy*, one of my favourite instrumental pieces by William Byrd, while Thomas listened. I could tell that he was restless, though, because he would not sit still and this began to irritate me a little.

'Oh, do stop it, Thomas, I can't concentrate.'

'Wait!'

'Pardon.'

'I can hear a rider approaching the house.' He was on his feet in an instant, striding towards the window. 'You know, it might be a message from Overbury.'

This was enough to cause me to break off my playing and come to Thomas's side.

'Yes, my word, it's his clerk!'

I struggled to remain composed as Overbury's letter was soon delivered into my hands. 'Is it good news?' I asked.

'M'lady, I'm pleased to say that it is. The contents of the letter will tell you more.'

'That is wonderful, indeed. Be sure to express my profound gratitude to your Master for his services to me.' I then proceeded to break the seal.

My Lady, it gives me pleasure to inform you that the Sheriff is persuaded of the merits of issuing a warrant for the arrest of Master Turnbull on a charge of ravishing the young woman, Melanie Tunnicliffe. Once apprehended, he will also be questioned concerning the other ravishments as well as the murder of Mistress Hodge, and, depending on his answers, other charges may yet follow. I am therefore confident that following this decision he will be indicted on at least one charge of ravishment and thus brought to trial. I must respectfully continue to caution you as to its outcome, but the fact that the blacksmith's and victims descriptions of what he was wearing are consistent with one another, must aid the prospects of his conviction. I need hardly add that if found guilty, even on a single charge of ravishment, he will most assuredly be hanged for his crime.

'Will the warrant be issued and acted upon today, do you think?'

'I would imagine so, m'lady. The decision reached us late yesterday afternoon.'

'And will you take your ease awhile, before returning to Exeter; I imagine you've ridden hard and are in need of some refreshment?'

'That would be most kind of you, m'lady.'

'I'll lead you through into the kitchen then.'

Once I had done so I then returned to Thomas, where, full of smiles, I showed him the letter.

'Allow me to offer you my congratulations. I'm delighted that all your endeavours have not been in vain, my love,' he

279

said graciously.

'I'll not rest easy in my bed, mind, until he's sent to trial and convicted. And I must let James and Olivia know the good news. I'll ride over to Fetford this afternoon, if you don't mind.'

'Why not send a messenger with the good news. Perhaps, Master Overbury's clerk might be willing...'

'I imagine he'll want to return to Exeter without delay and I'd rather go myself...I feel well enough.'

'We could go together, couldn't we?'

'That's surely too dangerous. You're safe enough within the confines of this estate but beyond it, and especially in my company, I do not think so...'

'So I must be left to fester here while you ride wherever you please.'

It was now plain to me that his mood had hardened since our conversation that morning. 'It's for your own safety..., our safety indeed,' I insisted. 'I know it's frustrating for you, of course I do.'

'I feel such a prisoner!'

'We have each other, don't we...'

'Yes, when you're not disappearing to Exeter or Fetford, or God knows where.'

'You make it sound as if I spend hardly any time here, and you know that's not true.'

'No, I suppose it's not...'

'Look, let's not quarrel. If I leave soon, I can be there and back in no time.'

'I doubt that. And tomorrow?'

'I told you, that depends on how well I am in the morning.'

46

The chase

Within the hour I set out for Fetford Hall. The news Overbury's clerk had brought me had been cheering indeed, but this was tempered by Thomas's mood and his evident dislike of being left to his own devices, even for a few hours. Of course, I understood that the situation he found himself in was a difficult one, but the alternatives seemed to me to be far worse. So long as I was well enough to ride, I was also unwilling to spend all my time at Altringham Manor, even if that meant upsetting Thomas, and for all that my conscience nagged me that I was behaving selfishly. Nor did I want us to ever part on poor terms and made a point of kissing him lightly on the lips and promising him again that I would not be gone for too long.

As a matter of preference I would always have ridden astride, but bearing in mind my somewhat delicate condition decided that riding side-saddle would have to suffice. Thomas's last words to me had been to take care and remembering the child I was now carrying I made a point of keeping to a slower pace than usual. The weather still being clement and the ground dry, I was nevertheless able to make fair progress and thought that I would be able to reach my destination in less than half an hour. However, my route took me through a wood, and it was as I entered this that I first became aware of a rider coming towards me at a canter, the cloak that he was wearing billowing out behind him a little.

At first, I could not make out his features but then as he came closer I realised that he was wearing a mask. The sight was enough to make me gasp and as quickly as I could I turned Hera round and encouraged her into a gallop. I felt constrained, however, by the use of the side-saddle, and decided that my best hope lay in reaching open ground before I was overtaken as the moment I did so there would come a prospect of being seen by men working in the fields. What was more, any cries for help would be more likely to be heard, even at a distance. The trouble was that I had already travelled about a quarter of a mile into the wood and in turning Hera round I had lost precious seconds. Glancing back I could see that my pursuer was now coming ever closer.

The thought struck me with a sickening sense of dread that if the man behind the mask was indeed Turnbull, he would want more than mere amorous gratification. Rather, he had surely come just as much for revenge, and having already strangled one woman, might well not hesitate to dispatch me in the same manner. Once knocked from my horse, I would also be stunned and utterly defenceless. Above all, I realised that I had to stay in my saddle or face the prospect of death.

I could sense, too, that veering off the road into the woods would only bring disaster a step closer as they were far too overgrown. True, there appeared to be a few gaps through which Hera might pass, but only surely for a short distance, whilst I might all too easily be felled by the branch of a tree before I had gone a few yards. All that I could therefore do was encourage Hera onwards and pray that she was the faster and stronger horse.

With every stride, however, I sensed that my lead was diminishing and even as the entrance to the wood came ever closer one more glance told me that my pursuer was almost alongside me. I screamed out in fear expecting at any moment to be overtaken but Hera just managed to hang onto her lead until we emerged into open countryside once more. At that very moment I sensed that my pursuer was giving up the chase and when I looked round I could tell that he had abandoned it.

Still, I continued to hold Hera to a galloping pace, until the wood was out of sight and I began to see men working in the fields, whereupon I slowed to no more than a trot. The realisation that I had come so close to ravishment and murder made me shake a little and then feel such a wave of nausea that I feared I was about to throw up. Gradually, though, this sensation abated as I took several deep breaths, all the while stroking Hera's mane.

'Well done, my beauty, well done.'

I then returned to Altringham Manor as quickly as I could, still feeling quite shaken, and also rather tired.

'Has something untoward happened?' Thomas asked me anxiously. 'You look very pale and why are you back so soon?'

'I never reached Fetford Hall. Turnbull, I believe it must have been him, chased me through the woods not far from there, but I managed to elude him. Now I fear he may avoid arrest.'

'You're certain it was him?'

'As certain as I dare be . He was masked and well-attired. He could have spotted me coming by chance, I suppose, and quickly donned his mask, but I think that unlikely. It's far more probable that it was a planned attack. After all, he knows that I am responsible for making accusations against him. He must have been keeping a watch on the road from here to Fetford Hall from some vantage point and managed to get ahead of me. Then as I entered the wood he charged me, and but for Hera's speed I know he would have tried to knock me off my horse and kill me, either with his own hands, or perhaps a knife.'

'And do you think he's aware that the Sheriff is prepared to issue a warrant for his arrest?'

'I don't see why he should...'

'In which case I expect he'll soon return to Exeter.'

'I can but hope so. In any event, the Sheriff should be informed of what has happened.'

'You're surely not proposing to travel to Exeter today?'

'No, that's out of the question, I'm much too tired, but I still hope to go in the morning. I'll call first on Master Overbury to thank him for his efforts, and also tell him what's just occurred.'

'Whatever happens, you must not go alone.'

'No, I agree. I'll take Mary with me.'

47

Bad news

'I have bad news for you, I'm afraid,' Overbury said sombrely, looking me in the eye. 'I have received a message from the Sheriff. It has still not been possible to arrest Turnbull. It's clear he's still not in the city.'

'It's just what I feared. He was surely the masked man who pursued me through the woods yesterday when I was on my way to Fetford Hall. I thought then that he probably had no intention of returning to Exeter.'

'The Sheriff has sent constables to Harpford, in case Turnbull's with his sister.'

'That's possible, I suppose. But if he's not there, then he must have fled, which would be as good as an admission of guilt.'

'I would agree.'

'And what chance do you think that he'll ever be apprehended?'

'If he manages to flee the country, none at all. Otherwise, if he's able to hide his identity, he may be safe enough.'

'To commit more crimes, you mean?' I asked.

Overbury looked uncomfortable. 'I would sincerely hope not, Lady Jane.'

Very well, I would ask you to keep abreast of events on my behalf and to write to me as soon as you hear whether or not Turnbull has been arrested?'

'I will do that with pleasure.'

I felt another wave of nausea come over me and was desperate for fresh air. When I had woken that morning I had felt well and that had continued to be the case even when I and Mary set out on our journey. However, we had barely ridden a mile when I had first begun to feel sick.

Twice, we had had to bring our journey to a halt so that I could throw up, and the second time it had happened I had seriously considered turning back. I wondered, too, if the drama of the previous day had had an adverse effect on me, but in the end, gritting my teeth, had decided to continue, fortunately feeling somewhat better even as we reached Overbury's chambers. Once there, we had then waited while he had sent his clerk to the Sheriff to find out if Turnbull had yet been arrested.

Now, I realised that I could put off a visit to my sister no longer, and that the moment was fast approaching when I would have to finally summon the courage to tell her both of my marriage and my pregnancy. Of course, I might find John at home, and that would give me an excuse to still say nothing, but I was minded to seek out an opportunity to whisper a few words into my sister's ear on the matter even if he was.

When I knocked on the door of my sister's house with Mary at my side, a young maid, looking barely sixteen years of age, whom I had never set eyes on before, answered it. However, the sound of my voice carried upstairs to where Caroline was and she rapidly appeared.

'This is an unexpected pleasure, dear sister.' She then embraced me with a measure of affection, which I found encouraging.

'I have been with our lawyer, Master Overbury, on an important matter, but thought that I would take the opportunity of also paying you a visit,' I told her. 'Is Michael well?'

'Very much so, at present. He has a healthy pair of lungs and has been exercising them a good deal of late, although at present he's sound asleep, I hope.'

'And your husband, John, is he home?'

'No, he is out on his rounds. I imagine it could be another couple of hours at least before he returns. Will you take some refreshment? I have beer.'

'Yes, that would be most welcome.'

Caroline urged me to take my ease while I gave instructions to the maid to bring us each jugs. I then decided that I could not tolerate any small-talk before coming to the point, having dispatched Mary out of the room to find her own refreshment in the kitchen.

'Caroline, there's something important that I need to tell you. It's also not news that I believe would please John so I would prefer it if you would be willing to keep what I'm about to say between ourselves.'

Caroline looked at my curiously. 'What on earth do you want to tell me that I can't share with my own husband?'

'The fact that I am pregnant.'

Caroline seemed utterly appalled by the very idea. 'How could you? I mean how is this possible?'

'I took a man to my bed, of course, but not just any man. We are wed.'

Now Caroline looked totally stunned. 'Who is he?'

'I think it would be best if I do not tell you who he is, for all our sakes. Suffice it to say that we wed by marriage contract.'

Caroline looked at me sharply. 'If you are not even prepared to tell me his name, I can only assume that he is a renegade.

After all, I know where your sympathies lie.'

'You may assume what you wish, sister.'

'And when are you expecting to be delivered of this child?'

'In the spring.'

'And will you seek to hide its existence?'

'Not hide, exactly. It will be given baptism, of course, and I have a wet-nurse in mind. We wish only to live in peace, I assure you.'

'So you will not come again to Exeter?'

'No, I think I might. However, once my time grows nearer that will not be possible. But once I have recovered from the birth, I will endeavour to make the occasional visit.'

'Whilst we will never be welcome at Altringham Manor, I suppose?'

'In the circumstances that would be difficult but do not say never. Perhaps, one day, when times are changed.'

'You still imagine that the monarchy will be restored?'

'I pray for that day whereas I imagine that John prays that it never will.'

'Oh Jane, is it not sad that our nation is still so divided?'

'Of course it is, but we cannot but be true to what we believe in, and both of us were raised to be loyal to our King, and to value that loyalty above all others.'

'You think me some sort of traitor then?'

'I did not say that...I understand that you must also have a loyalty to your husband.'

'Yes, and so I do.'

At that very moment I glanced out of the window. To my irritation it was John returning early for some reason or other, and there was no avoiding him as he hurriedly entered, calling out to Caroline as he did so, only to break-off in mid-sentence when he realised that I was present. His face conveyed more loudly than any words his evident disappointment.

He was polite but curt, not deigning to convey even a hint of smile, and I could not resist informing him that my endeavours, which he had done so much to belittle, had now been vindicated.

'You see, the Sheriff has been minded at last to issue a warrant for Turnbull's arrest and now it appears that he has fled the city, in which case he's as good as admitted his guilt. I only hope that he is apprehended.'

'So you have come here have you to boast of your victory?'

'No not at all. I'm here out of affection for my sister and also Michael. But if a murderer and ravisher has been exposed thanks in anyway to my endeavours, then yes I am proud of that.'

Unfortunately, even as I had begun to speak I had felt a rising wave of nausea and this rapidly became completely overwhelming.

'Forgive me, I need the privy, I am feeling sick.'

Ten minutes later, having wretched several times, I was able to recover in a chair, and attempted to pass off what had happened as being of little consequence.'

'I expect something that I have eaten disagreed with me.'

'If you wish I can prescribe a physic for you,' John suggested 'It should help to settle your stomach.'

'Thank you, but I feel much recovered.'

As I looked into his eyes, I worried that he was already suspicious of the real cause of my sickness, and felt a mounting desire to be gone as soon as possible. I could not be sure, either, whether I could trust my sister to keep the truth secret if he started plying her with questions, but was still satisfied that I had done the right thing in telling her what I had.

48

Gone abroad?

Five days later, I received a letter from Overbury informing me that the constables had returned empty handed
from Harpford. Upon questioning Turnbull's sister, she had
told them that he had visited her only the previous day and
then departed, giving her no indication that he intended to
do anything other than return to Exeter. It remained apparent,
though, that he had failed to do so, while his whereabouts
remained unknown.

'What frustrates me is that he has so easily escaped justice
and, so long as he remains at large, is free to strike again,' I
declared to Thomas.

'But by choosing to flee, he's surely lost his trade, and may
well be reduced to penury.'

'That's something, I suppose, but then again it could just
make him yet more vengeful.'

'You're saying then that we should still be on our guard?'

'Yes, until he's swinging at the end of a rope , every woman
most certainly should be.'

'If he's any sense, he'll have gone abroad.'

'And so he might but what's to stop him slipping back into
the country unnoticed, six months from now. He was also far
from poor and I can imagine him having a pile of gold and

silver put to one side, which he's now taken with him. It might not be a fortune but still enough to live off for quite some time.'

'Well, having fled, I struggle to believe that he'd ever be unwise enough to return to these parts again. Mind you, I accept that he remains a danger to womankind, wherever he decides to rest his head, but we can do nothing about that.'

'Nothing, I accept. I pray, too, that my sister will keep both my pregnancy and my marriage a secret from John.'

'If the risk of that concerns you so much, you should never have told her in the first place.'

I felt irritated. We had been over this same ground so many times before. 'I had to tell her. It would have been wrong to keep such a secret from her. Haven't I stressed that to you often enough?'

'Yes, you have, but I just fear that if she did reveal anything to him he would then be able to establish my identity.'

'I really doubt that, my love.'

'But you admitted that she guessed I must be a renegade. He could easily do the same...'

'But then what? Even if he were to surmise who you might be, you would still be just a name to him.'

'No, I would be more than that. The very fact that you have married me would declare that you may very well be sheltering me as well. It could bring another search party to our door, and interrogators, too.'

'But would he really be so... so vindictive as to report you. I mean it is one thing for him to dislike our politics, but I am still his sister-in-law and if he hurts me does he not also hurt Caroline?'

'But have you not said yourself he's too self-righteous to give much thought to others feelings?'

'Yes... I'm afraid I have. We can but hope that my sister keeps my secret.'

'And, too, that we have seen the last of Master Turnbull.'

'Amen to that.'

49

Revenge

A month passed and I decided that I would make one more visit to Exeter before my pregnancy together with the advance of winter weather made that impossible. I was uncertain about visiting my sister, Caroline, but there was still Master Overbury's account to be settled. Further, as a consequence of my pregnancy, I wanted to purchase materials for the making of both a suitable maternity dress and clothing for the new born infant.

Olivia, too, expressed the desire to make certain purchases so we agreed to undertake a further expedition together, hoping that autumn rains had not reduced the road to too much of a quagmire. The limited amount of daylight available to us also made it imperative that we set off at dawn so Olivia had arrived at Altringham Manor the previous afternoon and stayed the night. Fortunately, we then found the road to be perfectly passable, the previous twenty-four hours having seen no rain, and the weather continued to be fair for the duration of our journey.

Having left our horses at livery stables, upon arrival at Master Overbury's chambers, his clerk informed us that he was in court, and that so far as he was aware nothing further had been heard of Turnbull.

'We must assume he's gone for ever,' I commented before

paying the outstanding account and asking the clerk to again extend my warmest thanks to his Master for his services. Then, arm in arm, our friendship still feeling as strong to me as ever, I and Olivia proceeded to go shopping. My morning sickness had now abated, and I was beginning to feel in perfect health again, so I was determined to enjoy the day. Only once did I allow myself to think that if I were to die in labour, this would be the last time that I would ever see the city, but I quickly cast such a reflection aside, deciding it was needlessly morbid. All the while I and Olivia were shopping, I was also able to put-off making any decision about a visit to my sister, but once this task was completed, I knew that I could do so no longer.

'Are you willing to run the gauntlet with me, Olivia?'

'I came prepared for that probability, so of course I am.'

'Very well, we need not stay long, and nor would I wish to do so if John is present.'

As we then approached Caroline's door it was not without some feelings of unease on my part. Fleetingly, the thought that this might be our last meeting on earth came to mind but if anything this only served to strengthen my resolve not to walk away and I knocked firmly with my gloved hand.

As on my previous visit it was the young maid who came to the door, and I thought I saw a look of such anxiety on her face, that I wondered what on earth might be wrong. A moment later, however, I heard the sound of an infant's pathetic screams and imagined that Michael must be ill.

'It's the colic, Mam...M'lady,' the maid explained. 'The little mite's right poorly with it.'

As Caroline came to greet us I was shocked by her appearance, thinking that I had never seen her looking so tired. I could also see fear in her eyes.

'Is Michael very ill,' I asked.

'I think he may die... ' At that Caroline began to cry and I embraced her, offering what comfort I could.

'And John's on his rounds, I assume?'

'Yes, he is... He'd not...' There was a long silence and Caroline seemed to give me a guilty look.

'He'd not what?'

'... Be happy to see you here.'

I almost laughed. 'When has he ever been happy to see me here?'

'It's more than that... You see, he knows...'

'Christ in heaven, I swore you to secrecy!'

'But he's a doctor and nobody's fool. When you were so sick he was suspicious and you'd no sooner left than he started plying me with questions. Then he actually said I wouldn't be surprised if she isn't with child. I didn't say anything but he just took one look at me and said my God, she is, isn't she, I can see it in your eyes. I was still struck dumb but then he asked me if I knew who the father was and I shook my head. 'Oh come now, she must have told you,' to which I replied 'no,' only that you were married. I'm sorry, but it wasn't long before he came to the same conclusion that I did. It made him angry and he shouted that he never wanted to see you under his roof again.'

'Well, have no fear, we'll leave immediately. I only came to say farewell. I doubt if I'll be fit to even think of returning before next summer. Indeed, if all does not go well, you may never see me again.'

'But you are a strong woman, Jane, and blooming now, I can see that. Your morning sickness is behind you, I take it?'

'Yes.'

'Then you will be safely delivered of your child, have no doubt.'

The two of us once again embraced and I struggled to contain my emotions; still fraught by the notion that we might never set eyes on each other again.

'Before you go there is also something else you should know...'

'Oh, and what is that?'

'John knows or thinks he knows who your husband is...'

I was stunned by this revelation. 'Oh, really. And has he shared the name with you?'

'He thinks it might well be Thomas Sumner...'

'Oh does he now!' My brain was now racing, wondering how he'd managed to hit the mark with such accuracy.

'Look, I don't expect you to admit to this even if it's true. He was all for going to the Justices with his notion but I managed to persuade him against doing so. I said it would be too cruel on you, especially as you are with child, and upon me as your loving sister as I could not bear it if any ill befell you through any action on his part.'

'Well, I thank you for that, dear sister. But tell me on what grounds did he come to the conclusion that Thomas Sumner is my husband?'

'Merely on the basis that his family home is not that many miles from Altringham Manor, that you have spoken of visiting there on occasions, and because he is a notorious renegade whose whereabouts are currently unknown.'

'I see... Let me be clear then... I admit to nothing, nothing at all!'

'Of course, dear sister, of course...'

50

Fire

'Thomas shall be perfectly entitled to admonish me for ever having told my sister I was with child in the first place,' I declared to Olivia as we rode home from Exeter. 'If only I had not been sick in John's presence...'

'The truth might have slipped out anyway. Your brother-in-law can read your sister as if she were a book, I would imagine.'

'He's shrewd, I'll give him that. I only pray he keeps to his word and reports nothing to the Justices. The thought that he might still do so is like a veritable sword of Damocles hanging over us. At any moment it might fall...'

'If he has any love for your sister, he'll surely say nothing. In any event, it remains only a suspicion on his part, and would he really be so... so spiteful.'

'I can only pray not.'

By the time of our arrival at the gates of Altringham Manor it was already growing dark, and the weather closing in, with a hint of rain in the air as well as a penetrating wind, which was gathering pace, so Olivia was grateful to avail herself of my hospitality once more. I was also relieved that my marriage to Thomas had in the event done very little to damage our former intimacy and that Olivia found him not only handsome and gentlemanly in his behaviour towards her but also possessed of a relaxed temperament, which was devoid of any arrogance. Most of all, he gave every appearance of welcoming her presence when he could so easily have resented it, making Olivia happy, so she told me, to think of him as a friend.

At the same time, I was conscious of the fact that he was growing increasingly frustrated with his 'genteel captivity' as he chose to describe it. A man of action, he was easily bored, and what worried me most was that to console himself he had begun to drink large quantities of beer and wine. It wasn't making him incapable but it was causing him to be short tempered at times and thereby damaging our otherwise loving relationship.

Consequently, I was wary of what state we might find him in, and, depending on that, how angry he might become when I told him what had transpired in Exeter. It made me think, indeed, that if I smelt liquor on his breath, I should refrain from making any mention of it at all until he was more sober and likely to be in a better humour.

'Leave me to make any mention of what my sister told me,' I therefore counselled Olivia.

'Naturally. Tell me, though, are you thinking of not saying anything to him on the matter?'

'No, it's more a question of picking the right moment.'

We had barely dismounted from our horses when Harry appeared, looking deeply concerned.

'M'lady, I have some unfortunate news for thee.'

Thinking that some grave accident had befallen Thomas, I felt my stomach turn over.

'Oh dear.' My voice sounded distant to me as I struggled to remain calm, dreading what he might say next.

'Two of our sheep have been found dead. They've been killed.'

'Really!' For a moment I felt as much a sense of relief as anger.

'Tis true, m'lady.'

'Do you think it was a dog running wild?'

'No, m'lady, stab wounds did for them. Only a knife, or maybe a sword, could have inflicted such wounds. I can show thee the bodies, if y've a mind…'

'No, I believe you; but tell me, are they still where they were found?'

'No, m'lady, I've had 'em moved undercover.'

'And you've no idea who might have been responsible?'

'No, m'lady, I can't see why any poacher would do such a thing. Only a while after ye left this morning, they were just found lying in a hollow on the pasture where they're usually left to graze. The shepherd, Seth, reckons they'd not long been dead, so whoever killed them probably did so just as it was getting light.'

I and Olivia, both puzzled by such a wanton act of violence against dumb animals, made our way indoors where we were quickly met by Thomas.

'Harry's told you what's happened?' He look bleary eyed and I thought I could smell liquor on his breath but at that moment in time I was far more concerned about the fate of the two sheep.

'Yes, I don't understand who would do such a thing unless…'

'Do you think it might have been someone with a grudge against me? In God's name, it could even have been Turnbull?'

Thomas looked at me sceptically. 'That's possible, I suppose, but if it's him he'd be taking quite a risk coming back to these parts.'

'He'll have taken some precautions, I imagine. Perhaps

shaved off his beard, changed the garb he wears, much like you. Even changed his name, I wouldn't be surprised.'

'And, I fancy, he might not stop at killing a couple of sheep.'

'So what's to be done?' Olivia asked.

'If it was him, someone must be giving him shelter, and not all that far from here either. Find where that is and you'll find him,' Thomas said. 'Chances are he'd still have a horse with him, too.'

'He could be holed up on his own somewhere,' I postulated. 'An abandoned cottage, or even a house. There are a few around, after all, especially since the war.'

'But if that's the case, someone's likely to know about it. For a start, with winter setting in, he'd need to build a fire... And he'd need to stable his horse.'

I looked Thomas in the eye. 'Well, we can't be certain he's got one. In fact, we can't even be sure it's him at all.'

'No, of course you can't, but whoever it was I think they may well have come close enough to the house to set the kitchen dogs off. It was in the dead of night, too, when they started barking and roused me from my sleep.'

Supper was eaten mainly in silence while I fretted on the very possibility that a ravisher and murderer might still be threatening us. I was in no mood, either, to inform Thomas what my sister had confessed to me, and nor did Olivia fail to respect my express wishes on this account.

It was only when we all retired to bed and I and Thomas were alone together that I decided to tell him. He was fortunately not as angry as I feared he might be and relatively unperturbed.

'It's what I feared all along might happen but if she's truly persuaded him to take no action against me, we hopefully

301

haven't too much to fear.'

'There's still a risk he might change his mind,' I conceded.

'It's there, of course it is, but soldiers have come searching for me before without success.'

'Except if they were to come yet again, I would expect to be closely questioned and I imagine so would probably every man and woman living on the estate. It might not require too much intimidation for someone to give you away.'

I was too exhausted after what had been a long and tiring day to agonise any further about either this possibility, or, for that matter, the threat we might still face from Turnbull and quickly fell into a deep, seemingly dreamless sleep. However, at some point in the early hours, I was startled out of my slumbers, by the sound, emanating from the kitchen, of dogs barking. Thomas was already out of bed and putting on his breaches, while the wind was strong enough to be rattling the windows, although I could hear no rain.

'You're not thinking of going outside, I hope?'

'No, but I mean to check that the house is secure. The dogs surely aren't barking without good reason.'

'Well, take care.'

'Of course, I'll light myself a candle from the embers of the fire, and there's that old sword in the library...'

'What's that?' Sitting up in bed, I had thought I heard a crackling noise, and even though the bedroom curtains were supposedly closed, there was a sufficient gap between them for me to be able to see that the night sky had lit-up a little.

Thomas's response was to walk straight to the window where he threw back the curtains.

'Christ in heaven, I believe it must be the stables. They're on fire!'

This brought me to his side in an instant. 'The horses must be saved!'

As quickly as he could, Thomas donned his shirt and doublet, before putting on his boots, while I began to dress as well.

'I'd rather you stayed here,' Thomas said. 'it may be too dangerous...'

'No! You'll need my help... Without it you'll struggle to get four horses out on your own.'

'Oh, very we'll, but there's not a moment to lose...'

'Go then, I'll follow as soon as I can.'

51

Burial

As Thomas ran heavily down the stairs, I succeeded in throwing on the plainest and oldest dress I could find in the gloom before searching around for an equally old pair of shoes. I then decided to rouse Olivia and went to bang loudly on her bedroom door.

'Hello, who's there? Is something amiss?'

'It's me, Olivia,' I shouted. 'The stables are on fire! Thomas has already gone ahead to try and rescue the horses.'

'Oh my God!'

'Dress yourself as quickly as you can and come and help.'

'Yes, of course!'

I then ran down the stairs as quickly as the length of my dress would allow, the chilling coldness of a windy November night penetrating to my skin the instant that I left the house. It made my shiver, and cross my arms, but my eyes were fixed on the blaze that confronted me as the flames from the burning stables leapt into the sky.

It was small consolation that the powerful westerly wind was carrying the flames away from the direction of the house, which was separated anyway from the stable block by a good twenty yards. The choice which faced me was also whether to immediately run on towards the blaze or waste time in summoning aid from the likes of Harry. However, seeing just how far the flames had already spread, I barely broke my stride in racing to Thomas's aid, desperate at the notion that my precious Hera might already be beyond saving.

As I came closer I could hear the whinnying of the horses as if it was a desperate scream for help and quickened my pace, only to see Thomas emerging from the stables as if from the mouth of hell, bringing with him one of the horses. To my dismay, it wasn't Hera but his own horse, a stallion named Duke.

'The pony, Persephone, is already down, I'm afraid,' he shouted at me. 'The stable lad, Toby, is bringing Olivia's horse out...'

'I must save Hera!' I yelled and darted past him.

'No, Jane...'

What confronted me as I entered the building was a wall of heat along with gathering smoke and flames that made me cough and splutter and feel a rush of dread. Coming towards me was Toby, leading Olivia's horse, while to my left Hera was still in her stall, whinnying terribly, and understandably in a state of deep distress. I went straight to her.

'I'm going to get you out of here , my beauty, have no fear.' God knows, though, I felt plenty of that myself.

I then started to throw a bridle over her and in that very moment Thomas appeared at my side.

'Here, let me help you, the roof's about to cave in!'

Together, we did our best to encourage Hera towards safety, even as the beams above our heads began to give way and flaming sparks fell upon us. Never in my life before had I felt such dread, and even as we emerged into the open air, with Thomas carrying a saddle with girth, which he had managed to grab hold of, I could not help but scream when I saw that his doublet was on fire.

Desperately, he yanked it off, before throwing it to the ground and beating out the flames with his boot. Meanwhile, behind us the roof of the stables had given way with a crash. The building was beyond saving but I still felt an overwhelming sense of relief that we had been able to rescue three of the horses , especially my beloved Hera.

'Lord Almighty, Jane, your hair's on fire!' Thomas exclaimed even as he picked up his doublet from the ground and used it to put the flame out. My thick and luscious hair was, I sometimes thought, my most precious physical asset, and the thought that it had been badly singed was enough to overwhelm me with emotion and bring tears to my eyes. In hell's name, I wondered, was this calamity a mere accident, or was there an evil hand at work, possibly even Turnbull's.

Looking about me, I could see a number of people, whom I recognised, including Alice and Mary, all of whom had risen hastily from their beds upon hearing the cries of alarm, which I and Thomas had raised. However, one familiar face was absent.

'Olivia! Where's Olivia? Has anyone seen her?'

'M'Lady, she came outside, that I know,' Alice said. 'I was just making m'way down the stairs, having heard the commotion, when I saw 'er in the hallway. She turned to me and said there was a fire in the stables and then went outside...'

'But weren't you right behind her?'

'I would 'ave been, m'lady, but I got this awful twinge in m'leg and it pulled me up short.'

'Olivia! Olivia!' I cried out, filled with an almost paralysing sense of fear that something terrible might have befallen her. 'Olivia!'

There was no response, so, closely followed by Thomas, I walked back towards the front door of the Manor, still calling out Olivia's name, until I heard a muffled cry.

'D'you hear that?'

'Yes, I think it came from the copse.'

'That monster's seized her. He must have started the fire, too!'

'Harry, Toby, come with me...'

'He'll likely be armed, don't forget!'

'All right, I'll fetch the sword from the library.'

He then raced inside the house and it probably took him less than thirty seconds to return, flourishing the cavalry sword, which had once belonged to Paul. However, to me, it seemed like an eternity.

'Come on then, follow me!' he shouted, gesturing to Harry and Toby. 'And remember, we must stay together.'

The three of them disappeared into the darkness, again leaving me to fret, dreading the possibility that my dearest friend could already have been ravished and even murdered. I began to pace up and down, looked towards the horses, and made an immediate decision.

Seizing hold of the saddle, which Thomas had rescued from the blazing stables, I took it to Hera and threw it over her back before securing it. I had no stirrups and my long skirt was a considerable encumbrance but I was still determined to mount Hera. First, I attempted to rip my skirt, but it refused to give, so I decided that I would have to forsake all modesty even if it meant baring my arse to the cold night air. At least there were only women present and there was only the glow from the blazing stable to give any light.

'Mary, Alice, help me, will you.'

With their assistance, and thanks to my own agility, I managed, albeit in the most unladylike of fashions, to clamber onto the saddle, before catching my breath.

'Where be ye going, m'lady?' Mary asked me.

'No further than the gates. I'm going to stop that monster from escaping, if I can.'

I urged Hera into a canter, using all my skill as a horsewoman to ride her, even without the benefit of stirrups. The main gates to the estate stood open, as they always did, and whilst there were other ways out of it this was still by far the most obvious. I therefore intended to close them and so cut off the most likely escape route.

The distance from the manor house to the gates was barely a quarter of a mile and it had been on my mind to run to them if I had not managed to mount Hera. As it was I reached the gates in about a minute before dismounting from Hera and racing to close them.

Even as I pulled them together, I then heard the sound of a horse galloping towards me. Anxiously, I still completed my task before turning round, only to be confronted by a rider coming ever closer.

'You're trapped!' I screamed. 'You can't escape!'

'You cursed bitch! the rider snarled, his voice sounding as if it might well be Turnbull's, although in truth I could not be sure especially as I could now make out that he was wearing a mask. He had also brought his horse so close to mine that it reared up, making me back away in fear that the hooves of its forelegs might strike me, and then to my consternation he quickly dismounted and advanced towards me. I could tell that he was holding a knife in his right hand and I was prepared to run for my life if I had to. First, though, I decided to scream for help, hoping that in the night air my voice would carry some distance.

'Thomas! Thomas! Help me! I'm at the gate! He's attacking me!'

This was enough to make my attacker lunge at me with his knife. He might have struck home, too, if I had not managed to sidestep his attack and then run behind his horse so that it stood between us, all the while tossing it's head, and clearly ill at ease. I naturally hoped that I could continue to use its body as a shield until help came but when it decided to trot away there was nothing I could do to prevent it.

'Bitch!' Bitch!' the masked man snarled as he came at me, wielding his knife, and forcing me to run in fear for my life in Hera's direction. Once more I cried out.

'Save me! He means to kill me!'

Hera was only a few yards away but I was certain that I would be overtaken if I tried to remount her, so instead I continued to run, only to see a figure coming towards me. 'Thomas! Is that you?'

'Yes!'

My pursuer was now so close that I thought he might overtake me at any moment. However, at the sound of Thomas's voice, he altered course, running instead towards his horse, which had come to a standstill nearby. I could then only stand and watch, my chest heaving as a consequence of my exertions, as Thomas attempted to head him off. At first it looked to me as if he might fail in this endeavour but then the horse decided to trot off in the direction of the Manor House, and seeing that Thomas was now gaining ground on him, the masked man again changed course, this time fleeing in the direction of some trees.

'Surrender, or I'll run you through,' Thomas cried out.

I could now barely make out what was happening, but in response to Thomas's command I heard a snarl followed moments later by a scream that seemed to come to an abrupt halt as if it had stuck in the throat. Moments later Thomas came towards me out of the gloom and I ran into his arms, the sheer trauma of what had just happened causing me to break into tears.

'My love, you should not have put yourself or our child in such danger,' he gently chided me.'

'I thought if I did nothing, he might succeed in making good his escape. Is he dead?'

'Yes. He turned and came at me with his knife. It was as if he wanted to die. I had no choice but to defend myself and my sword penetrated his chest...'

'And have you removed his mask? I'm sure he was wearing one.'

'No, I have no reason to believe I'd recognise the man even if I did.'

'But I would... , if indeed it is Turnbull.'

'Whoever he is... , good riddance to him.'

'And Olivia... , She's not?'

'No, thank God, although had I not arrived when I did he would surely have succeeded in ravishing her.'

'I need to see the man's face then.'

By now both Harry and Toby had arrived on the scene and the four of us walked over to where the man was lying on his back. His body lay still and as I knelt beside him I could detect no sound of breathing. Summoning my courage, I then pulled back the mask, wondering what on earth we would do if it turned out to be someone other than Turnbull. I also appreciated that the darkness would not make it easy to distinguish the man's features but nonetheless as I looked at him intently I saw the tell-tale scar on his cheek and was certain that it was him.

'Is it Turnbull?' Thomas asked.

'Yes... , yes it is.'

'It's over then... He can do no more harm.'

'But the body... What are we to do with it? We can hardly admit you killed him.'

'It was self-defence. He attacked me; I had every right...'

'Thomas, That's hardly the point...'

'Of course it's not. I understand that perfectly well...'

'Begging your pardon, sir,' Harry interjected.

'Yes...'

'Why don't we just bury him. He was a devil come to earth, that's for certain, and on the run from justice. For all anyone knows he could have gone abroad or...'

'... Thrown himself off a cliff into deep water.'

'Except that he must have been living somewhere over the course of the last few weeks,' I pointed out.

'True enough, but as you've said yourself, my love, it could have been somewhere half-derelict, or perhaps just lodgings in an inn, miles from here. I also doubt if anyone's going to miss him sufficiently to want to raise any sort of search, especially if they had any knowledge of what he was accused of. No, Harry, I think your idea's a good one, although he'll need to be six feet under with the minimum of delay.'

'Why not in the copse then, where he tried to ravish Olivia.'

'All right, so long as the ground is suitable.'

'And now I must go to Olivia,' I declared. 'I just pray she's not too affected by what he tried to do to her.'

I found her in a state of deep shock but otherwise only bruised.

'I struggled with him and even managed to break free,' she told me. 'Then he caught me again and was about to have his way with me when he realised that someone was approaching. I'm just exhausted and need to sleep.'

I left her to do so, feeling totally exhausted myself. The events of the night had been dramatic indeed, the stables were now a gutted ruin, and there was still a body to be buried, but at least I now felt safer than at any time in nearly seven months.

52

Aftermath

Christmas was now almost upon us, it was snowing outside and had been so for an hour or more. I reflected that it was now eight months since that pleasant spring day when the first ravishment had taken place and some six weeks since we had buried Turnbull in the nearby copse without the benefit of even a prayer, save, perhaps, muttered under at least one person's breath, that he could rot in hell for all we cared. But then he had been a murderer and a ravisher who had deserved to be publicly executed so I felt absolutely no sense of guilt for what we had done.

It had anyway been a hard toil for Thomas and Harry to dig a six foot deep grave, but they had managed it in the end, and Turnbull's clothed body had then been tossed into it along with the knife he had used. In the absence of any coffin, it had also been decided to cover it in rubble taken from the ruined stables before piling on the earth, and it had thankfully remained undisturbed ever since.

All that remained above ground in evidence that Turnbull had ever been anywhere near the Manor was his horse. The burning down of the stables also meant that all the horses we now possessed had had to be accommodated in a barn, whilst I could see no prospect of being able to afford to rebuild unless and until better times returned. I could but count my blessings, however, and most especially that my pregnancy was continuing to progress without any alarms. Both Becky and Olivia also seemed to be recovering well from their ordeals and if I had any concern it lay in Thomas's growing tendency to drink too much. When in an inebriated state he was also now becoming not only short tempered but loud, too. However, I was determined to make allowances, understanding full well his frustration at so much enforced idleness, which had only been exacerbated by the coming of winter.

What had most shocked me was the news that Olivia had given me only the previous day when I had paid one of my weekly visits. James had been in Honiton the day before and learnt that Oliver Cromwell had now given himself the title of Lord Protector of a so called Commonwealth of England, Scotland and Ireland, advised by a Council of State

'My God, he's now King in all but name,' I had exclaimed

'And I say, the Lord protect us from him,' Thomas had quipped.

'And may your prayer be answered, my love. After all, he's already delivered us from one demon and may yet do so again.'

Now, as I turned my back on the winter weather, Thomas walked towards me with a ready smile on his handsome face, and I decided that I must be grateful for such good fortune as the Lord had seen fit to bestow upon me, whatever the future might hold.

THE END

About the author

The author is a retired lawyer living near Canterbury, Kent. He is married with two sons and three grandchildren.

Other books by James Walker

Ellen's Gold

My Enemy My Love

I Think He Was George

Shamila

Acknowledgements

My sincere thanks to James Essinger and Charlotte Mouncey for all their help in the creation of this novel.